DEATH IN MY REFLECTION

DEATH IN MY REFLECTION

A REESE CLAYTON AND EMERSON LAKE NOVEL

BARBARA FOURNIER

The characters and events in this book are a work of fiction.
Names, places, and incidents are the product of the author's
imagination. Any similarity to real persons living or dead is
coincidental and not intended by the author.

Copyright © 2022 Barbara Fournier
All rights reserved

Cover and interior design by Caroline Teagle Johnson

DEDICATION

I dedicate this book to my greatest gift in life and to the man who helped me to create that gift.

Our incredible daughter Crystal and my loving husband Al.

PROLOGUE

Timothy Cole sat in his cell, waiting for his demise. The cold, damp, gray block walls of death row reminded him of the psychiatric facility he practically grew up in. Only now this would be his last day in what he called captivity. This was his last chance. He had to figure out a plan. He was one of only two prisoners on death row. Tim couldn't have cared less about the other inmate.

The glaring bright lights dimmed, signaling lights out, yet they were never truly off. Tim heard the heavy footsteps approach his cell, then saw the silhouette of the guard. Tim tensed, not knowing what abuse lie ahead for him tonight. What he knew was this time would be the last time this six-foot, overweight, ugly prick would tell Tim to lower anything in his life. He was still in shackles as the guard shoved his face down onto the musty mattress. In the rush to open his fly, the guard's uniform pants fell suddenly to his ankles. Hearing the belt buckle hit the concrete floor, Tim knew this was his opportunity. Tim jolted upright and, in one swift motion, swung his cuffed hands over the top of the guard's head, twisting until he heard a crack. The guard's body went limp in his arms.

Tim closed his eyes for a moment and let out a long sigh as his body shuddered, releasing the built-up tension. He then gazed into the guard's bulging eyes, remembering that same look, the look of fear, in the eyes of his family. That look when he stabbed them all, one by one, wiping the blood from the blade after each one died, wondering how they felt now about sending him away. Then burying them all those years ago. That was a good day, he thought.

Tim held the guard up long enough to remove the keys to the cuffs from his belt, then removed his shirt, badge, and gun. He let him down gradually and maneuvered around so he could unlock his shackles. He then removed the rest of the guards' clothing and exchanged them with his own colorful suit of orange. Tim knew there would be no camera footage. The guards conveniently turned them off during their exploits.

After dressing himself in the uniform, Tim Cole smiled, spinning around, rather liking that feeling of power in blue, always did. This is a good look for me, he thought. He then picked up the guard and placed him on the cot facing the wall. Timothy Cole walked out of the prison that day, head held high, badge on his chest and hand close to his gun. Free yet again! Now it was time to settle a score.

CHAPTER 1

The dress made for a princess. White satin and lace covered with Swarovski crystals. Her train was not long, but right for a wedding ceremony by the lake. Hair pinned in place by an artist's creation topped with a tiara.

"Well, are you ready for your big day?" he asked.

"I'm as ready as anyone can be, Dad. I have waited a long time for this day."

"Me too, my baby girl. You look beautiful. A single tear ran down his cheek. If only your mother were here with us. I guess it's all parents' dream to see their child grow to be a woman and walk down the aisle. I am so proud. I love you."

"Love you too, dad. I'm ready."

The music played softly, the breeze gently coming off the lake, the perfect backdrop for a wedding ceremony. After giving his daughter away to her husband-to-be, he took his place of honor as officiant for his baby girl's wedding. The ceremony began.

"Welcome all. I am incredibly pleased to have the privilege of officiating at my lovely daughter's wedding. The bride and her groom, as well as I, are delighted to have all of you here to witness their union. Thank you for being here on this special day. Jennifer and Alessandro have requested to recite their own vows. Alessandro, you may begin."

"Even though we have only known each other a short time, I feel we were born to be together." He reached for her hand and placed the ring on her finger. "I love you, Jennifer. We have been through so much already, which is why I know we are meant to be. We can do anything together. I promise to be supportive and to always make our family a priority. I am so proud to call myself your husband from this day forward."

After he finished, the officiant nodded to his daughter.

Jennifer placed a ring on his finger. "I know in my heart that we will always be able to find our way together. Thank you for always supporting and loving me even when I haven't made it easy. I believe in you, the person you will grow to be and the couple we will be together. You are more than any man I could ever have dreamed. From this day forward my heart is yours."

The judge proceeded. "Do you Alessandro take thee, Jennifer, to be your lawfully wedded wife?"

"I do."

"Do you Jennifer take thee, Alessandro, to be your lawfully wedded husband?"

"I do."

The judge turned, facing the bride and her forever to be, a sparkle in his eyes. "By the power vested in me by the State of South Dakota, I now pronounce you..."

Before he could finish his sentence, blood splattered outward in every direction from a gaping hole in his forehead, peppering his little girl's gown like a Jackson Pollock painting. The crystals no longer shimmering in the sunlight.

Jennifer shrieked, "Daddy!" Her tears mixed with the blood streaked across her cheeks as her father, the Honorable Judge John Orrick, fell to his knees. No one heard the shot.

CHAPTER 2

"So, are you going to the execution Lake?" Reese asked her partner.

"Someone has to be present to verify they injected him." Emerson replied as he repeatedly tapped a stack of report papers on his desk. "I have said throughout these appeals that I want to be there when he takes his last breath. I would like some company though, Reese. It's a long drive down to the state prison. Will you come with me tomorrow?"

Detectives Reese Clayton and Emerson Lake had taken the lead in solving a bizarre serial murder case that had consumed their city of Cromwell, South Dakota, as well as the neighboring town of Jade. It had taken nearly three years, but the day had finally arrived when justice would prevail.

"How about it? We could take our time coming back, maybe take the whole day off to explore the sights. I know it's not the easiest job to watch a man take his last breath, Reese, but I feel it's important that we finish this case. See it all the way through to the end. What do you say? Are you in?"

"Yes," she sighed. "But only if you promise me a nice dinner sometime this week. You know, a suit-and-tie kind of dinner. And before you make a smart-ass comment that I don't need to wear a suit and tie; remember, partner, I carry a gun at all times."

"Why are you creeped out by Tim Cole's death sentence? He is a convicted serial killer, and too far gone to help himself or to be helped. A genuine threat to everyone."

"I know, but I kind of felt a little sorry for him. I know he needs to die, but I also wonder if they could have helped him, as a child maybe? There is a heart there somewhere. You saw how he tried to protect Kei Lien from her father. Probably the only friend she had until Daniel Nyung came along."

"I hear you, but remember this: he could have stopped the abuse that poor girl endured long before Kei Lien took matters into her own hands. Instead, he watched her being raped by her father and others repeatedly. He's an animal, Reese. An animal."

Reese shrugged and gazed out the window. They sat silently for the rest of the trip.

Arriving at the prison, they pulled into the visitors parking lot. The enormous brick penitentiary was surrounded by rolls of razor-wire covering the tops of the walls.

The two detectives made their way through the gates to security. It was nearing 11:30 pm. Like most executions, this one, scheduled for midnight.

Their firearms were placed in holding, their identification verified. They were patted down and instructed on what to expect during the procedure.

They approached the viewing room and took their seats behind the glass partitions. The only other people in attendance were guards and prison officials, including Warden Daniels.

There were no relatives of his victims present, nor anyone for the prisoner.

Timothy Cole was already strapped to the table with one of the two IV tubes in his arm. A cloth mask covered his mouth and nose to keep him from spitting at anyone. The first of three injections, the one to relax him, had been administered. It didn't work. His body twisted fighting against his bindings as the second injection rushed into his vein. He coughed and vomited; he still had a lot of fight left in him.

• • •

A young Catholic Priest stood near the convicted murderer. He wondered how this could happen and was distraught that administering the last rites was his first assignment as a man of the cloth. The prison guard lifted the sheet that covered Tim's body to make sure his restraints were still in place. They were. Reese leaned forward toward the glass; straining to get a look at Tim's leg. She turned toward Emerson and whispered, "We have a problem. That is not Timothy Cole."

Before Emerson could respond, Detective Reese Clayton screamed at the top of her lungs. "Stop! Stop! Don't proceed!" She grabbed her shield, slamming it against the glass, waving it back and forth to let them know who she was and to make them stop the execution.

The priest and the guards on the other side of the glass, shocked by the outburst, looked toward the warden for answers.

Emerson grabbed her arm and looked straight into her eyes. "Reese, what are you doing?"

"That's not Tim Cole," she repeated.

"What the hell are you talking about?"

"Look Emerson! Look closely. There is no brand on his leg. That insane asylum hell hole had branded his right leg for some fucking reason. I saw it when he was in our jail cell. It wasn't a tattoo. It was a circle with an X in the middle, burned, not ink. That's not him!"

The warden was sitting near a phone, a phone that was connected directly to the Governor, and was positioned only five feet from Reese Clayton.

His jaw tensed and his brow furrowed as he signaled the guards and the doctors to stop the administration of the lethal injections. He reluctantly picked up the phone. "Governor, we have a problem. The detective that was part of Cole's capture is here. She claims the inmate on the table is not Cole."

"Put her on the phone and stop the procedure!"

The warden held the phone receiver out to Reese. "You had better be right, lady, or your badge will be on the line. You got that, Detective Clayton?"

Reese put the phone to her ear and listened as he unleashed on her. "Yes Governor, I got it." She handed the phone back to the warden so he could hear the governor's instructions.

Reese was shocked. Why would the governor reprimand her for not only saving the life of the guy on the table, but also saving him and the warden from a huge embarrassment? It made no sense.

Emerson held onto Reese's arm, partly because he loved her, but also not sure of what the hell she was doing.

She pulled Emerson aside and told him what the governor

had said to her.

"What the fuck?" he whispered. "Wait till the press gets ahold of this?"

"Let's keep this between us until we speak with the captain."

The warden hung up the phone and took a deep breath. "Guards, please remove the covering from this man's mouth and nose. NOW!"

Emerson gasped, "Oh, dear God!"

They would not be executing Timothy Cole tonight.

CHAPTER 3

The man on the table began spitting and gagging until he vomited.

The warden yelled at the man on the table. "Who the hell are you and why are you in this part of the prison? There are only two inmates on death row, and you are not one of them!"

"I'm Jerry Owens," he finally replied in between gasps for air. "I was in a completely different cell block. Why the fuck am I on Death Row?"

"Guards, sit him up before he chokes to death on his own vomit." The warden was clearly angry at this whole mistaken identity fiasco.

The inmate, still trying to breathe and vomiting on himself began to share his story.

"Some guard came into my cell and dragged me out of bed. Removed my clothes and replaced them with underwear and a t-shirt. Then, once out of sight of the other prisoners, he duct-taped my mouth." He gagged again. "He threw me on a gurney and as he pushed me down the hall, he covered my face with the sheet. I have no clue who the hell he was. Never saw him before. What the fuck is going on? Why am I in this room and why is a priest giving me my last rites?" He peered down at IV in his arm, and it finally registered, his eyes widened. "I need to see a lawyer right now! I'm in here on a drug charge, albeit a big one. It's not a life sentence but, for fucking sure, it's not a death penalty offense." It sank in how close to death he was while under that sheet. He began gut wrenching vomiting. Blood was now oozing out of his nose and mouth. "What did you give me in that IV?" he said yanking it out of his arm. He tried to get off the gurney, but got dizzy and fell back, landing on the floor.

"Guards take this man to the infirmary," the warden ordered. "Get him checked out and then contact his lawyer at once. I want round-the-clock security on him, got it? Anything else happens to this guy, your asses are mine! Now move!"

"Sir, this prison needs to be put on lock down immediately!" Reese demanded.

The warden spun around. "Detectives, this is *my* prison." His face was beet red. His blood pressure climbing through the roof. "If orders are to be given," he gritted his teeth, "I will be the one to give them. I am in charge here; do I make myself clear?"

"Very clear, Warden," Lake replied. "But with all due respect, change the attitude. Without our help, your ass would have also been on the line for allowing a prisoner to escape and for nearly giving the wrong prisoner a lethal injection. Are we clear on that, Warden? The press will have a field day with this, and you know how quickly that will happen. Warden, it might be wise to inform the governor that his own reputation is on the line as well. Not exactly good press or a positive campaign advertisement when ultimately the prison is his responsibility. But we all know, it doesn't matter whose fault this was. Shit flows downhill, and that means you, Warden Daniels. I suggest you have a little more respect for Detective Clayton and myself."

CHAPTER 4

Reese got on the phone to Kimimela Brown, the first female and first Lakota Sioux to hold the distinguished title of Captain of the Cromwell P.D.

"Captain, Timothy Cole has escaped from the state penitentiary. Another prisoner was drugged and placed on the execution table. I stopped them just in time to let them know it wasn't Cole."

"How the hell did they not know that?" asked Captain Brown.

"Exactly. It's already one in the afternoon, Captain, and no one at the prison has slept or even had time for coffee and a hard roll."

"Detective, as disturbing as that is, we actually have bigger things to worry about back here."

"Bigger than an escaped death row inmate?"

"I was just notified of a murder that took place at a wedding in Jade."

"Who was the victim?" Reese asked.

"Judge John Orrick."

"No way! That's the judge that son-of-a-bitch Cole said would be next."

"It gets worse, Reese. The judge was officiating over the wedding ceremony. Whoever did this shot him from behind, hitting him in the back of the head, landing him in front of the bride. His own daughter."

"Oh my god! She must be devasted."

"I can take a guess where our escaped convict is right now."

"I agree. I hardly doubt these two incidents are a coincidence, Captain."

"Everything else is on hold, Detective. You and Lake head to Jade. I'll be in touch."

"Captain, if I may say something?"

"Go ahead."

"We need to run a full investigation into this prison. Something is not right, and I've got a feeling this goes farther up the chain of command than we think. You can call it a gut feeling if you like, but something is not right."

"Noted, but first you and Lake head to Jade. See if you can find any clues or evidence. Maybe the gun, fingerprints, notes to the judge, anything that will connect Cole to this murder."

"Yes, Captain, I'll contact the authorities in Jade."

But Reese already knew she wouldn't be calling the shots. This was now a federal offense; FBI would be on it as well as state and local police. Great, she thought. Now, I not only have to deal with an escaped convict, but also the influx of testosterone from the FBI and my partner. My worst nightmare. Shit!

CHAPTER 5

Lake and Clayton arrived on the bloody scene late in the afternoon of what should have been the best day of a bride and groom's life. The idyllic setting featured a crystal-clear body of water known by the Great Sioux Nation as Enemy Lake. The South Dakota state flower, the American Pasques, covered the wedding ceremony arch in beautiful shades of blue with just enough greenery to enhance the look.

The guests had been interviewed, Judge Orrick's body removed and sent to the morgue, and the bride and her groom had been taken to the hospital in shock. All that remained was the hustle of agents and the forensics team. State Police and local K9 teams were busy searching the area for evidence as the daylight was disappearing quickly.

Reese and Emerson had one thing in their favor: they knew Timothy Cole; they knew his threats were to be taken seriously. He operated in a way that they understood. They also knew he murdered the judge.

"Those were his last words to the judge at sentencing, Reese said. 'When I get out, you're next.'"

"I know. It seems he kept his promise."

"How is it that no one heard the shot? The only way that I know of is with an assault rifle. A Kate is what the marines call it. Maybe a 308 or 338. Probably used a silencer as well to cut down on the flash. But how?"

"Lake, where the hell would someone like Cole get an assault rifle? It makes no sense. I mean, he has been on death row for quite a long time now, no outside visitation. How could he arrange for one to be waiting once he escaped? It would have to be an inside job, but who? There were only two of them on death row. The other guy is still there."

"Sorry to eavesdrop detectives, but I'd say we need to scour those rocks across the lake. Pretty easy to hide behind any of them." Officer Clark worked for Jade County and was glad to see the detectives that captured Cole on the scene. The entire precinct was grateful for their help in solving the murders of Cole's entire family and having him sent to prison. "Detective Lake, that weapon, whatever you called it, could easily be hidden in any of the crevices up there. Those formations jutting out onto the lake are a beautiful backdrop for a wedding, but certainly could have been a perfect cover for someone."

Emerson grabbed a pair of binoculars. "How far is it across the lake? Doesn't look too wide."

"I'd say possibly three or four football fields." Clark calculated. "I could be wrong. There are areas that are not as wide because of the rocks, but if the shot came from the other side of this lake, the wedding arch was directly across from there. They shot the judge in the back of the head. It must have been high caliber to blow a hole like that in him."

●　●　●

Two FBI agents entered the crime scene with their typical swagger and authority.

"Evening detectives, I'm Agent Rob Olden," he extended his hand. "And this is my partner Agent Michael Wells."

"Nice to meet you. I'm Detective Emerson Lake. This is my partner, Detective Reese Clayton," he replied, all four shaking hands.

Reese gestured to the officer from Jade. "This is Officer Clark. I'm sorry, Officer, I forgot your first name."

"It's Calvin, detective." He nodded a thank-you for the introduction.

"We finished speaking with all the guests and no one saw or heard anything except the scream from the bride. And then all hell broke loose." Agent Olden continued. "The strange thing is no one here heard anything resembling a gunshot."

"We were just talking about that with Officer Clark. We're thinking a Kate with a silencer. Perhaps, high caliber round to cause that much damage." Emerson explained their theory about the position of the shooter on the rock formations as well.

"Whoa, c'mon detectives," Agent Olden interrupted. "Let's not get ahead of ourselves. This isn't a ridiculous action movie. Let's be realistic. I'm thinking of a high-powered rifle. Doesn't look *that* far from the arch to the other side of the lake."

"Really? Are we seriously going to do this?" Reese rolled her eyes. "How about before we confirm who's got the bigger dick or smallest vagina, we see what happens with the search. Shall we?"

Officer Clark snorted, trying to stifle a laugh. Agent Olden shot him a dirty look.

"Besides the K9 units," Reese continued. "We will also need to have divers in the water."

"They are already on their way," Agent Wells confirmed. A much more polite manner to his voice.

Emerson tried to smooth things over. "Agent Olden, Agent Wells, I think we're getting off on the wrong foot. Detective Clayton and I are tracking a death row convict that escaped from the state pen. He was to have been executed last night, but that didn't happen. We believe the two cases are connected.

"Exactly," Reese chimed in. "Timothy Cole is a danger to society; we believe he kept his promise to kill the judge."

"It would probably be in our best interest to come up with a plan for sharing information," Lake suggested.

Agent Wells' phone rang, interrupting the conversation. "Yes. Ok. Got it." He shoved the phone back in his pocket. "Well, we have a weapon. The local K9s found it beyond the rocks on the other side of the lake. It's a Kate. Hidden in the tree line, not in the rocks. The perp must have just left it there, but the shell casing is missing."

"Reese, I'll bet that crazy bastard Cole kept it as a souvenir." It pissed Lake off. Cole eluded them once again. He vowed it would be the last time.

"Emerson Lake," Reese said, "let's go find us a psychopath."

CHAPTER 6

"We're here to see the wedding couple that was brought in earlier today. I'm Agent Wells, FBI. This is my partner, Agent Olden." Both presented their shields to the nurse at the fourth-floor desk of Jade Medical Center.

"Right this way. We have them in the same room. They didn't want to be apart. I'm sure you understand. No injuries to either of them, at least not physically." She stopped outside the room where a guard stood watch. "Her wedding gown is still here. We weren't sure where to send it. We were trying desperately to get it off and far away from her so she would stop screaming. We gave them each a mild sedative to calm them down a bit."

Agent Olden gave the guard in front of the hospital room specific instructions. "Do not, under any circumstances, leave the entrance to this room. If you need to eat or take a leak, contact one of us and we will send in a replacement. This is now an FBI investigation."

The guard nodded.

"I want everyone that walks into this room," Agent Olden barked, "or even onto this floor documented. That includes law enforcement, nurses, doctors, relatives, anyone. Understood?"

"Sir," the nurse replied, "we don't have the resources on this floor to track and document all visitors. Can't keep everyone from coming and going."

"Then I want them both moved to a secure location in this hospital. I am sure there is a wing set aside for visiting dignitaries in case of emergencies. Where would you put the President of the United States if something happened?"

The head nurse was now getting pissed at being told what to do on her watch. "Well, that depends on which President, Agent Olden."

Agent Wells snickered at that remark, trying not to, but he just had to.

Olden shot Wells a glare.

Agent Wells cleared his throat. "Maybe someone like Nixon or Reagan. Please do the best you can."

The nurse liked that Agent Wells had a bit of a sense of humor. "I will," she smiled.

"Let's just get this moving," a pissed off Olden ordered as he shoved the door open.

Jennifer and Alessandro lay in their beds, both in hospital gowns, looking like deer in headlights, wanting to run, but frozen in place. Neither knowing what would happen next.

The FBI agents introduced themselves to the couple. "We would like to ask you a few questions. Are you up for it?" Wells asked.

They both nodded in agreement.

"Jennifer, do you know of any threats recently made against your father? Has anyone been hanging around the house that perhaps you didn't recognize? Did he mention he was uncomfortable lately for any reason at all?"

Jennifer Orrick did her best to hide her anger and her tears as she sat facing the window. She turned slowly toward the agents, wiping away her tears, but the vision of her father was just too much to manage, and there were no drugs to relax her, no matter what the nurses told her.

"Agent Olden, are you a father?" she sniffled. "Obviously not," she growled, "or you would not be asking such a fucked-up question? Fathers protect their children. They do not give them things to worry about. Besides, he is a Judge. He put many people away over the years. Does that answer your question? Idiot," she mumbled.

"Jennifer! What the hell is wrong with you? These guys are just trying to help us find out who murdered your dad. Give them a break," Alessandro pleaded. "I'm sorry for her outburst. Jennifer is normally a sweet person, and she would never talk like that. It must be the drugs they gave us."

"Stop it Alessandro! Don't you dare apologize for me. My father is dead!" her voice rising, her fists clenching. "His brains and blood are all over my wedding gown!" She let out a blood-curdling scream. "We're not married! Get out! Get out! You're not my husband! Did you kill him? Did you murder my father?"

The nurse raced into the room. "Leave! All of you. We need to stabilize this young lady before she has a stroke." She hit the call button for help. "I need someone to come in here now and take Mr. Rossi to the adjoining room."

"No!" Alessandro begged. "I want to stay with her; she is not herself. Please let me stay and try to calm her down. This has been an awful shock to us."

An aide appeared in the doorway. "Maybe it would be better if you leave for just a little while." Alessandro reluctantly sat in a wheelchair as they escorted him out of the room.

Agent Olden called for another guard as he followed the groom into the next room. He watched as the nurse tucked the young man into his bed. "Mr. Rossi, we know this is difficult. What do you remember about the ceremony?" Olden asked. "Anything unusual? Anyone out of place that didn't belong there? Anyone on the lake, swimming or in a boat trying to get a glimpse of the ceremony, maybe?"

"No, nothing out of the ordinary. I answered these questions before. It was my wedding day. My focus was on Jennifer." his voice trailed off. "She should be my wife right now, and we should be getting ready for our honeymoon. Shit, I need to make a call to let the resort know we won't be there tomorrow. I also need to contact the air..." Mr. Rossi fell asleep mid-sentence.

"Well, I guess I'm not getting anything more out of him tonight," Olden sighed.

CHAPTER 7

As they drove toward Jade Medical, passing through Pierre, Reese and Emerson could see the Capitol building buzzing with reporters waiting for a statement from the governor

"I hope they have a field day with that arrogant bastard," Reese hissed. "Threatening to take my badge. Who the hell does he think he is? He should be kissing my ass right now for stopping that execution."

"Yikes, that's a lot of anger, little lady," Emerson chuckled.

"Yeah, well, shit happens. I'd like to see him sweat a little for this. He's not the best choice for the office. Not sure how he even got elected."

"You want to stop for coffee or something? I'm worried about you, Reese. Seriously, are you okay?"

"I'm fine. I could use a cocktail though," she joked, "I don't think we could get away with that. Do you?"

"Not today, partner."

Local and national news teams surrounded the hospital when they arrived, looking for anyone that would give them a statement. Emerson Lake was correct. The press would have a field day with the murder of a judge and the escape of a death row prisoner.

As they exited the car and made their way to the hospital entrance, the microphones swarmed them.

"Detectives, can you tell us anything about the couple brought in today? Are they hurt? Do you have any suspects?"

"What about the death row inmate?" another reporter shouted above the din of the crowd.

Emerson placed his hand on the small of Reese's back and guided her quickly through the sea of reporters. "No comment."

CHAPTER 8

"Detectives Clayton and Lake." The two displayed their badges for the nurse at the desk. "We are here to see the bride and groom that were admitted earlier today."

"I remember who you are," the nurse remarked. "I'm sorry, but they are both sedated. They need quiet and rest right now. The FBI agents just left. I think you should hold off on any more questioning until tomorrow."

"We understand. Where are they? I do not see any security guards around. The FBI would never allow them to be left unguarded."

"They are in a private wing, you might say."

Emerson smiled at the nurse. "Thank you for the help. We'll be back in the morning. Let's go Detective Clayton."

"Are you still calling her detective?" the nurse asked with a grin. "I thought for sure it would be *Mrs.* Detective by now. At least that was the scoop on the street that you proposed."

Emerson leaned in toward the nurse's ear, "Not yet. I am still waiting for you."

The woman gave Emerson a big smile, stood and straightened

her white skirt. A rare wardrobe choice these days when most hospital staff wore slouchy scrubs. "Oh, stop it! You know I'm too old for you. Besides, you couldn't handle me," she winked.

"You got that right, young lady," Emerson chuckled. "But you can't blame a guy for trying."

Once outside of the hospital, they headed for a diner nearby. It had been hours since food entered their minds. "The food is always good here," Emerson said, rubbing his belly.

"That's if you can get past the grease stuck on the menu," Reese added. "It's certainly not five-star dining."

"Well, I wasn't planning on getting lucky tonight anyway, after I had to postpone our little getaway."

"Emerson Lake, you idiot. You still had a chance until that remark." She tossed the menu at his chest like a Frisbee.

CHAPTER 9

Jennifer Orrick awoke with a terrible headache. Drug related; she was sure of that.

"Well, good morning," the nurse cheerfully greeted her. "How about we open the curtains and let a little sunlight in here? Breakfast is on its way up. Do you want to take a shower before breakfast? Or we can wait till you're finished eating."

"I'm not starving yet, so probably shower first. I have no clothes here."

"We will get you a clean gown." The nurse regretted her choice of words the second they fell out of her mouth. "I didn't mean..."

Before the nurse could finish apologizing, Jennifer went into a wild rage. "You bitch! Where is my wedding gown? What did you do with it? Where is my husband? What did you do with him?"

"Miss Orrick, please calm down." She rang for help.

"My name is not Orrick, it's... Oh my god, what do I call myself? What's my name? Who am I?"

The door swung open as the staff and guard at the door

rushed in to help.

"Miss please," the officer pleaded. "Let these people help you."

The male and female aides each took an arm, gently easing Jennifer into the overstuffed leather chair. "You're going to be fine," the young male attendant reassured. "My name is Roy. Can you tell me yours?"

"Jennifer."

"Take your time. Breathe. Would you like a glass of water, Jennifer?" the female aide asked.

"Um, yeah. I mean, yes, I would."

"There. All better now." Roy said, smiling at her. "Now, let's get you cleaned up and ready for the day. Is that okay with you?"

"Yes, will you help me?"

Roy looked at the floor nurse. "Evelyn, is it all right if I help?"

"Of course, I'll help you shower if that's comfortable for you and then Roy can help you get into your clean pajamas."

Jennifer nodded.

The guard turned to return to his post. "Anything else you need, I'll be right outside this door, okay?"

"Thank you." Jennifer whispered. "I am sorry if I am causing trouble. I'm so confused."

"It's okay, young lady."

CHAPTER 10

The FBI was first to arrive at Jade Medical Center later that morning. Detectives Clayton and Lake were right behind them. Olden was not exactly happy to have them in his space.

"Agent Olden, Miss Orrick is asking to see her fiancée." The guard on duty said as all four approached the door to Jennifer's room.

"Look," Reese commented. "This is a lot of law for anyone to handle. Why don't Lake and I check in at the nurse's station, see how things went last night, while you and Wells question them both. After you finish, then Detective Lake and I will ask our own set of questions. We can meet or text after, to swap results."

"Sounds good to me," Olden said. "I'll take the groom, Wells, you take the bride."

"Good thinking, Reese," Wells winked at her.

Reese showed her credentials to the nurse at the desk. "How was everything last night with Ms. Orrick and Mr. Rossi?"

"Says here," the nurse replied, looking down at the chart, "everything was quiet."

"Thank you." Lake said to the nurse. "Reese, let's grab a cup of coffee and give the agents a little more time with the couple. When they are done, I'll take the judge's daughter. You check in on Alessandro."

The nurse notified detective Lake when the agents had left the rooms.

The questioning began.

"Mr. Rossi," Reese asked, "do you remember anything you may have seen yesterday, before, or during the ceremony? Anything unusual? Think hard. This is especially important."

"Of course, it's important, Jesus. I'm not an idiot, Detective. No, for the umpteenth time, I saw nothing. I'm sorry for being so rude to all of you, but my eyes were on my bride to be, who now is acting out. I think she could deal with all of this if we were at home. When can I leave here? I want to take Jennifer home. I want to be married to my Jennifer. I want this to be over, Detective Clayton."

"Our patient needs to rest. Detective, you can come back later." His nurse helped Alessandro up from the recliner and back into bed.

"Just one more question, Mr. Rossi. What was your relationship like with the judge?"

The machines attached to Alessandro Rossi began to beep rapidly. His nurse glared at Reese. "I said it is time to leave. Now!"

Reese complied. She turned the corner into the waiting room and was greeted by the FBI Agents and Emerson. She could tell by the looks on their faces, something was wrong. "What is it?"

"We have new information." Wells said closing the door. "It appears you are no longer needed in this case."

"Why is that?" Reese asked biting her lip.

"The prints on the murder weapon do not match those on file for Timothy Cole."

CHAPTER 11

"It has been a pleasure working with you both," Wells shook the detective's hands.

"Same here," Detective Lake responded, noticing it was a rather long handshake between Reese and Agent Wells. One of those where Wells' left hand cradled his over Reese's.

"Have a safe trip back to Cromwell." Wells smiled.

Reese and Emerson headed to a café around the corner from the hospital. Reese desperately needed coffee before she made the call to Captain Brown.

"Well, that was interesting," she said as they grabbed a table by the window. "I could have sworn it would be Timothy Cole's prints on that gun."

"Me too. Let's call the captain."

Captain Brown was just as shocked as everyone else that the prints did not match the escaped convict. "There is no reason for you to stay in Jade. Let the FBI handle the Judge's murder investigation. I need you back in Cromwell. We still need to find Tim, but I highly doubt he is still in Jade, or if he ever was."

"Understood Captain, but before we return, we would like to

question the couple again. We really did not get a lot of answers from either of them. Reese and I thought it best if we interview both of them together this time, instead of separately. The judge's daughter seems to fly into a rage anytime she's talking about her groom. She says things about Rossi that are puzzling. For example, she asked him if he killed her father. Why would she say such things about a man she was moments away from marrying? Something doesn't add up. Maybe it doesn't have anything to do with Cole, but let us just close this loop and then we'll head back."

"Okay Lake. But I want you both back here later today unless you come up with new information. Got it?"

"Yes, Captain. Thank you."

"Lake, I'll contact Agent Olden and let him know we're going back to Cromwell later today, but we want one more shot at interviewing Rossi and Orrick before we leave. We promised to keep them in the loop."

Once again, both detectives arrived at the hospital, this time determined to get answers.

"Nurse, would you mind having Mr. Rossi join us in Ms. Orrick's room? We would like to speak with both, if you don't mind?" Lake was being exceptionally respectful.

"Of course."

"Good morning, Jennifer," Reese smiled as she peeked in the room of the once radiant bride. "How are you feeling today? I'm detective Clayton, this is my partner Detective Lake."

"I could be a lot better. How soon can I get out of here? I feel like I am a prisoner."

"You are not a prisoner; the doctors just want to make sure

you are well enough to go home. You have been through a great deal, Jennifer, much more than anyone should have to go through."

•••

The guard knocked on the door and entered Jennifer's room. "Detectives, could I see one of you in the hall for a moment?"

"I'll go, Reese." Detective Lake followed the guard into the hallway.

"Detective, Mr. Rossi is not in his room and the guard is no longer there either. Don't ask because I have no clue where they are, or how they got out of here without being seen. This is a secure wing."

"Well, obviously not that fucking secure! Contact the FBI agents and let them know what is going on. Lock down this hospital. I want a full search *now*! I'm contacting the locals to put out a BOLO on both. Do you know the guard that was on duty last night? I'll need a name and a photo."

"No, he wasn't one of ours. We thought he was local PD."

"Since when does the FBI not check the credentials of a guard on a secured floor? You make that call now, and if you move three feet from this door, I will have your pension. Got it?" Emerson went back into Jennifer's room.

"Detective, what's going on?" asked Reese. She could see the concerned look on Lake's face. "Where is Alessandro?"

Lake ignored Reese's questions and strode over to the bedside. "Jennifer, when was the last time you saw Alessandro?"

"During the night, maybe two, three o'clock in the morning.

He came in to kiss me good night. Why? What's wrong? Is he okay?"

"No more holding your hand, Ms. Orrick. We need answers. Now! Why were you accusing your fiancée of killing your father? Do you think he had a hand in all of this? Your beloved Alessandro and his guard are missing. Would you possibly know anything about this, Jennifer?"

Jennifer propped herself up on the bed, straightening her hospital gown and then fluffing her pillows before responding to the detective. Her voice taking on a more enlightened tone. "I think I should have my attorney present if you are going to treat me like a criminal, Detective Lake."

"I think that might be the smartest thing you have said since being brought in here."

Lake tilted his head, motioning Reese toward the door. Once out of the room, he pulled Reese over toward the lounge area. "We have a fake guard watching over Rossi and a bride that does not want to cooperate. She knows more than she lets on."

"What makes you think she knows something?"

"I didn't," he said, "until she just mentioned the attorney. Did you see how her demeanor changed dramatically? From scared little girl to defensive smug woman. I am going to take a wild guess here and say Daddy's big bucks had a lot to do with his murder. Usually does."

"Jesus, do you really think she and her husband put a hit out on her own father?"

"Anything is possible Reese, especially when money is involved."

"Ok, let's see what else we can find out about this Rossi family, and the judge's daughter. I'll call the captain and let her know we may be late."

"Hold that thought, Reese. Our FBI friends have just arrived. Let's fill them in."

Wells was the first to react. "I knew there was something going on with these two. On the way over, I had my team run a search on Alessandro Rossi. Turns out there is a mob boss on the radar, same name, from New York City. Involved with gun running and drugs. Kind of low level on the list, but if they murdered a judge, it would bring their status up in the syndicate."

"Thanks for the help, detectives," Olden once again offered his hand to both detectives.

"You're welcome," Reese responded. "Thanks for letting us tag along to see if there was a connection with our case. Good luck." Wells gave a nod to both of them.

The detectives headed toward the exit.

"Let's go find our escape artist, Reese" Emerson said. "Cole has to be somewhere between here and Cromwell."

CHAPTER 12

"How about you stay at my apartment tonight, Reese? By the time we get back to Cromwell, it will be late."

"No, I think it will be easier if you drop me at my place. That way, I'll have everything I need in the morning. I'll pick you up around eight and bring some bagels and coffee."

The drive back didn't feel as long as the way there. Arriving in Cromwell, Emerson pulled up to Reese's place and kissed her passionately. "I'm sorry my original plan for the romantic getaway didn't work out."

"We can do it another time," she smiled at him.

He walked her to the door. Kissed her again. Watched as she let herself into the building and took the stairs instead of the elevator, as she had done many times before. Then drove off after he saw the lights come on and she blew a kiss to him through the picture window.

The moment Reese closed the drapes, the hair on the back of her neck stood on end and an eerie feeling swept over her. It felt like someone was in the room or had been there. She removed her service pistol from its holster and slowly began turning on all the lights and checking the windows. Everything was secure.

"That was weird. I'm just tired." Shaking it off, Reese changed into her pajamas, brushed her teeth, and fell into bed. It didn't take long for sleep to come.

The alarm startled Reese awake. She had been in such a deep sleep. She rolled over, rubbing her eyes, trying to knock the cobwebs out when she realized she had just an hour to get ready, pickup breakfast and meet Emerson. She stepped out of her pajamas and into the shower. The warm water felt good pouring over her body, but as she reached for her loofah, she sensed she wasn't alone again. She stopped and stood still, listening intently for any audible clue that someone was there. She quickly snapped the shower curtain back, water droplets flying all over the bathroom, but she was alone.

"What the hell is wrong with me?"

She dried off, got dressed and left the apartment, still not able to shake off that creepy feeling. She knew she wouldn't be staying there tonight, at least not without Emerson.

As she drove down her street on the way to the bagel shop, it hit her like a ton of bricks. Before she had left for the trip to Jade, she clearly recalled having burned her breakfast and cracking a window open to air out the apartment then forgetting to close it. But when she checked the windows last night, they were all locked.

"Shit!" she gasped.

CHAPTER 13

"Welcome back, detectives," the desk sergeant greeted them at the Cromwell P.D. "Crazy couple of days, huh?"

"Thanks. Every day is a challenge," Emerson was just making small talk, but wanted to be quick about it without being rude. "Hey, is the captain in?"

"Yes, I'll let her know you're on the way up."

The new layout of the precinct was much more modern. The captain's office was now sitting up in a loft. It had a large glass wall along the front and was solid brick along the back, except for one arched window that overlooked the street. Remote powered electric shades provided privacy when needed. There was a small conference table in the corner, and her desk, at her request, was simple oak. The rest of the office was just as basic.

"Welcome back. You both look tired," remarked the captain. "I have a job for you that needs to be tended to right away. There was a break-in at the Bank of Cromwell late last night. The media has not gotten wind of it, not yet anyway. The odd thing about it, it wasn't your typical bank robbery."

"What does that mean not typical?" Emerson asked.

"As far as we can tell, nothing is missing, but it appears someone tampered with a safe deposit box."

"Just messed with it?" Reese chimed in. "The suspect didn't take anything. Why would someone not take the contents or the entire box?"

Emerson asked, "Who's safe deposit box?"

"That's the odd thing. Someone named John Tenison. I spoke personally with the family of Mr. Tennison. He has dementia and his children have the power of attorney. They can't fathom why or what anyone would want from their father's safe deposit box. They said all it contains is their late mother's diamond ring, his last will and testament, and the deed to the house. Nothing of any real value. And it was all still there. The family is terribly upset, of course, and wants answers, otherwise they threatened to contact the press. They're also hiring an attorney."

"Didn't the security cameras pick up anything?" Reese asked.

"The person who broke in was on camera. He had on what appeared to be a police uniform."

"Shit," Emerson grunted, "just what we need. There isn't enough trouble between the public and law enforcement these days. Now they're going to portray us as thieves. We need to get a search going and find out more about this Tennison guy A.S.A.P. There's got to be something that connects him to this break in."

"And don't forget," the captain reminded them, "you two also still need to find our escapee. How was he able to escape a state prison without a trace?"

"We're not sure, Captain, but I suspect he had help from the inside," Reese theorized. "Like I told you over the phone;

we need to investigate that prison. I certainly didn't like the attitude of the warden. If nothing else, they need a better procedure for executions. How do you not confirm the right person is being executed? That guy they had on the table with a needle in his arm has got one hell of a case against the state. I'm guessing he's got himself an excellent lawyer by now and will be out sooner than expected."

"Well, you two certainly have your plates full. Keep me informed. Now get to work."

Lake started a background check on Tennison. "No outstanding warrants, and this Tennison guy isn't young, he's an old man," he said.

"How is it possible there is nothing on this Tennison guy, not even a parking ticket? Emerson, do you think we are looking at this all wrong? Suppose just for a minute, I know this is a long shot, but what if this "officer" that broke into the bank was looking for the wrong safe deposit box? A case of mistaken identity. Just look at the numbers. 211 vs. 277, simple mistake."

"It's not the craziest idea I've ever heard, Reese, but here's something else. This guy has not renewed his driver's license in the last eight years. I'm taking a wild guess that he's too old to even drive."

Reese pulled up the video footage to take a closer look at the suspect. "Um Emerson, I don't think that's a police uniform. Take a look." She swiveled her monitor in his direction.

"Holy shit, that's a corrections uniform!"

"I'm contacting the warden. We need to review the video footage from the prison the night Cole escaped. I'll bet you there is a guard at the prison missing a uniform."

CHAPTER 14

"Hello, Detective Clayton. I was actually just about to call your captain."

"Really, Warden Daniels? About what, if I may ask?" Reese knew she was going to have to play nice if she had any hope of getting that video. She quietly put the call on speaker and signaled to Lake to come over and listen in.

"We came across the body of a missing guard. His uniform removed and replaced with an orange jumpsuit."

"That's good information," she replied as she jotted BINGO on a post it note and showed it to Emerson.

Emerson jotted a question on the post it for Reese to ask.

"What about the prisoner that was sent to the infirmary? Did he remember anything? Did you show him a photo of Cole?"

"What kind of question is that? Of course, we questioned the other prisoner. I was just going to tell you he identified Cole as the guard that pulled him out of his cell. You know this is not my first rodeo, Detective. You had better check your tone of voice when speaking with me. I know people in high places in this state and if you want to keep your job, you little princess, then you better treat me with the respect I deserve. Got it?"

"You listen to me, *Warden Daniels*. You ever threaten me with shit like that again, I will have your fucking head on a platter. You just broke every conduct code imaginable. Now we can either work together on this case, or apart. The decision is yours. What's it going to be?"

Click.

"Guess I got my answer."

Emerson laughed, "Whoa, those were some mighty enormous balls, lady."

"There are even bigger ones where they came from. What an asshole!"

"Well, at least we know it was Tim Cole that broke into the bank. He probably just forgot that the judge who sentenced him was from Jade, not Cromwell."

"Emerson, do you think Cole was looking for the judge's address?"

"Possible. Probably shocked the hell out of him when he found an old man who didn't know if he was on foot or horseback. I'm sure Cole was in and out. You know how creepy he is. Gets in and out of places unnoticed."

"Yes, I certainly remember how sneaky he is. Speaking of which, Emerson, we need to talk. In private."

CHAPTER 15

"Sweetheart." Reese turned to face the man she was going to marry. "I have to tell you something."

"Jesus, Reese, what's the matter? You're as pale as a ghost, and that's not a good look for you."

"Last night when you dropped me off at my place," she paused.

"Yeah, what about it?"

"I think there may have been someone in my apartment."

"What? Why the hell didn't you call me? What happened? Did you see who it was?"

"I checked everywhere. I didn't see anyone and believe me; I checked every nook and cranny. But I still had that eerie feeling that someone was there, or maybe they had been there and left before I got home. Even this morning when I showered, I still had that creepy feeling."

"Damn it, Reese! What were you thinking?"

"Just listen to me, please? When I was on my way to pick you up this morning, I remembered that when I searched my place last night, all of my windows were closed and locked."

"And how is that problematic?"

"When we left to go to Cole's execution, I left one window open a crack to let some fresh air in. Not the window near the fire escape. The one on the opposite side of the building, in the alley. It was closed when I got home. Emerson, it was closed," she repeated as a chill ran up her spine. "Someone was in there."

"Are you sure?"

"I'm telling you; someone was in my apartment."

"You won't be staying there without me, that's for sure. Not until we find out what the hell is going on. It's not as though we haven't had threats before. That comes with the job. But this guy is a psychopath. We need to find him, and fast. We should also notify the captain. But first, let's get someone over to your apartment to search for fingerprints."

"Emerson, we made a mistake, assuming Cole murdered the judge. We should know better than that. Now he's got such a big head start and we're stuck playing catch up. We need a new plan of attack. Step 1: There's already a BOLO out for Tim Cole in Jade, but we need to get one out here in Cromwell, too."

"Agreed."

"Step 2: We need to figure out how Cole is getting around. He can't just be on foot. Did he steal a car?" Her eyes widened. "Or a cab? Jesus Emerson, we know he's killed a cab driver before."

"Shit. You're right. This sick fuck wouldn't think twice about doing it again. When I get the BOLO started, I'll make sure they send his photo to all the regional transportation companies. Maybe we'll get lucky, and someone will recognize him."

"Ok, sounds good. Step 3: We need to visit Mr. Tennison.

Talk to his caregiver and his children. See if they've noticed anyone out of the ordinary in the area. Anyone fitting Cole's description."

"I'll get the BOLO going and meet you at the car."

Reese punched the Tennison's address into Google Maps on her phone, slipped into the driver's seat and started the engine.

Emerson approached the driver's side. "What do you think you're doing?"

"I'm driving this time. You had all the fun driving to Jade," Reese quipped.

"Deal! I'll take a nap." He hopped in the passenger side and reclined the seat.

"Bullshit Emerson Lake. We still have a lot of work to go over. Plus, at some point, we need to plan our own wedding. We don't even have a date set. Maybe after this case is over, we can take a couple of weeks off and head to the beach. Give us some time to figure out our plans."

The only thing Reese heard from her dear Emerson Lake was the sound of his snoring.

"You son of a bitch."

She didn't notice that he opened one eye and smiled at her.

Reese's phone rang. It was the captain. She put it on speaker loud enough to make her partner jump. "Yes Captain, we're just on our way to the Tennison residence to see if they noticed anyone hanging around the house."

"Okay, good. When you finish up there, I want you to go to the Cromwell mall. Someone just used a debit card at the ATM in the Big C department store there. The name on the card is Alessandro Rossi."

"We're heading that way now, Captain. We'll make that visit to the Tennison residence later." Reese disconnected the call, flicked the switch for the flashing red lights and stepped on the gas, throwing her partner back in his seat.

"Geez, do you think I could get a little warning there, hotshot?"

"What did you want me to do? Stop and put you in a child's car seat in the back? You're damn lucky I didn't launch your ass right through the windshield."

"Reese, I heard every word you said before. I was just messing with you, sweetheart. And by the way, it's not nice to call my mom a bitch."

They both laughed, and Emerson leaned over and kissed her cheek. "We will plan our wedding, I promise," he said.

Uniformed officers were at every entrance to the parking lots, the inside of the mall, and Big C department store when the detectives arrived.

"Detectives." A female uniformed officer from their precinct approached them. "We contacted the bank that operates this ATM. They will get us the footage from the camera. I highly doubt Rossi is still in here, but a complete search of the mall, as you can see, is underway, much to the dismay of all the shoppers. Of course, no witnesses so far or description of anyone using the ATM. Why does no one pay attention to their surroundings anymore?"

"Beats the shit out of me. Thanks, Officer Brennen, excellent job." Reese liked this new officer. She was feisty, and if people were smart, they wouldn't mess with her.

CHAPTER 16

Timothy Cole was walking on a dirt road that led out of town. Whistling a tune, talking to himself. Getting no responses. A black Lincoln Town Car sped up next to him, kicking up a cloud of dust.

"Cole?" asked the man driving.

"Who wants to know?"

"I do," came a voice from the rear seat. "Get in. We need to talk."

Cole slipped inside. As soon as he closed the door, the driver took off.

"Look at me Cole. You said you could finish the job and get the hell out of this state. My guard told you if you could find the address of the judge's private residence, we would look the other way. We got you out of prison and saved your sorry ass from death. One job and you clearly fucked it up. And here you are still roaming around Cromwell where anyone can find you. What are you still doing here?"

"Hey! I got myself out of prison. That guard, that asshole of a guard, would not be doing those things to me ever again."

"True, you may have gotten yourself out of that cell and off death row, but there is no way you could have just walked through the front gates without my help."

"You're pissed at me?" Cole stared icily at him. "You got what you wanted anyway." Tim gritted his teeth. "I'm the one who waited all this time to kill that fuck." Tim turned toward the window. "I wanted to watch him squirm as I put the knife to his throat. Just like my father did." The corner of his mouth turned up into a disturbing smile as he relived the moment. "I wanted to see his eyes bulge a little, hear him beg for forgiveness for putting me away somewhere...where they hurt me. Just like my ole man put me in that bad place." Tim's eyes darted back and forth "The blood oozed right out him when I slit his throat. The warm blood felt nice on the cold blade when I wiped it with my bare hands." He licked his lips. "I should have been the one to see the judge slowly die. I should've…"

"Snap out of it!" He slapped Tim hard across the face. "We got him all right, no thanks to you imbecile. One of my men hired a hitman. I couldn't trust you to get the job done."

Tim rubbed his cheek. "I don't like being called names," he growled. "And I don't enjoy being in a room with gray walls either. That won't ever happen again." Cole pulled a knife from his belt, leaned over the driver's seat. "Stop the car!"

The driver hit the brakes, tossing Cole backward. He regained his balance and with the swiftness of a cheetah on the hunt, lunged and slit the driver's throat. He reached for the door handle of the car, opened it, and pushed the driver out onto the ground. Cole wiped the blood off the steering wheel as he climbed into the front seat and regained control of the vehicle.

"Where to?" His dark eyes stared into the rearview mirror at the man in the back seat. The man responsible for everything related to the state prison.

Cole's passenger, scared enough to piss his pants, jumped from the moving vehicle as they approached town. Cole sped away, singing along to a country tune playing on the radio.

CHAPTER 17

News 7 Sioux Falls South Dakota

Breaking News

ALESSANDRO ROSSI MURDERED

The future son-in-law of the late Judge John Orrick was found murdered. The body of Alessandro Rossi was discovered by runners along County Highway 102, three miles from the Sioux Reservation, leading out of Cromwell, South Dakota. Stay tuned to News 7 for the latest on this developing story.

Officer Carly Brennen had returned to her normal position on the front desk at Cromwell P.D. She preferred being on the street, but at least her foot was in the door, a step closer to her new career. Officer Carly Brennen was a transfer from Sioux Falls who had been with the department almost a year. Mostly on the desk, but with aspirations of being on the street. She loved the job.

Captain Brown, upon entering the precinct, began giving orders.

"Officer Brennen, get the Governor on the line. I need to meet with him A.S.A.P."

"Yes, Captain. Should I tell him what this is regarding?"

"No, I'll take care of that. Also, get Lake and Clayton on the phone. Actually, I want to speak with them first."

"Yes, Captain, right away."

Carly patched the detectives through to the captain's office as soon as she got them on the line.

"Captain, this is much bigger than originally thought," Reese advised. "I still think this goes up the ladder, if you will. I think the Warden is involved and possibly the Governor. They both had a problem, with me in particular, especially after I told them they had the wrong guy on the table."

"That's what I want the two of you to investigate. This is still under FBI authority, so caution is vital here. Governor Cramer is notorious for his casino dealings, I've even seen him on the Reservation a few times, and that could very well be a factor in all of this."

"Meaning?" Lake asked.

"Money. Everything is always connected to the almighty dollar."

The Reservation police department handled law enforcement activities and the casino was off limits, in part anyway, to local law enforcement. It was an unwritten agreement, but being Lakota Sioux herself, the captain had some unique insights and privileges.

"I want the two of you to find out just what Judge Orrick may have had in common with our governor. We also need to find out if the judge's daughter is involved."

"Captain, when we met with Jennifer Orrick at the hospital," Emerson said, "she was like Jekyll and Hyde. One minute she portrayed this hurt little girl lost without her father and the next she was a nasty bridezilla accusing her fiancé of killing her father. I suppose the stress of a devastating personal loss could cause anyone to act out, but I'm not so sure in this case."

"I'll contact Agent Wells." Reese said, "see if they have found anything new in the case. They can clue us in on the judge's daughter. Emerson went after her pretty hard, just before we left Jade."

"No need Reese, I already contacted the FBI myself," Captain Brown said. "Agent Olden claimed they had nothing to hold Jennifer on and told her as soon as she felt better, she could leave the hospital. Now that was before the love of her life died."

"What about our escapee, Captain?" Lake interjected. "He obviously has a few bucks now to buy clothes and food and possibly a way to leave the state. Assuming he is the one using Rossi's debit card at ATMs. I doubt he's even still in the area or even in the state. He must know the entire country will be looking for him. He is smart enough to lie low."

"Captain, I disagree with Lake. I think Tim is still in Cromwell,"

"Do you have a reason for this assumption, Detective Clayton?"

"No actual proof, but I think he may have been in my apartment sometime yesterday. And if not him, someone else."

"Captain, we already sent forensics over to the apartment to search for fingerprints. Nothing is missing, as far as she can tell, anyway." Lake added.

"I'll send an officer to watch your place in case your hunch is correct. In the meantime, find somewhere else to stay, detective."

"I'm already on it, Captain."

Captain Brown shook her head as she hung up. Having an on-the-job relationship isn't prohibited, but she did not approve. They were playing with fire.

"Captain Brown," Officer Brennen interrupted, "I tried to reach Governor Cramer. His secretary says he is out of the office, and she will have him contact you as soon as he returns. She didn't say how long that would be."

"Thank you. I'll be back shortly, Officer Brennen. If he calls while I am gone, which I highly doubt, patch me in."

CHAPTER 18

"Hi Donald, have you seen Will in here today? I've been looking everywhere for him."

Donald had been the hotel's concierge and Casino host since it opened. His job was to keep the high-roller elite happy at all costs. If they were happy in their suites, more money crossed the poker tables. A win for all.

"No, not today anyway," Donald replied. "Is there anything I can help you with?"

"No. I just wanted to see if he was available for lunch, that's all. Thanks anyway." She turned to exit the casino.

"Hold on a minute, let me check again." Donald picked up a cell phone and hit just one button. He whispered a few words then hung up. "Mr. Cramer will see you now, Kim."

"Thanks Donald. I owe you one." She winked at him and headed for the elevator.

She had changed into a short skirt and high heels before heading to the Reservation Casino.

Governor Cramer opened the door to his suite and politely ushered Kim into his lavishly furnished penthouse abode.

"Thank you," she purred, moving closer to him. "What do you have for me?"

"That depends on what you have for me, my dear. Come here and tell me what it is you want, and I will oblige, like always."

"I need a shipment of assault rifles, Kates. Preferably .338 caliber. Delivered to this address," she said handing him a slip of paper."

"That is a tall order. It will take a while to get together. The cost alone."

"Do not hand me that bullshit. I know better," she stared directly into his eyes.

He knew she would not back down. "Okay, if I do this for you, what do I get?" He looked her up and down seductively.

She smiled playfully as he threw her on the luxurious bed and took her in every way he could. When he finished, he remarked, "I don't recall you being this good."

She refrained from saying what she wanted. Instead, she went to shower, got dressed, and returned to the bedroom.

"So, when can I expect the shipment?"

"Frankly, I doubt this request is possible, Kim. FBI agents and a couple of detectives are watching me. So, I'm sorry, my little Indian Princess," he grinned smugly, "maybe next time.

Kim's body tensed.

"You can let yourself out." He motioned toward the door. "I need to rest. I have a busy night." He rolled over on his side and closed his eyes.

Kim reached around the back of her skirt and pulled a switchblade from a leather sheath.

CHAPTER 19

"Emerson, I need to make a stop at the store before we get back to your place. We need to buy some decent food to cook. I am not eating lunchmeat and potato chips. I know that's your staple, but it's not mine."

Before Emerson could respond, his phone rang. "Lake here. What can I do for you, Agent Olden?"

"We have three print matches from a black Lincoln Town Car we found in a parking garage at Sioux Falls Regional Airport. They match the prison warden Steven Daniels, Alessandro Rossi, and your #1 escapee, Timothy Cole.

"How did you match the prints to Rossi so fast?"

"Rossi's passport," Olden confirmed. "It appears he was planning a honeymoon in Paris or perhaps a getaway of a different kind. So, the judges' murder and Cole's escape seem to be connected after all."

"We've thought there was link right from the start. Fast work Olden. I doubt Cole is going to fly anywhere though, too risky. He is smarter than you think. My partner and I still think he is back here in Cromwell. Have you been able to have a chat with the bride-to-be?"

"That's the other reason for this call, Detective. We've had a tail on her since she left the hospital. She was last seen entering the home of someone from your precinct. Someone named Carly Brennen."

Reese had been listening to the call on speaker and jumped in. "We will get right on that one, Agent."

"Hello detective," Agent Wells spoke up. "How are you?"

"Just fine, Michael. Yourself?"

"Good, Reese, I'm good. See if your captain can put a man on her. We'll pull our guy. Track her every move."

"Got it. We will let you know what we come up with."

Lake ended the call. "Since when are we on a first name basis with the FBI, Reese?"

"More flies with honey...*Honey*," she winked. "Actually, I shouldn't have even dignified that question with a response. Wait, is my fiancé jealous?" Reese nudged him lovingly in the arm.

"No! Let's just stay on task, shall we?"

"Fine. I'll let it go...for now. Really, Carly Brennen? How would the judge's daughter even know her? I suppose they might be close in age. Perhaps they hang around in the same circles."

"They could have gone to school together, Reese."

"It's possible, but if they were friends why wasn't Brennan at the wedding?"

"Who knows? I think we should pay Carly a little unannounced home visit. If Jennifer Orrick shows up there again, we can question them together."

"Good idea. See if someone in records can do us a favor and get her address. I'll drive."

Lake made the call and jotted down an address. "Got it!"

The static of the police radio crackled as a 911 operator dispatched a call for Fire and Police to respond to a fire in progress at an apartment building on the corner of Quail and Connors.

"Oh shit!"

"What's wrong?"

"Step on it, Reese! That's Carly's building."

CHAPTER 20

"Captain Brown, I still haven't been able to reach the Governor," Officer Brennen informed the captain when she returned to the station. "His office claims he is attending meetings regarding some bill that's coming up for a vote. That's all his secretary would say."

"I figured he wouldn't want to speak to me. He knows enough to be unavailable to anyone after this execution fiasco."

"I doubt I would want to speak to anyone either, Captain. That's not exactly a feather in his cap." Her private cell rang. "This is Carly Brennen. Holy shit!" she hurriedly grabbed her belongings nearly tripping over her desk chair. "Captain, my building is on fire. I need to go."

"Of course, Go! I'll put someone else on the desk. Keep me updated."

As officer Brennen pulled up to her apartment building, detectives Clayton and Lake were there to greet her, along with Cromwell fire department and other emergency responders.

"What is going on, Detectives? Why are you here?"

"Because Emerson always wanted to be a firefighter and when

the alert came over the radio, we were nearby, so he insisted we join the cavalry. Seriously, though," Reese continued. "The fire seems to be contained in the basement, mainly storage boxes and some electrical wire damage. It's under control, but the fire department will investigate what caused it." Reese was playing the good cop.

"That still doesn't tell me why the two of you are at my apartment, detective? Again, what is going on?"

"Well, we were actually already on our way over to see you when we heard the call go out over the radio."

"I'm working today. Why didn't you just come to the station? And now that I think about it, how did you even know where I live Detective?"

"We're detectives Carly. Finding people is kind of what we do for a living," Reese smiled.

"Look, Officer Brennen, the FBI has been tailing Jennifer Orrick, and they saw her entering your building yesterday. They asked us to check it out," Lake said.

"Wow, so instead of coming to me directly, you sneak around behind my back illegally getting my home address, treating me like I'm some kind of criminal. You know I'm an officer of the law too, right? We work on the same side."

"So, you didn't go to school with Jennifer or maybe meet her through friends?" Reese continued.

"Look, I don't know her personally. What I know is only through the case the two of you are working on. What does she have to do with this fire? Damn it, detectives, we're on the same fucking team. I work with you, not against you. For the last time, tell me what the fuck is going on here, or my next call will be to the FBI. Maybe they can tell me."

"For the last time, the FBI is curious how Jennifer knew where you lived, and why she would show up here," Lake informed her. "They asked us to keep an eye out to see if she would return."

"You know, all you had to do was come to me directly to ask for my address and any other questions you may have had. Not sneak around behind my back, like I am a criminal. This is bull-shit! Do I need to notify my union representative?" Carly took out her phone and dialed the captain. "Hello Captain Brown, were you aware detectives Lake and Clayton were investigating me?"

"Boy Reese," Lake whispered, "she's got guts talking to us like that. I like her. Anyone else would be shaking in their boots by now."

"I like her too. She's smart. Let's just keep our ears and eyes open. One never knows."

"Officer," the captain replied, "tell Clayton and Lake I would like to see them in my office after you check your apartment. I want you here as well. If you feel the need for representation, invite them along."

"They can hear you, Captain. I have you on speaker. Thank you."

As she hung up, the fire chief approached. "Chief, when can I get into my apartment to see if there is any damage?"

"It appears the fire was caused by faulty wiring, ma'am. It's all clear to go inside."

As Carly continued chatting with the fire chief, Reese whis-pered to Emerson, "Hey, back off a bit. Let me handle this." Emerson nodded.

"Carly, is it ok if I go with you into your apartment just in case someone has been in there and you were not aware of it? For your own safety."

"I think I can take care of myself, detective. But I have a feeling you're not going to let this go, so knock yourself out if you want to come on up. I don't have a clue what you think you might find, but I have nothing, and I mean nothing, to hide."

Lake and Clayton weren't so sure about the faulty wiring, more like someone destroying papers that were not for public viewing was more likely.

Once inside, Carly looked around, going room to room. Nothing seemed out of place. Reese followed, not wanting to invade their newest officer's space, but also wanting to see any telltale signs. Signs that Brennen might not be telling the truth about knowing Jennifer Orrick. Reese noticed how nicely decorated the apartment appeared to be. Nothing out of place either. "You have a lovely home, officer Brennen," Reese said and meaning it.

"Stop, Detective. Do you smell that? That sweet odor?"

"No, not really. All I smell is the smoke from downstairs."

"Come over here, next to me. Now, can you smell it?"

"Yes, but it just smells like perfume to me."

"Exactly, detective. I don't wear perfume. I don't even use scented soaps. Unless one of the firefighters is a woman, and I did not see any, then I think you might be right, detective Clayton. Someone was in here. Why the hell would somebody break into my place? Better yet, how did they break in? Shit, the door was unlocked. I assumed the building manager unlocked it for the fire department, but maybe not. We need forensics to check for prints, detective. Now, before anyone else touches anything. We also need to find out which firefighters were up here."

"Carly, do you notice anything missing? Credit cards or bank statements? Cash? Anything that could be used for identification, like a passport?"

"I have a passport, but that's in a safe deposit box at the Bank of Cromwell. I used it when I took a trip to Paris before I got this job. A gift from my parents for being hired at the Cromwell P.D."

CHAPTER 21

The detectives and Officer Brennen entered Captain Brown's office and took a seat at the conference table. No union rep.

"Let's start with you, Detective Clayton. What is the reason for the visit to Officer Brennen's apartment?"

Reese recounted the events of the FBI tail on Jennifer Orrick and the connection to Officer Brennen's apartment. "Captain, we don't have any reason to believe that officer Brennen has anything to do with the events of this case. We would, however, like to accompany her to the bank to see if her passport is still in her safe deposit box."

"Are you serious, Detective? Do you really believe I would lie about that?"

"Absolutely not Carly. We just need to verify that it wasn't stolen. If that's ok with you. If you like, contact your union rep or an attorney. We are fine with either or both. What do you think? Do you trust us?"

Carly softened. "I do trust you; we are a team at this precinct. But I also have to cover my ass here. I'd like to have representation and Captain Brown present. I worked too damn hard to get where I am today not to protect myself."

"I told you, partner," Reese whispered to Emerson, "she is smart." Then she replied to Carly. "That is perfectly fine with us. Captain, are you in?"

"Officer, get your rep on the phone," the captain ordered. "Tell him we will meet him at the bank in an hour. We need to make this happen fast before they close."

The four of them jumped into one of the squad cars. Captain Brown drove. Carly calling shotgun.

They pulled in front of the bank. As they exited the car, all you could smell was the pizzeria on the same block. "Boy, I could go for a slice," Emerson inhaled the scent of marinara sauce hanging in the air.

"Me too." Carly said.

The bank manager escorted them to the safe deposit boxes and asked if he could be of further service.

"No, thank you," Carly answered, "we won't be but a minute. I'm almost afraid to open this." The key went in the lock and the lid flipped back and there it was, her passport with a stamp from Paris, just as she had said.

"Carly, sorry, Officer Brennen," Emerson corrected himself. "When you were in Paris, did you run into anyone by the name of Alessandro Rossi? He was Jennifer Orrick's fiancé."

"I know who he is, Detective Lake. I sit at the front desk of the precinct. Not a lot gets by me unless I am out on the street, where I eventually want to be full time."

"We need you to think back," Lake continued. "Did you run into anyone possibly that looked like him or maybe the names were similar?"

"I see what you are getting at, Detective, but I do not remember him. I'll look at the photos again when I get back to the station."

"Okay," Captain Brown chimed in. "Let's get to work on this. Detectives, how would you feel if I assigned Officer Brennen to work on this case with you?"

"I'm good with that," Clayton replied, "how about you Lake?"

"Fine with me."

"Officer Brennen, I want you in plain clothes. People are reluctant to speak to uniformed officers. Are we all good here?"

"Yes, Captain," they all replied in unison.

Back at the precinct, Lake approached Captain Brown in her office. "Captain, are you assigning Brennen to this case to keep her close? See what she does, or perhaps, doesn't know?"

"No, I actually want to see her in action with the two of you. I think she has some excellent skills and will be an asset to the precinct. It doesn't hurt to keep her within reach in case we find out she has a connection to Rossi and Orrick. Keep me in the loop. You have my private number."

Detective Lake nodded and left the office. On the way out, he passed Carly. "Hey Brennen, see you tomorrow."

CHAPTER 22

"There is still no match in the database for the fingerprints found at your officer's residence."

"Damn," Lake replied. "I was hoping there would be something by now. What about the hair?"

"Really, detective Lake? I am doing everything possible to find answers as quickly as possible for you, but I'm only one person." William Oosterhout worked hard to fill the shoes of his predecessor Sara Hunter. She had lost her title as Chief Medical Examiner during the trials connected to the Timothy Cole case. Since then, he had made it his mission to be the best he could be as the current Chief Medical Examiner. And had since added forensic investigator to his credentials.

"I know Bill, I'm sorry. Let me buy you a cup of coffee. I'm just eager to get a hit on these prints. If they belong to the judge's daughter, then we have a strong case for a warrant to search her home."

Officer Brennen walked into the lab mid conversation. "The prints in my apartment aren't Jennifer's. On a hunch, I checked the county clerk's office. She has a concealed pistol permit.

Judge must have pushed it through for her. Her prints would have popped up already if there was a match. Her prints are in the system."

"If I were the judge," Bill interjected, "I would have insisted my daughter be packing heat as well. There are some crazy people out there. Some hairs we recovered from the apartment are yours, Officer Brennen, but there were a few that weren't even human."

"What, were they alien?" Lake joked.

"No, they're synthetic. They are most likely from a cheap wig. Do you own a wig, Officer Brennan?"

"That's a hard no, but if we could find it, we could lift some skin cells from the scalp of whoever was wearing it."

"Well, aren't we just a wealth of knowledge, Officer Brennen? Where did you learn that from," Lake laughed, "Beauty School 101?"

"Car and Driver Magazine, smartass." Carly jabbed back. "Actually, I wanted to be a Forensic Scientist. I took a few courses in college, then decided if I were going to be handling dead bodies, I would rather be the one trying to catch who killed them."

"Yes," Bill interrupted, "but although DNA can be on scalp tissue, it is more likely to be discovered on the human hair inside the wig. When you remove the wig, it's likely some of your own hair comes out with it. Might be a long shot, but worth the try."

"Now," Officer Brennen said, "we need to see if anyone dumped the wig near my apartment. I'm heading back to my street to start searching the trash cans. It's not due to be picked up for a couple of days."

The skills and hustle of the young recruit genuinely impressed Emerson Lake. He just nodded and said, "Nice. Keep us informed, Bill." As Detective Lake held the door for officer Brennen, he yelled back, "I'll have that coffee sent down."

CHAPTER 23

"So, now that I am in street clothes, what am I allowed to do while I'm working with you?" Carly asked. "Do I have any value as a cop, or am I just supposed to stand around and look pretty?"

"Funny," Lake replied. "You take on the role of an officer in this precinct, just like any other day on the street."

"Oh, so it would be normal for me to hop out of this vehicle while stopped at a traffic light and run over to that illegally parked car and write him a ticket? Seriously, detective, in street clothes?"

"No, Officer Brennen," Reese jumped in, "what Detective Lake meant is that you follow our lead. You ask questions. You take notes. Just like we do. You're right that you will have to be mindful that you're not in uniform, so it's possible someone might ask for your ID. Show them your badge and tell them you're an officer with the Cromwell Police Department. If things get heated, use your training. That's pretty much it."

"Got it."

Carly appreciated the opportunity to work with Lake and Clayton. Her goal was to move up fast at the department, and she knew she could learn a lot from the detectives.

Carly's phone rang. "Brennen. Yes, thanks Captain. Oh, ok, that's interesting. Thanks for getting back to me, Captain. I appreciate the call."

"What's going on?" Lake pounced.

Carly laughed. "Not that, captain. It was the captain from the fire department. You should see your face, Lake. Don't get your panties tied in a knot."

"Hey, watch it," he said. "You're still a rookie."

"I called the firehouse asking if there were any females on the truck when they took the fire call at my apartment yesterday. There weren't, but one of his men saw a female firefighter in the building on the upper floors, but he didn't really pay attention to her. I am guessing detective Clayton; the perfume odor came from her."

"Possible, very possible. Do you know if there were other firehouses that answered the call? If so, maybe they had females on their trucks that day."

"That's just it, only one house responded, so they don't know who that could have been."

Carly Brennen left the station after the shift was over and headed back to her apartment. It was still under lock down. Forensics doing their best to find evidence. There was minor damage to the apartment building.

"I'm officer Brennen. I live here, and I am trying to find out who was in my apartment. It appears the only place left to look for clues is the garbage cans. Do you mind if I have a look?"

"Actually, we do mind officer," one of the team explained, "this has to be done by the book."

"I understand that, but I am looking for something specific. A wig. A blonde wig."

"Well, officer Brennen, we actually did find a wig, but we have already secured it and we will send it to the state labs with all the rest of the evidence. I am sorry, but that is all the information I can give you. Now, unless you want to take a chance on evidence being tossed out in court, then I am going to have to ask you to leave. The team will finish in here later today and someone will notify you when you can return to your apartment."

"Thank you," Carly responded. "I appreciate everything you are doing."

CHAPTER 24

"Captain, there is a call for you from the Bur Oak Casino. Guy says his name is Donald Albano."

"Put him through." Captain Brown enjoyed having Deputy Allen Manning on the desk this morning. Not his usual job, but today is where she thought he would be of the most value to the department.

"Yes," she said as she picked up the line. "What can I help you with, Mr. Albano?"

"You can start by telling me what the fuck is wrong with you?"

"I'm sorry. What did you just say to me?"

"You know exactly what I said. Are you out of your fucking mind to pull a stunt like that?"

"I'm sorry, Mr. Albano. I don't like your language, nor do I appreciate your tone, and I'd suggest you change both fast and speak to me with a little respect. I do not know who you are or what you're referring to. You're from the Reservation, Bur Oak Casino, correct?"

"Look, Kim, I really don't enjoy being in the middle of your little escapade. Did you think you were going to get away with what you did to him? He isn't dead, you know. Well, not yet anyway. But damn close. We had him flown to a hospital. Reservation cops are crawling all over the place asking questions. I don't know what happened in there and don't want to, but I can't cover for you. There were quite a few people in here who saw you talking to me."

"Number one, Mr. Albano, my name is Captain Kimimela Brown. I do not go by the name of Kim. I'll call the Reservation police myself."

"Be my guest, bitch, but they won't be happy, and neither will the Feds when they find out you were banging the Governor before you took a knife to his throat."

CHAPTER 25

Captain Brown, rarely shocked at anything that happened on the job, was reeling. She grabbed at her throat, gasping for her next breath.

"Captain, are you ok?" Deputy Manning was just outside the captain's office and had heard how upset she was on the call. "You look like you could use a glass of water. Please sit down. I'll get you a cold washcloth. Sit down before you fall. What happened?" Manning grabbed a hand towel from the captain's private bathroom. Placed half of it under the faucet, leaving the rest dry. When he came out, he closed her office door and pulled down the blinds. "Here," he handed her the half-soaked towel, "wipe your face off. Take a drink of water. Now talk to me. What just happened? Someone get hurt over at the Casino? Did someone die? What?"

"No," the captain replied, taking a gulp of water. "Well, not yet anyway. I need to get over there right now. I need back-up. Put someone else on the desk, Manning. I need you with me. Find Lake and Clayton. Tell them to meet us at the Casino. There has been an attempted murder over there."

"But Captain, we have no jurisdiction over the Reservation; you know that. I know it's your tribe, but..."

"We'll see about that!" she stood up, regaining her composure. "I was just accused of trying to murder the governor. Now let's move before the Feds decide to take over."

"What?! You've got to be kidding me. Who the hell is this Albano guy, Captain? Is he the one who just gave you this information?"

"He's the Casino host. Do you trust I had nothing to do with this?"

"Of course, Captain. But don't you think you should let Lake, Clayton and myself handle this for now? Maybe you should try to get a handle on what your rights are before busting in there, ready for heads to roll. Did he say the Reservation police were looking for you?"

"No, he just said he can't cover for me. Perhaps you're right. Maybe I am being too hasty. Let me think for a moment." She slid back into her chair. "Get Lake and Clayton back here. We need to huddle on this A.S.A.P."

CHAPTER 26

The two detectives and Officer Brennen arrived at Cromwell P.D. in fifteen minutes, greeted by Manning.

"Officer Brennen, take over the desk. You two, come with me to the captain's office."

As they entered, Emerson asked, "Captain, is there new info on Tim Cole?"

"No, have a seat. All of you." She recounted the details of the phone call she received from the casino. "I had absolutely nothing to do with this. You trust me, right?"

"Yes, of course," Emerson reassured. "But remember, Captain, if any of these accusations turn out to be substantial, then we have to advise you of your rights like anyone else. This is some serious shit."

"Who the hell is this Donald Albano, anyway?" Reese asked with a bit of fear in her voice. "Do you know him personally?"

"No, not at all. All I know is he works at the Casino. He's the guy who, how do I say this? He hosts the elite. He takes care of their needs while visiting the casino, compensates the high rollers for money spent on the floor. When the Reservation planning board was deciding whether to allow the casino to be built on Native American land, I heard his name come up. He was just one speaker promoting how good this would be for jobs and all that bullshit. I work and live off the Reservation, but I still know most of what's going on. Until about an hour ago, that is."

"Captain, I am going to ask you, as a friend, two questions." Lake took a deep breath. "Do you have or have you ever had a relationship with the Governor?"

"None." she replied matter-of-factly.

"Is there anyone on the Reservation police force you trust, and I mean really trust, with your life?"

She pulled a piece of paper from her desk, printed a name on it, and passed it to Detective Lake.

There was a knock on the captain's office door. Officer Brennen peeked her head in. "Captain? There are two men here to see you. They say they are from the FBI."

"Let them in, officer Brennen."

She opened the door wide and waved the two men in, and closed the door behind them.

"Captain Brown, this is Agent Olden and I'm Agent Wells, FBI. We'd like to ask you a few questions?"

"I know who you are. We've spoken on the phone concerning our escaped serial killer, Timothy Cole. What can I do for you?"

"This has nothing to do with Timothy Cole, ma'am." replied Agent Wells.

"Where were you this past Thursday?" Olden inquired.

"Excuse me?" Lake jumped in. "What the hell is this all about?"

Both agents sat silent. Eyes focused squarely on Captain Brown, waiting for her to answer.

"Everyone, please take a breath. Gentlemen, pull up a chair. Agents, we need to work together on this situation. I received a phone call a short while ago from the host at the Bur Oak Casino. His name is Donald Albano." She continued to tell the agents the same story she told her officers and detectives. "I have never met Mr. Albano. I'm only aware of him from the meetings on the land deal for the Casino construction."

"Captain," Wells stated, "the Governor is in critical condition. His throat was slit. He's lucky the concierge sent someone to his room; he was late for a poker game. Now, this Albano guy claims you were the last person in his room, "having lunch." He said that's code for a booty call. He also said you have been in the governor's suite frequently."

"Hey!" Lake pounced. "That's enough! You'll show our captain some respect!"

"Captain, don't you think you should have an attorney present?" Manning suggested. "Shouldn't you have legal down here like anyone else on the force?"

"Calm down, all of you," the captain reprimanded.

"Captain, you still have never answered my original question," Olden reminded her. "Where were you last Thursday?"

"Agent Olden, that's enough!" Reese bellowed. "Captain, I'm serious. Don't say another word until you have an attorney present. Agents, where's your warrant?"

"This is just a courtesy visit, Reese," Agent Wells reassured. "We would hope for the same if the situation were reversed. If anything turns up on those casino videos, we'll be back with a warrant. Personally, Captain Brown, I would listen to your officers. Get counsel."

CHAPTER 27

"Well, did you arrest her?" Donald Albano asked as the FBI Agents walked into the casino.

Agents Olden and Wells ignored the question and headed to the penthouse suite with Albano in tow.

"Listen, Mr. Albano," Wells said as they strode along the corridor. "We really need that camera footage. All entrances to the casino. Footage from the lobby and elevators, as well as the gambling floor."

Albano was not happy about the orders being barked at him.

"We're working on it, Agent. You are aware we have some pretty high-end guests at this hotel? They will not be happy to have their names and faces splashed everywhere. Let alone the faces of the people they are keeping company with here. We like to keep things discreet for our top clients, if you know what I mean."

"Look, you little weasel." Agent Wells spun around and poked Albano in the chest. "I don't give a rat's ass who stays here, including the governor. You are accusing a very prominent law enforcement official of a profoundly serious crime and you're worried about who sees the guest list. Let me warn you, I would tread lightly, or your career might not be the only thing at stake."

"Agent Wells, are you threatening me?"

"No, that's a promise."

Albano backed down. "Fine. I will go check on how the footage is coming along."

The agents arrived at the Penthouse suite, ducking under the crime scene tape, pleased to see the forensic team hard at work.

"What have we got so far?" Olden asked the team.

"Well, we have bodily fluids from the sheets, blood of course, no knife, no signs of a struggle, just the bed is pretty messed up. There are wine glasses, two of them, an empty bottle of wine, one cigarette butt, no lipstick on it, so probably from the governor. Everything is being bagged and tagged and sent to the Forensics labs. Some hairs on the soap and in the shower."

"Okay, thank you, all of you."

Albano appeared in the Penthouse doorway. "The footage is ready."

The Agents followed the Casino host to the room where video cameras were always running.

"Here you go, agents, the footage you requested, including from the night Captain Brown was here. Chuck here will pull them up for you."

Chuck was ready to shit his pants, hands shaking. Chuck was Lakota and scared out of his gourd right now. He hated when the Feds came around, it wasn't often, but when they arrived, it would always cause a scene. Chuck knew what he had to do, no matter how nervous he was about the FBI being in his space. He rolled the footage.

"Stop it right there," Agent Wells commanded. "Zoom in on her. Closer, damn it!"

Olden and Wells looked at each other, dumbfounded.

Olden spoke first. "If I knew she could look like that, I may have asked her out."

"Oh my God," Wells responded. "What the hell? Look at this."

"The captain is a very good-looking woman," Olden commented, "but this version is drop dead gorgeous."

"The next clip," Chuck's voice quivered, "shows her in the elevator and getting off at the door of the governor's suite."

"Look at this." Wells pointed at the screen. "The time stamp on the film coincides with the attack, but the captain would need to be living dual lives."

"Do you have cameras in the suite?" asked Olden.

"No sir. That would be un-ethical."

"Really, Chuck? Do you think any of this is ethical?"

"No, Sir."

CHAPTER 28

"Carly, if you need a place to stay while your apartment is being violated, you are welcome to stay with me."

"Thanks Deputy Manning. I appreciate the gesture, I really do. Violated apartment. That's funny and sad at the same time."

"Seriously, you are welcome. I'm not seeing anyone, and you could have the spare room all to yourself. Has its own bath."

"Thanks again, but I've already rented a hotel room. It shouldn't be that long before forensics finishes going through my apartment. I'll just hire a cleaning service when they're done to give it a good scrub down. It's been a long shift, just going to chill for the night. After I call my parents and tell them I'm not dead. They always worry. Why is that?"

"Because that's what parents do. So, I'm told anyway. Where do they live?"

"Florida. Have a good night, Allen, and thanks for the offer."

Once at her hotel, Carly took a nice hot bath, ordered room service, and put her feet up to watch mindless television. Suddenly, she jumped out of a half sleep/wake moment. "Oh, shit!" she exclaimed aloud. She picked up her cell phone and dialed a number.

"Reese, meet me at my hotel room. I'll text you the address and room number. Bring Lake with you. We need to talk."

"What's wrong?"

"I'll tell you when you get here."

Emerson and Reese changed into jeans and t-shirts before heading over to the hotel, both confused about the phone call.

"Come in. Sit," Carly held the door as the detectives filed into her room. "I have nothing but water in the mini fridge. Sorry."

"That's okay," Lake said.

"This is a nice little set-up you have here." Reese looked around the spacious room. "All you really need for a few days, anyway."

Carly interrupted the pleasantries. "I remembered something, and I hope to hell it's nothing, but it just jolted me out of a nap."

"Well, are you going to make us guess?" Emerson hovered over the food tray sitting on the bed. "Hey, you don't mind if I snack on a few of these wontons, do you? They're just sitting here calling my name."

"No, help yourself. Listen, I was at the desk the other day. I was trying to reach the Governor on the phone for Captain Brown. His assistant claimed he was out of the office on business, working on a bill coming up for a vote. The captain didn't seem too surprised that he had been avoiding her."

"Well, of course he's avoiding her. He has egg on his face after this whole execution debacle" Emerson threw a soggy French fry back on the plate.

"But wait, there's more. I remembered the captain left the

station right after that and told me if he called, to patch him to her cell."

"So?" Emerson scoffed.

"Knock it off Lake! Let her finish. Carly, are you thinking the captain may have had something to do with the attempt on the Governor's life?"

"Reese, I don't know what to think, but I have a very eerie feeling about all of this and thought you should know."

"Brennen, I get where you're coming from," Emerson interjected, "but I'm sure there is a logical answer. Remember, the Captain isn't thrilled with how the Governor treated Reese and me. I'm guessing she was trying to reach him to give him a piece of her mind."

"Can I ask you both a question?" Carly knew this was tricky territory, but just had to lay it all out there. "What do you really know about the captain other than she's Lakota? Does she have a husband? Children? Where does she live? Does she have a life outside of the precinct? What kind of life?"

"Emerson and I have known Captain Brown for a couple of years. Beginning shortly before the Tim Cole case broke. She's really been a wonderful addition. She's even been responsible for setting up some innovative community policing programs to bridge the gap between John Q. Public and the law to help improve relationships and trust. Captain Brown is a good woman and a positive leader in this department and community. Carly, listen to me," Reese clasped Officer Brennen's hands. "You cannot say a word about this to anyone. At least not until we figure out if this has anything to do with this case. Our Captain is a good person and deserves our respect and the benefit of the doubt. Maybe she was following up on leads in the Tim Cole case, or maybe she was running a personal errand." Reese could tell Carly was anxious and was doing her best to calm the situation before all hell broke loose.

"That's all really nice, but that's not really what I asked. What do you really *know* about her?" Carly looked at Reese and Emerson and raised an eyebrow.

Reese and Emerson got back to their car, both alarmed at the conversation they just had with officer Brennen.

"Do you realize what Carly said has merit, Emerson?

"I don't buy it."

"Just think about it for a minute. Captain Brown was trying to contact the Governor and she didn't tell Carly where she was going when she left the station. As a recent recruit, I would be a little concerned, especially if I were the only witness that knew the captain was trying to reach the governor. That perhaps there was a connection between them. Carly is savvy. She may have this all wrong, but what if on some level she's right, Emerson?"

"I really don't have a clue what would happen if she were? What I do know is our workload just exploded. Now we not only need to find Tim Cole, but it looks like we need to investigate the private life of our beloved captain and that, my dear, sucks. I think I may need a beer. This is some strange shit, Reese."

CHAPTER 29

The next day, Reese and Emerson made it a point to be at the precinct a little early. They weren't the only ones with the same idea.

"Good morning, Manning. You're early. What are you doing at the desk? Where's Carly? You're pretty and all, but well, you know, not my type."

Reese gave her partner a slap up the back of his head. "Seriously?" she snickered. "I think Allen looks perfect behind that desk. He certainly looks smart and extremely easy on the eyes. If you know what I mean?"

"Thank you, Detective Clayton, right back at ya?"

"Okay, that's enough," the three of them turned to see Captain Brown standing behind them. "I assume all the cases on the docket today are already solved, with all this time to horse around." There was just a hint of a smirk on her face. "Where's officer Brennen?"

Allen cleared his throat, embarrassed to be caught in the antics with the detectives. "She'll be here shortly, Captain. She called to say something had come up and she would be a little late. Also, the FBI Agents that were here yesterday called and asked that you contact them when you arrive."

Reese shot a quick glance at her partner, neither wanting to believe the worst.

"Thank you, Deputy. I'll call them now."

"Uh, no need Captain," Lake advised. "They're walking in the door." His heart dropped to his stomach.

"Captain Brown," stated Wells. "We would like to speak with you in private."

"About what?" she glared.

"Please Captain," Wells continued, "I think it would be in your best interest if we met in your office... alone."

"I will be the judge of that, Agent Wells," the captain folded her arms across her chest.

Wells sighed, "Okay, have it your way. Captain, we pulled the footage from the casino security cams. We have images that place you at the Bur Oak Casino at the time of the Governor's assault. In fact, one shows you exiting the elevator directly in front of the Governor's suite."

"That's ridiculous!" Reese exclaimed. "Captain, you really should have an attorney present before you say anything."

"Detective, I'm aware of my rights," the captain scolded Reese.

"We have the screen shots from the video. Have a look for yourself."

The captain's brow furrowed as Agent Olden handed her his phone. Her eyes widened with fear as she stared at the pictures. "That is not me. I told you before, I have never been to that casino. Ever!"

"Captain, may I look?" Lake asked.

She handed the detective the phone.

Lake's mouth fell open as he swiped through the images. "What the hell?" His gaze moving back and forth between the Captain and the images of the woman on the screen.

Reese leaned over Emerson's arm and had a look for herself. "Really? This is what the FBI has come up with?"

"Wait just a damn minute!" Lake was ready to pounce on the agents. "All you've got here are some images of a woman getting off an elevator. Last time I checked, that isn't evidence of attempted murder. If this is Captain Brown, and I truly question if it really is, how does this involve her? This just shows she may or not have been a guest at the Bur Oak. It is none of your business, nor ours, how she spends her free time. It's a public place. She has every right to be there. If, again, it is even Captain Brown."

"Everyone, just calm down, please," Agent Olden urged. "My partner and I don't like this either. Believe me. However, we have to follow the agency protocol. The images aren't the only thing we found at the scene, Captain. We have something else." He handed Captain Brown a piece of paper. "Captain, your DNA is a match to the fluids found on the sheets in the Governor's hotel suite. You are now officially a person of interest in this case. We're going to need you to come with us, Captain."

As the agents took Captain Brown into their custody, Reese reassured her friend and boss, "We got your six, Captain."

"I know you do Clayton. My attorney's contact info is on my desk, pinned to the inside of my calendar."

Reese nodded.

As the FBI agents led her toward the door, Detective Lake

removed his jacket and placed it over Captain Brown's shoulders. "Show her some goddamn respect."

The captain silently nodded in appreciation. Thankfully, there were no press or paparazzi in sight.

As they placed her in the car and drove away, Agent Wells was first to start an interrogation of sorts. "Captain, would you care to explain any of this?"

Captain Brown just turned her head toward the window in silence.

"Captain, off the record, those images damn sure look like you. You really can't disagree with that."

Captain Brown's steely eyes met the gaze of Michael Wells, through the rear-view mirror. Calmly, almost matter of fact. "First, I will wait to speak with you when my attorney is present. Second, there is no such thing as *off the record* with the FBI."

CHAPTER 30

"Manning, find out where the hell Officer Brennen is," Reese commanded, "and, in the meantime, ask someone else to sit the desk. Lake and I are going to need your help."

"Sure. No problem. I can do whatever it is you need."

Reese hurried into the captain's office and opened her calendar. Inside was the info for her attorney, just as she said. Reese made the call and explained the situation.

"I'll be there in approximately two hours, Detective," the attorney reassured. "Do you know if Captain Brown has any friends left on the Reservation? We have no authority there. We need to find a way in. If you get what I'm saying, detective?"

"We have a name, and yes, I get what you are saying. Thank you."

As Reese hung up, Carly strolled into the station.

"Where the hell have you been?" Lake slammed his fist on the desk.

It startled officer Brennen. "Excuse me? Despite what you may think, detective, I don't answer to you."

"Oh, really?"

Reese had enough. "Hey, you two, knock it off! Lake, we've got enough shit to deal with right now. And you," Reese turned toward Carly and glared, "I'd suggest you check the attitude. With the Captain out of the station, you answer to us."

Carly wasn't intimidated by too many people, but Reese was no one to mess with. "What's up with the Captain?" she muttered.

"She's been detained by the FBI, newbie. Oh, but you would have known that already if you were on time for work." Lake just couldn't let it go.

"You're kidding?"

"No Carly, he's not kidding. So, while we're tied up with this, we need you and Deputy Manning to stay on Judge Orrick's murder case for us. If you think you're up for the challenge?"

"Yes, of course I'm up for it. What do you need me to do, Detective Clayton?"

"Check his daughter's travel plans. Get depositions from friends and family. Find out if there were any tension or problems that may have arisen from Jennifer's marriage to Alessandro. Perhaps daddy didn't approve? Just keep in mind this is technically an FBI case, but we have a stake in it as well, so discretion is going to be key. Do you think you can stay under the radar and not step on any toes here?"

"Absolutely. You can count on us." Carly felt the butterflies of excitement. This would be her first real case.

"Good. Allen, you're the lead here. As savvy as our Officer Brennen is, she's still green. Make sure you're following protocol, otherwise all our butts will be on the line. Got it?"

"Yes, ma'am. I got it. We will be on our best behavior, right

Carly?"

"Absolutely," she responded. "Detective Lake, I apologize for my behavior, sir."

"Apology accepted," Detective Lake took a piece of paper from his pocket and handed it to Reese. "For safekeeping partner. Captain Brown thought we might need a bit of information at some point."

She glanced at it quickly and placed it in her pocket "Okay, let's get moving. We have less than two hours before the attorney arrives."

CHAPTER 31

The piece of paper Lake handed to Reese contained Chief Maka's contact information. He was a good friend of Captain Brown and Chief of Police on the Reservation.

Reese made the call, "Chief Maka please."

"Who should I say is calling?" the voice on the other end of the line sounded much older than expected. Female.

"Tell him it's a friend of Kimimela Brown," she replied.

"And your name, please."

"Reese Clayton." There was no way of getting around this bright receptionist.

"Hello Detective Clayton. I am aware of who you are. Captain Brown left your number as a contact if needed. How can I help you, Detective?"

"Well, I'd like to speak to Chief Maka. Captain Brown left us his contact information. So, I'm guessing there is some mutual admiration and trust here."

"One moment please," the receptionist connected the call to the Chief's office.

"Chief Maka, how can I help you Detective?"

Reese explained their predicament with the captain's arrest. "We need your help Chief Maka. The FBI has taken over the case and has been at the Bur Oak Casino to collect evidence against the captain. All we have seen is the screen grab from the video taken from the casino elevator. Do you have a way of finding out more of what the feds have on her? Her attorney is on the way. We would like to get into the casino and do some investigating of our own."

"I've seen the videos and I do not believe it myself; Kim is a prominent leader of the police force. I know blood, hair and bodily fluid samples are being sent to the labs. I'm sure results will be expedited. I'm not sure how I can help. That's about all I know. I'm relying on the staff and a few regular patrons at the casino for my intel."

Reese found it odd that the Chief called the captain Kim. She never once heard her called by anything else but Kimimela. "Chief Maka, do you believe the captain was having an affair with the Governor?"

"I have known Kim since we were kids on the Reservation. I would have believed none of this, but that photo sure looks like her. Albeit a very spruced up version of her. Same features, hair, body type. Fit, built like Kim. Height and weight, I would guess the same. Love does strange things to people, detective. I don't want to believe she hooked up with that guy. He's a bastard. I will let you know if I get any more details. Her attorney will have access to all of Bur Oak evidence. Oh, and Detective, call me Jimmy."

Reese smiled. "Thank you, Jimmy. I will be in touch if I find anything else on our end and I appreciate your help. Our captain has a great deal of faith in you. She wouldn't have given us your contact info if she didn't."

CHAPTER 32

"Denton Hollingsworth, I'm the attorney for Kimimela Brown. May I see my client?"

The FBI headquarters was a much nicer establishment than the city lock-up. Denton had not been there since his early years as a lawyer and that was just to observe."

They brought Kimimela to a room for her to meet with her counsel. Standard room furnishings, metal table with a bar that ran across the top to handcuff the accused. Better than normal chairs. Denton thought maybe placed there for his client's comfort. Mirrored wall. Two- way, no doubt.

Captain Brown, not handcuffed, took a seat after shaking hands with her lawyer. "Thank you for coming, Mr. Hollingsworth. I am not sure how this all happened. The photograph they showed me looks like me, but it is not. That is what they are holding me on, a lousy picture."

Denton could see her changing attitude and strain on her face. "Ms. Brown, please say nothing more unless I ask you a question. Do you understand the charges against you?"
"Attempted murder?"

"Were you read your Miranda rights?"

"Yes, of course. These guys are not stupid."

"Ms. Brown?" he said in a reprimanding voice.

She gave him an apologetic glance, "Yes they read me my rights."

The door opened to the interrogation room. "I'm sorry to interrupt, Mr. Hollingsworth, is it? I'm Agent Olden. This is my partner, Agent Wells. We have the lab reports. Your client will remain in custody."

Olden handed a folder to Hollingsworth. "Kimimela Brown. DNA proves you were in Governor Cramer's suite the night of the attempted murder."

The captain didn't flinch. It was as if she expected the DNA would be a match.

CHAPTER 33

"Detective Clayton," Reese answered her phone.

"Reese, this is Mike Wells. Could you meet me at Paula's Diner in town for a cup of coffee? I have some information to share with you."

"Certainly. I'll be there in about a half hour."

"What's that about? Emerson inquired. His voice was up a few octaves, his eyes glued to hers. Meet who and where"

"Mike Wells at the diner. He has information for us. Are you having a jealous moment, my love?"

"Maybe. Maybe not," he shrugged.

Reese was rather enjoying this side of Emerson. "Maybe you better stay on your toes, detective," she teased. "You know what happens when you don't pay attention to the love of your life." He took her by the arm and escorted her to the break room. He then grabbed her around the waist, pulling her incredibly close to him. She could feel his erection. He kissed her passionately like it would be his last. "I love you more than life itself," he said. "Never forget that."

"I know you do, and I love you just as much. This is just a work meeting with another law enforcement agent. Learn to trust, dear Mr. Lake. I'll be back before you know it."

She arrived at the quaint little diner sooner than expected and asked for a booth near the back.

Agent Wells was running a little late and had called to let her know the situation. She ordered coffee and waited.

"Sorry about being late, Reese," he slid into the vinyl seat across from her. "You look lovely, as usual."

"Thank you, Michael."

He ordered a hard roll with butter and jam and a cup of tea. "I have some info about this situation with your captain. I think you should know Reese. Lab results are back. The captain's DNA is a match to the bodily fluid on the sheets in the Governor's suite."

"Damn it! What was she thinking?"

"But that's not all Reese. I also have the fingerprint report," he stared into her beautiful eyes.

"And? Why are you telling me and not her and her attorney, along with the rest of the precinct?"

"Because," he hesitated, "the fingerprints don't match. There's something she's not telling us."

"What? Michael, how did her DNA get on the sheets without her fingerprints? I suppose the prints you found could be from anyone, cleaning staff, room delivery service, or even other paid services provided by the casino."

"Exactly. Or, was there someone else with her at the time? In the photo, the captain was wearing gloves. Maybe to protect herself."

"Or, maybe it was just part of her outfit, Agent Wells."

"Why wouldn't she admit to us she was seeing the Governor? Why deny that? I don't think it's ethical to be dating a married man, but it's not against the law. We need her to map this out for us, Reese. Her entire career is at stake."

"I understand Michael, but when the public finds out about an affair, her career also goes down the toilet, so to speak. Trust issues. The press would have a field day."

"Well, they are going to anyway. This will be a headline that won't go away. It's top of the hour reporting. You can't stop it. Mark my word."

"Well, now what?" Reese asked.

"I want you to come and speak to your captain to see if she will reveal anything that we don't already know."

"Are you out of your mind? Why would I do that? She has an attorney, and a damn good one at that." She got up to leave. "The coffee is on you, Agent Wells. You know how to contact me if you have anything reasonable to say to me."

"Reese, wait a minute. Please," he grabbed her hand. Reese looked down in surprise. "I would like to see you again, outside of work. A dinner date perhaps. You are a very smart and sometimes hilarious woman, Reese Clayton. I think we have a great deal in common and I would like a chance to see where this could go."

Reese stared at him for longer than she expected. "First, there is no *this*. Michael, as flattering as your offer is, I must decline. I am engaged to someone else." She turned toward the door.

"Please wait Reese, let me walk you to your car," he threw cash on the table to cover the bill with a generous tip. He reached for

Reese's arm as he opened the door. "Look Reese, I'm sorry if I offended you. You can't blame a guy for trying, right?"

"Look Michael, let's just keep this professional. Okay"

"Yes, of course."

She got in her car while Michael stepped back waiting for her to start the engine. Before she could reach for the seat belt, he flung the door open, yanked her out by the arm, practically dragging her into a sprint. He threw her to the ground, landing on top of her, covering her head with his arms, just as her car exploded.

CHAPTER 34

Emerson Lake was one of the first on scene of the burning vehicle. Terrified at what he would find. Fire and emergency medical vehicles were pulling in at the same time. Grabbing the hoses and ordering the public away from the area. Everything stood still in that moment for him. The scurry of people around him shouting of orders, but the world for Emerson was silenced. Then he saw her on the ground, bloodied face and arms, paramedics tending to her. Ordering a stretcher, words coming out of them that Emerson could not hear. He just wanted to be with her. Kneeling next to her was Agent Michael Wells.

"Detective," Agent Wells wobbled trying to pull himself to his feet, "she's alright, just banged up from the force of the fall to the pavement. There was a bomb under her wheel well. I saw a flashing red light under her car as I was saying goodbye. She was already inside the car. I just reacted instinctively and yanked her out before it exploded."

"Agent Wells, sit back down," ordered the paramedic. "Let me check you out. Agent Wells, please?"

He swayed back and forth as he tried to stay upright. Blood

soaked the back of his suit coat. An 8-inch piece of metal was lodged in his back. Emerson Lake grabbed him before he fell and eased him to the ground. "Thank you, man."

Emerson let the paramedics tend to the agent as he got on the ground with Reese, breathing a sigh of relief knowing she was okay. "I'm right here. I got you, sweetheart. You have some scrapes and a few bumps and bruises will certainly follow, but thanks to your friend you're alive," he gently stroked her hair.

Paramedics placed Reese on a stretcher and loaded her in the ambulance. Agent Wells was a different story. The paramedics propped him up in a sitting position on the stretcher next to Reese to avoid touching the projectile impaled in his back. They worked diligently taking his vitals and pushing IV fluids into his arm. Wells' eyes were open, but it was obvious he was not alert to what was going on around him.

"Detective Lake," the paramedic shouted above the commotion, "we are taking Detective Clayton to Cromwell Medical. Agent Wells is going there as well. I'm not sure what organs that piece of metal may have pierced, but we need to move fast. He's losing a lot of blood." The paramedic nodded at Lake to close the doors to the ambulance.

The blare of the sirens and red flashing lights snapped Lake out of his fog. "I'll be right behind you." No one heard him.

"Michael, can you hear me?" Reese asked, removing her oxygen mask "Don't you die on me, you got that, don't you dare die on me! I need you to fight. We have a lot of work to do." Reese suddenly realized someone wanted her dead. "Shit, Michael, someone just tried to kill me." Panic raised her heart rate enough to set off the machines. Her ears were still ringing from the blast.

Michael could see Reese's mouth moving, but he couldn't hear her. Just a muffled ringing in his ears. He could see the look of worry spread across her face. Words of encouragement formed in his mind, but he was unable to speak.

"Miss, please lie down. Let me put the oxygen mask back on you. Breathe, nice normal breaths."

The ambulance sped into the hospital ER drop off. The paramedics flung the doors open greeted by emergency room doctors and nurses barking orders.

"Take her to room four."

"They're waiting for Agent Wells in surgery. Go!"

CHAPTER 35

"What are we missing here? How is this even possible?" Captain Brown was baffled by the results of the DNA test. "I was not in his bed. Ever. What about the fingerprints?"
"Not back yet," Olden replied

Denton Hollingsworth, now more frustrated than ever, was trying to keep his client from saying anything incriminating. "Captain Brown, please allow me to ask the questions. You hired me for a reason. Let me do my job."

"Then do it, damn it! Ask the questions! You know they have no actual evidence to hold me. I need to get back to the precinct. There is a convicted killer on the loose in case all of you have forgotten that. I have work to do. The city of Cromwell gifted me with this job for a reason. I took the oath to serve and protect. I cannot do that from here."

"Agent Olden, do you have actual evidence to hold my client? Other than she may or may not have been in the Governor's room."

"I was not in his room!" Kimimela barked.

Denton placed his hand on her shoulder and squeezed hard. If that wasn't enough to make her stop talking, the rap at the door did.

"Enter," Olden ordered.

"Sorry to bother you, sir, but there is a problem."

"I'll be right back," Olden said. He returned minutes later, with paperwork in his hand.

"Captain, Detective Clayton and my partner Agent Wells are at Cromwell Medical. Seems he pulled Reese out of her car just before a bomb exploded."

"Oh my god," Captain Brown stood out of instinct, to go help her detective, only to be stopped by her attorney.

"You can't help them. You are here in connection to this case. Lake will oversee it."

Olden continued, "Reese is going to be okay. Wells is in surgery. He took a piece of shrapnel in the blast. We won't know his prognosis until he is out of surgery. Hollingsworth, your client is free to go for now." He handed him a piece of paper from the lab.

Denton looked at the paper, stunned.

"None of the fingerprints we found in the suite matched yours, Captain. Not the ones we have on file for you at least. Do you have an explanation, Captain? Anything you want to add?"

"Do not answer that question," Denton Hollingsworth advised his client. He was furious an FBI agent would even attempt such questioning.

"Captain Brown, I'll no doubt see you at the hospital. Correct?"

Captain Brown stood confidently and strode out the door being held open by her attorney. Never looking back.

CHAPTER 36

Officer Carly Brennen and Deputy Manning headed to the Cromwell Lab after receiving a call from their medical examiner.

"What have you got for us, Bill?" Manning asked not expecting much since the FBI had all the evidence.

"I have the results from the wig found near your apartment, Officer Brennen. There were human hairs found inside the wig. Two of them had the hair follicles still attached. She must have ripped it off her head, a hairpin still attached to the underside. The hairs definitely belong to Jennifer Orrick."

Manning's' phone interrupted the conversation. "Captain? Are you okay? Where are you? Yes, Captain, I got it. We're on it. Are you okay, Captain?" he repeated.

"I'll take care of me; you just do your job. Are we clear?"

"Yes, Captain," Deputy Manning had never heard that tone in her voice before.

"Carly, we have orders to get a warrant to search the apartment of Jennifer Orrick. Let's move before the judge leaves the courthouse. Thanks, Bill. Let's go officer, we have a job to do."

"Wait, what about the FBI? Aren't they going to have

something to say about all this?" Carly was confused. "Aren't they technically the lead on this case?"

"No, they asked us to start the tail on Ms. Orrick when they saw her near your apartment. So, we tailed. Apples and oranges. Now we will see just what she was doing in your apartment. Let's go."

They parked the squad car around the corner. They could see Jennifer's car parked in the open garage. The apartment was more of a duplex. Lovely tree-lined street. Neighbors appeared to take good care of their yards and homes. Upper middle class.

"Carly, go around back, just in case she tries to leave. I'll take the front. Remember, we are just here to ask questions. Let me ask them. You take notes. Got it?"

"Got it," she replied and slipped around the side of the house, trying to avoid the prickly shrubs.

Allen walked cautiously up the steps to the wraparound porch, noting there were no curtains on her windows. He knocked on the door, surprised when Jennifer answered it and offered him in without giving him a hard time.

"Come on in officer, what can I do for you? May I get you a drink, water, coffee, a beer perhaps?"

Allen stepped into the foyer and handed her the paperwork. "I'm Deputy Manning. We have a warrant to search your home."

"And by *we,* would that also include the young lady in my backyard?"

"Yes, it would."

"Please," motioning him toward the kitchen. "What is it you are looking for?" Her voice was as sweet as maple syrup.

She opened the back door and Deputy Manning waved his

recruit into the home. "This is Carly Brennen. She works out of our precinct. We have evidence that you broke into officer Brennen's apartment during a fire emergency. Would you care to explain?"

"Not really, but I did not break in, Deputy. I had a key. My fiancé gave it to me and asked that I go pick up a couple of things for him."

Carly couldn't contain herself. "What are you talking about? How would your fiancé get a key to my apartment? I don't even know him."

"Officer Brennen. Stop!" Allen urged.

"Oh, I think you do." Jennifer stepped closer to Carly, her hands now on her hips. "He told me you met in Paris and have remained close ever since. He said he held onto your apartment key since your college years. He said he left my passport at your place by mistake. He asked me to go pick it up. You know, to save him from having to call you." Jennifer took another step closer to Carly, her calm demeanor slowly evaporating.

Carly stood her ground never losing eye contact with Jennifer.

"You see, we were in a bit of a hurry. We made plans to honeymoon in Paris and I needed my passport to travel. He oversaw all the arrangements for our romantic getaway. But now I'm thinking that dead prick was no doubt banging you while he was engaged to me! You bitch!"

"Officer, back away!" Manning yelled. "*Now!*"

Carly did as she was ordered and reluctantly moved away. She knew better than to get into an argument with a suspect. But her own temper was next to none. Her fists clenched, ready to take down this woman accusing her of sleeping with her fiancée. She knew better, but wasn't about to have her own reputation destroyed by Jennifer Orrick.

Manning could see Carly's emotions bubbling to the surface. He certainly had his hands full with two pissed off women. "Where is the passport now Jennifer?" Allen already knew Carly's was secure in safe deposit box. He wanted to see if Jennifer would reveal anything else.

"I couldn't find it. That slut probably burned it or something."

"I'm not the one with a fire bug tendency. That would be more your style," Carly fired back.

"Enough, Damn it! Carly, go check the bedrooms. You, Ms. Orrick, come with me. Sit your skinny ass down on the sofa!"

They searched the home and found nothing of any value to the case.

"Miss Orrick, are you sure it was your passport you were looking for at Officer Brennan's home?"

Manning could see he hit a nerve with Jennifer. She paced back and forth, her head down, eyes tracing the floor. "He lied to me; said he would take care of everything. He asked me to meet him in Paris when things quieted down. We could get married there. He said he knew this girl who looked enough like me that I could get away with using her passport. Told me her address and everything."

"How did you get into my apartment?"

"I told one of the firefighters I was a cop and that I lived there and needed to grab my badge and gun. He didn't ask questions. They were too busy. The door was open."

"Really? The door was open?" Carly asked. "And how did that happen? Magic?"

"Carly!" Deputy Manning had about enough of Carly's attitude.

"I don't remember. I'm feeling a little anxious. I think I need to lie down and rest. I've been through a lot, you know. I just lost my daddy." Tears welled in Jennifer's eyes as if a switch had magically turned on.

"Well, Jennifer Orrick, you can rest in a jail cell." Deputy Manning removed his handcuffs from his belt. "Place your hands behind your back. You are under arrest for breaking and entering." He proceeded with reading her rights.

The ride back to the precinct was uneventful. No disruptions from Officer Brennen or their suspect. Carly was worried about being reprimanded by Lake and Clayton when they returned. She knew better than to act like a scrappy teenager.

Upon their return to the precinct, Deputy Manning confronted Officer Brennen. "It was a bad idea to have you on a case related to a break-in of your own apartment. But you will have to learn to control yourself when dealing with any potential suspect. What the hell were you thinking? I should write you up, teach you a lesson. But mistakes were made by the department putting you in that position."

"Deputy Manning, I have the utmost respect for you and the entire Cromwell P.D. I have no excuse even if it was a conflicting case personally involving me. But I promise it will never happen again."

"It better not, or it will be your last time. And that Officer Brennen, you can count on."

Once Jennifer was remanded to her a cell, Manning made the call. "Lake, we have Jennifer Orrick in custody. She admitted to attempting to steal Brennen's passport. The odd thing, she never gave us a real problem. She allowed us into her home. She got a little testy at one point, but, well, she goes from hot to cold. Do you know what I mean?"

"I do know. One minute she could bite the head off a snake and the next she was crying about daddy. That might be a ploy. Lot of money riding on the reading of the will. I'm guessing she stands to inherit a great deal."

CHAPTER 37

Emerson quietly opened the door to Reese's hospital room. It was a private room except for the guard outside of her door. Not knowing what to expect, he walked up to her bed, reaching for her hand. "Hi, beautiful. How are you feeling?" He was a little shocked to see the bruises on her face had appeared so quickly. "I just saw you an hour ago. Now you look like you tried to take on Ali in the first round and got your ass kicked."

"I feel like I went a few rounds," she chuckled, rubbing her forehead. "I hit that concrete with major force."

He kissed her gently on the lips. "I love you, damn it. Don't scare me like that again. Mike Wells saved your life, and I will be eternally grateful for that. You were correct, my love. He is a good man."

"How is Agent Wells doing? Anybody hear anything yet?"

"He is out of surgery; we are waiting to speak with the doctor. But I'm more concerned about you. This is serious shit. Someone tried to kill you. Do you want to talk about what happened?"

"All I know is, I got up to leave the restaurant. Wells paid the bill then walked me to my car."

'What was it he wanted to tell you about the captain?"

"He asked me to talk to her. See if she could explain to me what she was doing at the casino. Specifically, in the governor's suite. I told him, absolutely not. She has an attorney. It pissed me off he would ask me to meet him just for that. He then told me they had the fingerprint report and they were not a match. How is her DNA on his bed and not her fingerprints anywhere?"

"Okay Reese, remember he is an agent, and we probably would have done the same thing had it been us. Now think carefully, did you see anybody else hanging around your car when you parked it? Anyone in the restaurant that looked a little shady or someone you may have recognized from somewhere else. Maybe someone from another case?"

"Not that I can recall right now. I think that's pretty much all I have." She left out the small detail of Michael Wells inviting her out to dinner.

"Ok, well, the doctor wants you to stay here overnight, to be sure there are no head injuries. I'll be back later. You will stay with me when you're discharged. That's an order, detective."

Reese smiled and saluted wincing a little from the pain.

CHAPTER 38

Deputy Manning approached his new prisoner. "Were you able to reach your attorney, Ms. Orrick?"

"Yes, but he won't be here for a few hours. Can I get a ginger ale? I'm thirsty."

"I can get you a bottle of water." He signaled Officer Brennen to get her the water.

"I would much rather have a nice bottle of wine and a shrimp cocktail, Deputy. Could you arrange for that?"

Allen leaned into the bars of the cell. "How about you stop being a pain in the ass and answer my questions?"

"Oh Deputy, play nice with me." She walked up to the bars of the cell, getting as close to his face as she could, Manning didn't budge an inch. "You do not know who or with what you are dealing."

"Really? Why don't you enlighten me?"

"My daddy will tell you; I am a good girl and I have done nothing wrong. He will get me out of here and then I will get that shrimp cocktail and the wine."

"Good Luck with that, Ms. Orrick." He turned to Carly, who

was holding the bottle of water, took it from her, twisted open the cap and drank it down.

"Deputy Manning, I believe that was our last bottle of water," Carly smirked. "And I didn't see any wine in there either."

"Shit happens."

"My daddy will fix this!"

"Shut up and sit down!" Carly snapped. "Your daddy is dead."

"Well, I never!"

"I somehow doubt that."

Manning could see the two women were about to lock horns and stepped in to redirect. "Ms. Orrick, we still have some additional questions about this passport thing." He knew she could easily be out on bail soon being the late judge's daughter so they needed to get as much information as possible.

"What would you like to know?" Jennifer sat down on the hard bench inside the cell and crossed her arms and legs.

Carly saw the opportunity and turned on her phone to record the conversation. "Are you waving your rights to have an attorney present, Ms. Orrick?"

"You are aware you are being recorded?" asked Manning, signaling Brennen to back off.

"Yes, I am. I have nothing to hide."

"Are you admitting to breaking into Officer Brennen's apartment?"

"No, I didn't break in. The door was open."

"You claimed you had a key. Where is that key, Ms. Orrick?" Manning continued. "Do you have it with you by any chance because we didn't find it when we searched your apartment."

"I don't recall saying I had a key."

"What were you looking for in officer Brennen's apartment?"

"Proof that my dick of a fiancé was banging someone else."

Allen Manning knew this was a little game for her. He played along, using her first name to lull her into feeling safe to speak openly. "But, Jennifer, why would you stand up in front of your father and all of your family claiming your love for him if you suspected he was unfaithful? What am I missing here, Jennifer?"

"He killed my father."

"How could he have killed your dad? He was right by your side the whole time."

Jennifer's eyes began to glisten as small teardrops began to form and trickle down her cheek; not the full-on crocodile tears like before.

"He hired someone to do it. I thought he was just going to scare my dad, not kill him," she sniffled.

"Why would he want to scare your dad, Jennifer?"

"We wanted my inheritance sooner rather than later, to start our new life together."

"Do you know the name of this man he hired?"

"It was someone from the family."

"Who's family, Jennifer?"

"Alessandro's family, I guess. I didn't ask."

"Could you tell us where Alessandro's family lived? Was it close by, Jennifer?"

"No, I think in New Jersey or maybe New York. I don't remember."

"Did you ever meet this family member, Jennifer?"

"Yes, once."

"Jennifer, can you tell us his name?"

She drummed her fingers on her forehead struggling to remember the name "Steven...Steven," she paused. "Steven Daniels. That's it, Steven Daniels."

"Would you recognize this, Steven, if we showed you a photo?" asked Manning.

"Maybe."

"Officer Brennen," Manning asked, "would you mind looking for photos of people named Steven Daniels? Here and in New Jersey and New York." Manning already knew who they would search for. So did Carly. Someone right here in their own state of South Dakota.

"Absolutely, no problem, Officer Manning. I'm on it." Carly pulled up five photos with the name and printed them out, bringing them back to the holding cell.

"Do you recognize any of these men, Jennifer?" Allen still playing the role of good cop.

She shuffled through them one by one until she viewed the second to the last photo. "That's him!"

The deputy leaned into the microphone on Carly's phone. "Jennifer Orrick is pointing to Warden Steven Daniels, of the South Dakota State Prison."

CHAPTER 39

"Well, Deputy," said Carly, "this should be interesting. What do you think will happen now? Our suspect just said a lot of serious stuff, *without* her attorney present. Do you think any of this will hold-up?"

"I'm not sure," he said. "We went over the Miranda Rights with her again, so we should be fine on that level. I'm just not sure what her end game is going to be. Was she clueless about the murder of her dad? Did she really think you were having an affair with her boyfriend? And the other question, who unlocked your apartment door? If she were easily giving us all this other information, why would she lie about breaking in? Makes no sense."

"Is she attempting to get off by the crocodile tears and all the *daddy* stuff?" Carly rolled her eyes.

"We are about to find out."

"Officer Manning?" a young man approached the front desk with a briefcase in one hand. Cell phone secured in the other.

"Deputy Manning," Allen corrected.

"Apologies, Deputy. Colin Teasdale, counsel for Jennifer

Orrick. I would like to see my client."

"Absolutely," Carly replied. "I'll have her brought into the interrogation room for you."

Colin Teasdale was what you would expect of an attorney for the rich and famous. Very professional, polite, and definitely dressed for success. Italian-made suit and expensive watch. Allen noticed the watch because it was rare you saw this piece of jewelry anymore; everyone uses their cell phone to tell time these days.

Once settled in the interrogation room, Mr. Teasdale began. "Miss Orrick, were you given your rights in this matter?"

"I was," she responded.

"Did you fully understand those rights?"

"Yes, I did."

"And yet you gave these officers a statement, anyway? Why didn't you wait for me to arrive?"

"Because I did nothing wrong."

Colin Teasdale shook his head. "Please, say nothing more to the police unless I am with you. Do you understand the seriousness of this charge?"

She looked up at her attorney with sheer anger in her eyes. She stood up and poked her finger into his chest. "Don't tell me what to do. I am paying you, remember that. I am paying you."

"Yes, you are indeed. With daddy's money," he said under his breath.

Colin Teasdale emerged from the interrogation room. "Deputy Manning, I will need a copy of the recording of Ms. Orrick's statement. I will speak with Judge Canton."

"You can get a copy of this recording from the District

Attorney. Do what you have to do. In the meantime, Ms. Orrick will remain in custody."

CHAPTER 40

Reese took it upon herself to visit Michael Wells, while she herself was being kept for observation. The guard placed at her door by Emerson Lake was not about to allow her to go without him at her side.

"Detective, my ass is on the line here. You have 10 minutes before I contact Lake. Got it?"

"Officer, I'm a grown woman, a detective. I don't need a babysitter. Now get the hell out of my way before I shoot your ass. Got it?"

"No. I have orders and I will not lose my fucking job because you have a shield attitude. Now, we go together for the said 10 minutes or I handcuff you to your bed. What's it going to be?"

"Come on, let's go." She was not happy. "Wait till I get my hands on Lake. She mumbled."

Her guard at least allowed Reese to go into Agent Wells' room alone to visit.

Reese was finding it harder than expected to visit the man that saved her life; the man who kept asking her out on a date. She smoothed her pajamas and pushed her hair around as best she could. *I must look like hell*, she thought. She felt her stomach turn, and a lump in her throat. She took a few steps toward the bed and stopped as her eyes filled with tears. What the hell is wrong with me? Pull yourself together.

Agent Wells appeared to be asleep or maybe he was in a coma. Reese didn't want to think about the latter. "Michael," she whispered, "can you hear me?"

He didn't answer.

"It's Reese." She moved closer to him, leaning over his bed, taking his hand in hers. "Thank you for saving my life, Michael. I will be forever grateful to you. I'm sorry you got hurt. I wish I could take your pain away. When you wake up Michael, I need to know how you knew there was a bomb under my car."

All she heard was the hum of all the machines attached to her new friend, her new friend for life.

"Michael please don't die." A single tear fell from her eye onto his cheek. "We need to solve a lot of cases in our lives yet and maybe some of those cases together."

"Red. Flashing. Light," he muttered pausing between each word as though it were a herculean effort to speak. "Under. Wheel. well."

Reese breathed a sigh of relief that he wasn't in a coma and could speak. "Good catch, Agent. I didn't think the FBI was that smart," she quipped, choking back more tears while giving him a big smile. "Red light, huh? Why didn't it go off when I got in the car or started the engine?"

"You didn't start the engine," the words were coming easier for him now. "Some detective you are," he joked trying to laugh, but a cough replaced it.

"Take it easy, Michael. Stop talking." she gently put her hands through his hair. The cough sounded more like a death rattle to her.

"I figured you were going to die if I left you in that car. So, I took the chance. Does this tear I felt drop on my face mean you'll go to dinner with me?"

"Knock, Knock." In the doorway stood Emerson Lake. Emerson quipped. "Is there a party I'm missing in here? Hey Mike, how are you feeling? Ready to go out there and kick ass?"

"Maybe tomorrow, today not so much Lake." Michael coughed again and then took a breath. "I was just telling Reese about the bomb under her car. Haven't heard what kind it was yet. Have you? Appears the FBI is every bit as slow as the Cromwell P.D."

"At least we have something in common, Wells," Emerson chuckled.

"I was just telling Michael how grateful I am to him for saving my life. He's lucky to be alive."

"I know he is. I am every bit as grateful to him as you," Emerson said, grabbing Michael's leg and giving it a squeeze. "Even more than you know Mike. Reese is my fiancé. I couldn't live or love without her. That information stays between us, copy?"

"Copy. I guess dinner is out of the question then, Reese."

"Reese can have dinner with whomever she wishes. I have no problem with that at all. Hell, *I'll* go out with you sometime, Wells. I'll even pay." Emerson made the right call. Normally, his jealousy would have gotten the best of him, but in this moment, he was just grateful the love of his life was alive.

"If you don't mind, I'll decide who I have dinner with and

when." Reese was impressed with and grateful for Emerson's attitude. "I'm headed back to my room boys. Hopefully, I'll be able to leave here soon. Take care of yourself Michael. I'll be back to visit, I promise." She leaned over and kissed him on the forehead, once again running her fingers through his beautiful blonde curly hair. "Thank you again."

She grabbed Emerson's hand on her way out and gave it a gentle squeeze, "Come down when you finish up here."

Emerson winked at her and said, "Of course."

She opened the door, nodded to her guard, and walked out of the room.

"Smart play," commented Wells. "Taking the high road with your woman."

"Occasionally, I have a smart moment, my friend. I just have a few questions to go over with you about the explosion."

"I'll do my best to answer, but I really know nothing. Pulling her out of the car was merely a knee jerk reaction."

"What about uniformed police? Did you notice one of those around the area?"

"Now that you mention it, there was a uniformed officer on the street, up about a block from Reese's car. Closer to mine than hers. Looked like a local, checking windshields for expired inspection stickers, bald tires. Fuck! I saw him when I was about to enter the restaurant. You're thinking Cole, right?" Wells began coughing uncontrollably, struggling to catch his breath. He was gasping heavily, setting off his monitors.

The staff raced in yelling orders. Nurses rolled in a crash cart ready to use it if needed. "Please leave, detective," the head nurse demanded. "We need to stabilize him."

Emerson Lake did as he was told, but waited just outside the door to Michael Wells' room. He needed to make sure his new friend was going to be alright.

CHAPTER 41

Captain Brown returned to the station, ready for what was going to be another long day. She tossed her bag and the jacket she was holding on the desk.

"Welcome back Captain."

"Thank You Deputy Manning. What did you find out about Brennen's apartment?"

It did not surprise Manning she was all business. "Jennifer Orrick, definitely broke in. We're just not sure how. There were a couple of different stories she gave us. She admitted to searching for Brennen's passport. She also claimed she was looking to prove her fiancée was having an affair. We have all of it recorded on Carly's phone. And before you ask, yes, she knew she was being recorded. She also admitted to a hit that was placed on her father. Her attorney is aware of everything, too. The DA sent a copy to his office."

"Good work. And Brennen, how are things moving with her? On the job, I mean?"

"Captain, so far, so good. She's got potential. She is resource-ful. A bit of an attitude, but nothing we can't mold. Lake may butt heads with her because they are both cut from the same cloth. From my end, it all looks promising."

"Good to hear. Anything on Clayton and Wells?"

"Just keeping Clayton for observation. Wells is in tougher shape; we don't know his prognosis."

"And Cole, any sightings of our escapee?"

"Emerson and Reese seem to think he's still in Cromwell."

"He is. That crazy bastard." Emerson walked in just in time to join the conversation. "Sorry, I just left the hospital. Spoke with Wells. He saw what appeared to be a uniform on the street. We agree it was probably Cole still in the prison guard's uniform who likely planted the bomb. The FBI's team is reviewing all the evidence recovered at the scene. They'll be able to determine the type of explosive used. Hopefully, we'll get lucky, and they can find a serial number or other markings on the components that are traceable. Or maybe even a fingerprint to nail Cole."

"Okay good. How's Reese?"

"I will pick up Reese tomorrow morning. She's doing good right now, but I think she should take a few days, clear her head, maybe talk to someone about all of this. She's been through a lot."

The captain raised her eyebrows. "In case you don't know it, your partner has a mind of her own and a stubborn streak a mile long. I doubt she will do either of those things, but I'll insist she needs a couple of days to recover. It will be your job to keep a close watch on her, Detective. Someone is out to get her. Whoever it is, they are going in for the kill, not a scare tactic?"

"I know. Thing is, I don't think it's Cole's idea. If he planted the bomb, someone had to pay him big money or threatened him. Perhaps extortion."

"I'm with Lake on this one, Captain," Manning agreed. "I don't think Cole would want to kill Detective Clayton. The two of them bonded when he was being held in our jail. That is the only way I can describe it. You could see he had respect for her."

Emerson jumped in. "Yes, respect, but Cole would do anything to be a free man. I suppose I would too. I just do not think it was his idea. He might be on someone's payroll to get Reese out of the picture. I have a hunch who is holding the purse strings on this, Captain. Warden Daniels. He and Reese did not exactly hit it off at the botched execution. She has said all along there is more going on at that facility than we know. I am starting to agree with her point of view. The Warden's job is on the line for almost putting the wrong prisoner to death, and for allowing an inmate on death row to escape. That's a ton of shit flowing his way. And we all know shit flows downhill. The only one above the warden is the Governor. I suspect he's involved, too. He threatened Reese's badge when she stopped the execution. Why would he do that when she was saving his ass?"

"Okay," Captain Brown said, "let's reorganize. Manning, you and Brennen contact all available off duty. I'm mandating overtime. Lake, bring Clayton in as well. I want her close by."

"Got it Captain."

"No one is going to fuck with my team. I expect everyone to work through the night. I want an update by 7am with all the evidence you have. That includes what you have on me. Dismissed."

CHAPTER 42

"Manning, see what you can find on Warden Daniels," Lake ordered. "Background, home life. See if there may have been preferential treatment with appointing him to the position of warden by the Governor."

"You got it!"

"Like it or not, I need to do the same with the captain. Brennen can manage the desk here and any research we may have difficulty navigating. She is hot on that stuff."

"I think she has more contacts outside the precinct as well, Lake." Manning replied. "She's smart, that's for sure."

"Yeah, I think you're right. If we need her to go deep, call me. It's going to be a long night."

The activity at the precinct was at a fever pitch.

Manning brought Carly up-to-speed. "Officer Brennen, I'd like you to do some research on the Rossi family. See what you can come up with. We know they are lower end, mob connected. But see if the path they chose led them to South Dakota. If so, why?"

"Isn't this FBI jurisdiction?" Carly questioned. "They won't be happy about us stepping on their toes. I don't want to be disrespectful, Deputy, but is this going to land the rest of us in hot water? Because I'm not getting a warm fuzzy feeling about this at all."

"There is a lot going on, Officer, and we need your computer skills to find out things that otherwise would not come to the forefront. This is coming from the captain. And she may have you researching her life as well. Understood?"

Carly reluctantly nodded. She was not at all comfortable with what she was about to do, but she liked Officer Manning. Right from the beginning, he seemed to have more respect for her than any of the others. He always noticed and gave her positive feedback about her ability to solve problems, along with her knack for finding her way around the internet.

"Officer Brennen, we are a team here at Cromwell. We always have each other's backs. All law enforcement agencies have to work together on this one. It's up to you. What's it going to be?"

"I'm on it, Deputy," she smiled. This was the first time she felt like she belonged at Cromwell PD. The first time in a year. She smiled and thought, if I go to jail, I won't be alone.

CHAPTER 43

"When do I get to find out what my father left me in his will?" Jennifer yelled from her cell.

No one responded.

"I'm Jennifer Orrick, the judge's daughter damn it and I have rights!"

Once again, no one responded.

"I need to hire an excellent lawyer, one that will see I'm innocent in all this, and get me the money I'm entitled to. That money is rightfully mine. He owed me that inheritance. You know, I have to pay for things. I want that money and I want out of this place. Now!"

Deputy Manning had enough of Jennifer Orrick's tantrum. "Seriously, miss, you need to keep quiet. Would you like to contact your attorney? You know the one you *already* have. I can ask him come back here in the morning. That's if the poor bastard still wants to be your counsel. If not, sit your ass down and shut up!"

Jennifer Orrick grew up thinking the world owed her a living. She had everything a young girl would want. Designer clothes and shoes, a hefty allowance, which went up and down as her dad saw fit. Trips with friends to Europe and to islands whenever she decided she was bored. Judge Orrick didn't like what Jennifer was becoming and blamed himself for it. Her lifestyle of the rich and out of control. She never had to work and now it had become clear, she never would. When she told him she was going to be married, he reluctantly agreed to pay for the wedding and for the honeymoon in Paris. After all, she was his little girl.

She paced back and forth in the cell, getting more anxious by the minute. "Look at me you, freak. Don't you dare walk away from me when I'm speaking to you. What's your name again? I need your badge number, too. My daddy will have you fired for keeping me locked up like this."

Manning just rolled his eyes and continued with his work.

"I'm sorry," Jennifer apologized. Her voice softening. "Can you come over here, closer? I want to tell you something important. Please?"

Manning strode over to the cell. "What is it you want to tell me?"

"I like you," she flirted. "I think you like me too. Do you want to kiss me? I'm okay with that, you know. We could do lots more if you like."

Manning wanted to laugh, but instead moved in close to her face between the cell bars. "No thank you, Ms. Orrick. I'm not your type."

"Oh, but how do you know what my type is Officer," she asked demurely. Still trying to lure him in.

"It's Deputy, not Officer. And my dear, I am gay. Now for the last time, sit down and shut up!"

CHAPTER 44

"Well, Officer Brennen, how's it going?" Manning sat himself down on the corner of Carly's desk, peering at her computer screen.

"You will not believe what I found and please don't ask how I got this info. Deal?"

"Deal. Give it to me, officer, I can take it," he snickered.

"Warden Steven Daniels was a Marine way back in the day. He married while in service, to a young lady. They had a daughter, according to military records, just before his discharge and returned to his hometown in Kingston, New York. Daniels worked for the state of New York for a few years until a series of events sent him out of the state."

"What series of events?"

"Hold onto your hat Manning. This is where it gets interesting. Daniel's daughter was nearly eight years old and, according to police reports, she had gone to a sleepover at a friend's house. During the night, someone broke in and killed both Daniels's daughter and her friend. Guess what the friend's name was? Cramer! Governor Cramer's daughter."

"Wow! So, the Governor and the Warden definitely had a connection through this shared tragedy. How did you get all of this so fast? And dare I ask where?"

"I told you, don't ask. It's better you don't know, Deputy. There's more. There was an arrest made in the murder of the two little girls, but they threw the case out of court on a technicality. And the suspect was set free."

"What a nightmare. They never got any justice for their daughters. Why was the case thrown out?"

"The counsel for the Daniels family was a young attorney who apparently had a drinking problem. He was drunk on the job and made the mistake of giving jurors info they should not have received forcing the judge at the time to toss out the case. The judge allowed the attorney to keep his license, but he could no longer practice in New York State. It looks like the attorney entered a recovery program at the judge's suggestion and moved out of state, eventually ending up in South Dakota. He worked his way up the ladder here and was appointed as a judge in Jade County." Carly flipped the computer screen toward Manning. "The young attorney that blew it on the Daniels/Cramer murder case was none other than Judge John Orrick."

"Holy Shit!"

CHAPTER 45

7:00 am arrived at Cromwell P.D. headquarters and the big screen was up and running in the conference room waiting for the team's report. A long table at the center of the room was set with eight chairs. Coffee, water, and breakfast snacks were strewn across the top. Captain Kimimela Brown asked the officer at the front desk to see to it they had no interruptions while in the meeting. She walked into the room to see all four of them standing at attention.

"Please, sit," she said. "Welcome back, Detective Clayton."

"Thank You, Captain."

"Who wants to go first?"

Allen Manning raised his finger. "Captain, Officer Brennen has been quite busy all night. I think she should start."

Carly stood and pointed the remote at the screen revealing the discoveries she had shared with Manning the prior night. Both the story and how she tracked it all down stunned the detectives.

"Nice job, Brennen," Lake said.

"Go on, Officer," the captain requested, wanting to know just how much or how little she knew.

Carly continued. "My guess is, as time went by, both men wanted to avenge the deaths of their daughters. The only way was to first appoint Daniels to Warden after Cramer took office. Find the guy who had been arrested for the murders and then go after the attorney who made the mistake at the trial. That attorney, we now know, later became Judge John Orrick. One question that sticks out in my mind, Captain, is how did Orrick become a judge? His mistake was on his record, right? Appointing a judge is a very in-depth process. Who pulled what strings to get him on the bench?"

"Shit," Lake stated. "Great work, but that's a lot of hearsay, Brennen. We need something solid. Proof to take to a judge. And even then, the likelihood of a judge turning on another judge is slim. Especially, one that was just murdered by a sniper."

"Well, the murders were documented in New York State and didn't follow either of them to South Dakota." Carly continued, "It's proof Governor Cramer and Warden Daniels knew each other before they arrived in this state. Their kids were friends. It's not illegal to appoint a friend to a position I don't think, but is it ethical?"

"Good point," the captain noted. "Do we have a name for the person accused of their daughters' murders?"

"I'm waiting on that, Captain." Carly was beginning to feel part of the team.

"Reese jumped in. "That's not all. The Governor's finances appear to be a little off kilter. There is an ongoing investigation into his dealings with the Bur Oak Casino and his campaign finance fund."

The captain wanted to avoid discussion about what her team found out about her background and the governor, so quickly moved on to questioning the findings about the wedding couple. "So, how does this all tie into Jennifer Orrick and Alessandro Rossi? Why did someone want the groom dead?"

Detective Clayton's phone pinged. She looked down in surprise. "Well, as luck would have it, I may have that answer for you, Captain. Agent Olden just sent me the name of the suspect arrested for the murders of the two little girls. Benito Rossi. Next in line to take over the *family business* and the uncle of Alessandro Rossi, our groom. From what Olden is saying, they reported Benito Rossi missing from his home in the Catskills nearly a year ago. He hasn't been heard from since. Probably in the concrete of a high rise by now."

"And our bride, Jennifer Orrick?" the captain continued. "What is her role in all of this?"

Lake jumped in. "She is a spoiled brat looking for daddy's inheritance, but that's just a guess, ma'am. The reading of the judges' Will takes place sometime this week. One of us will be there with Ms. Orrick for the outcome. I'm guessing she knows more than she's saying."

"Good job everyone. Lots of information. Now we need the proof." She rose to dismiss them, but before she could, Reese stood to address the captain.

"Captain, I hate to bring this up, but you asked that we investigate you as well."

"I know what I said, Detective. Let's deal with me later. Dismissed."

Reese turned toward Emerson with a look of disbelief.

He looked at her intently, "Grab your things, let's go."

Once out of earshot, Reese began a tirade. "What the hell was that? We need to inform her of what we have. The information is overwhelming. It's going to take some time for her to process this, Emerson."

"That's if she doesn't already know about it."

"True. But I can't imagine she does. How did it not come up on a background check when she joined our department? Let's go back to your place, Emerson. We'll sort all of this out and take another look. We should also see if Chief Maka found out anything else. Time is not on the captain's side. The press will no doubt have this in a heartbeat."

When they arrived, Emerson opened the door and entered his apartment cautiously, just to make sure no one was lurking around. He did not feel comfortable letting Reese go back to her own place, especially knowing someone was trying to kill her. If Tim Cole broke into Reese's apartment, Emerson knew he could also worm his way into *his* apartment as well. Once he felt the apartment was secure, he grabbed her around the waist, pulled her close, and kissed her passionately, not realizing he was holding her too tightly. She put her hands on his chest and pushed him away. "What do you think you are doing, Emerson?"

"I'm sorry. I didn't mean to hurt you. I just haven't been able to tell you how worried I was about you. How scared I was of losing you. I love you and I never want to see you hurt. I couldn't live with myself, knowing I wasn't there to protect you."
"I know," she softened. "I love you too, but I'm still a little shaken and sore. Maybe later."

"I wasn't trying to get you in the bedroom, Reese. I'm not that sick. Jesus."

"Let's just drop it for now. Okay? Let's go over these documents."

"Got it."

CHAPTER 46

Reese sat in Emerson's apartment finishing the last few sips of her coffee when her phone rang. "Agent Wells, what a pleasant surprise. How are you feeling?"

"I'm good. Hope to be released in a few days. Question for you Reese."

"Okay, lay it on me?"

"Are you aware your Officer Brennen is treading on thin ice?"

"What are you talking about?"

"Her computer hacking skills are causing a great deal of concern. Rob and I are doing what we can to avoid a colossal headache and rift between the FBI and Cromwell P.D. We agreed to share information with you in solving this case. Sharing and stealing are two different things, Reese. You need to stop her or else she's not only going to lose her job, but she'll also wind up going to jail."

"Damn it," Emerson slammed a file folder on the table. "I knew something was wrong."

"Hey, Lake, I'm glad you are on too. Now, I don't have to make two calls. Both of you need to get on top of this, and fast.

Our careers are on the line as well. Just knowing Carly puts us in a tough spot. You know what I mean?"

"We do," Reese sighed. "How the hell did she get in?"

"She is extremely bright and could have a major career in the computer crimes unit. High-tech skills are a precious commodity these days," Wells laughed. "If she can keep her skinny ass out of trouble, that is."

"More like if we can keep her out of trouble," Lake replied. "Thanks for the heads up, my friend. Hope you are up and about soon."

"Thanks, Agent Wells," Reese echoed. "We appreciate the heads up about Carly. We'll take care of it," Reese reassured him.

"Wow, we went from Michael to Agent?" Wells said, disappointed. "I think we can all dismiss the formalities. Talk soon." The call ended.

"I knew she was hacking into something, Reese. I just never thought it would be the FBI. Pretty stupid move on her part. If it weren't for Olden and Wells, they would have had her in cuffs by now. What the fuck was she thinking? She's smart, but this was so out of line. Trying to make a name for yourself is one thing, but criminal charges against you is not the way to do it. What the hell are we going to do now?"

"How did she think she would get away with this? You know, when the captain finds out she is going to fire her on the spot. I don't know of any way to stop it, either."

"For now, Reese, I think we better handle Brennen ourselves."

"Agreed. In the meantime, let's keep going on the case. Number one. How was Orrick allowed to practice law after he blew the case against Benito Rossi? Who would have hired him after that debacle? And why did that black mark not follow him to South Dakota?"

"It was a different era. Think about it, Reese. The kids were little when all of this happened. By the time Orrick moved here, he was already up there in age. Who would question his ethics, especially in a small town like Jade? After all, he was coming from New York. I still have connections in upstate New York from when I lived there. Maybe I'll contact them and see what they remember about this old case."

"Yes, I know all about your connections to New York. It sounds like a plan as long as this brief trip down memory lane doesn't include a call to a certain reporter named Brenda. You remember her, don't you?" Reese quipped.

"Are you still jealous of her, Reese? That was an exceptionally long time ago. There is nothing between us. And why would I contact her? She is still in D.C."

"Oh really? And how would you know where she is, Emerson Lake? Unless you have been in touch with her?"

"Damn it, Reese. Knock it off. You know she's on the national news every day. It's always on at the station 24/7. I want you to go into the bedroom and lie down. Take a couple of aspirin, try to sleep."

"I'm sorry. You might be right." Reese rubbed her bruised cheek.

"I'll handle some of this for now. You need to rest and re-focus. You've been through a lot. Are you sure you don't want to talk to someone about what happened? Maybe with a professional?"

Reese glared at him, rolling her eyes as she walked into the bedroom, slamming the door.

CHAPTER 47

Detective Lake received the call about the reading of Judge John Orrick's last will and testament shortly after Reese went in for her nap. Not wanting to disturb her, he left a note on the coffee table explaining where he was and would return after he escorted Jennifer Orrick back to her cell.

Emerson led the handcuffed Jennifer into the building and escorted her into the elevator. Deputy Manning and Jennifer's brand-new counsel joined them.

"Where's Teasdale? Did he give up on you already?" Emerson teased.

Jennifer shot him a look that would shrivel your skin.

Emerson leaned into Manning's ear. "I wonder how long this guy is going to last?"

Manning muffled a laugh.

As the elevator made its ascent, Jennifer clenched her fists and raised her arms. "Are these really necessary detective?" she rattled the cuffs in front of Emerson's face.

"Yes, Madam, they are," he grabbed her elbow and led her off the elevator at the third floor.

The office assistant greeted them and escorted them to a small room where an attorney sat behind a desk. They took their seats and the reading began.

"Miss Orrick, your father had a sizable amount of money. He invested well over the years."

"Well, I am sure he did. Can we get on with it?"

"In his time as Judge of Jade County, he changed his wishes several times. When you finished college and decided you wanted to do charitable work with the poor your father was very proud. He asked that his fortune remain with you as his only heir."

"Aw, daddy. I knew he would take care of me."

"However, he came to see me six months ago asking to make a change to his Will. He said you had stopped helping others and become a doormat to Alessandro Rossi."

Jennifer frowned and shot an angry glare at the attorney.

"I'm afraid, my dear, Judge Orrick no longer trusted your judgement. He arranged it so you would have enough money for living expenses. In the amount of three thousand dollars per month. The rest of his fortune has been set aside to support a scholarship program in the name of Lisa Daniels, deceased daughter of Warden Steven Daniels."

"What?!" Jennifer slammed her hands on the desk in front of her and instantly winced as the metal cuffs dug into her wrists. "Who the hell is Lisa Daniels?" she screamed. "I've never heard of her. Did he have a fucking kid I didn't know about? Was he cheating on my mother?" She turned to her new attorney sitting next to her. "Do something about this!" she demanded. "Why the fuck did I hire you? Read that document and make sure it's right!"

"I assure you it is correct." Her father's attorney handed her new counsel a copy.

Jennifer's attorney scanned the paperwork. "I'm sorry Miss, but it does seem to all be in order."

Detective Lake was shocked and slightly amused at what had unfolded. He reached for Jennifer's arm to escort her back to the precinct. "I believe we're done here."

"Get your hands off of me!" She swatted her cuffed hands at him then turned and spit in the direction of her new lawyer. "You worthless piece of shit! You're fired!"

"I'll send you my bill, Miss Orrick. Have a nice day."

"Welp, another lawyer down the drain," Lake mused as he escorted Jennifer Orrick out of the building.

"I won't be in jail long, Detective. You can bet your ass on that."

"Really? Getting another attorney, are we?"

"Fuck off! I did nothing wrong. You can't hold me for anything."

"Haven't you heard breaking and entering is a crime, Miss Orrick?"

"I told you, I didn't break in. The door was wide open."

"And I suppose the owner of the apartment just left it open for you? Seeing how you and she are friends with the same guy, you know, the one you were supposed to marry."

"I want my lawyer," she screamed. "Now!"

"Which lawyer do you want now, Ms. Orrick? I will be glad to oblige you by allowing you to make that phone call." Emerson Lake was enjoying this a little too much. He was glad her father didn't leave her his entire estate. She didn't deserve it acting like such a spoiled debutante. There was one thing though that he couldn't quite shake though. A nagging feeling that she might actually be telling the truth that Carly's apartment door was open.

CHAPTER 48

Reese picked up her phone to call Emerson, but it rang before she could dial. "Hello, Captain."

"Reese, I have info on the bomb placed under your car. Our escaped prisoner has been a busy guy."

"So, it was Cole?"

"Appears that way. Forensics is trying to find out where the explosives came from, but could be anywhere. Not so sure they will be able to pinpoint that detail. I placed a call to Agent Olden to ask for his help. Their labs are better equipped."

"How do you know it was Cole?"

"There were prints lifted from the rear fender. He must have leaned on it as he was placing the explosive under the wheel well. His weren't the only prints found though. Yours, of course, but the others are still not identified. It could be anybody walking by the car. We will see what pops up as they continue their investigation."

"Thanks Captain, What now?"

"Well, we still have an APB out for Cole. Finding him is still problematic. Emerson was just here dropping off Jennifer

Orrick. The reading of the Will didn't go well for her, but Emerson will tell you about it. He's on his way to you. Reese, I want you to think about getting some counseling. Trauma just doesn't go away. Trust me on this."

"I hear you. I will think about it. Captain, there are still things that Emerson and I need to speak to you about. The information we uncovered about you."

"Not now, detective, *not now*," she said harshly. "When I say so and not before. Got it?"

"Yes, Captain." The call ended.

When Emerson arrived home, it surprised him to see Reese in tears. "Hey, come here. What's going on?" He held her carefully, not wanting another episode like earlier. "What happened? You can tell me anything, you know that, right?"

She blew her nose and explained the conversation with the captain.

"So, it was Cole that planted the bomb? I seriously didn't think he would do that to you. He is a sick person, a psychopath for sure, but I thought he kind of liked you, Reese. In some weird way."

"Don't forget, Cole loved his mother too and look what he did to her."

"Fair point." Emerson did his best not to laugh. He knew better this time. Normally, they would have both laughed at a comment like that, but this wasn't a normal situation.

"But that's not what is bothering me." Reese tried to explain to Emerson her phone call with the captain without falling apart again. Her emotions were still very raw and uncontrollable ever since the explosion. "The captain was adamant about not discussing the information we uncovered about her. Not until she said so. She doesn't even know what it is we found, but she gave a direct order. She never does that to us anymore. In the beginning, yes, but not after all this time. I think we should continue to dig deeper into her past."

"We will, but, right now, let's have dinner. Get dressed, we're going out. Time for you to live. I'm afraid you are getting depressed sitting here thinking of what might happen or could have happened. Don't worry, I won't let you out of my sight. Not for a minute. Come here." He brushed her hair aside, tilted her face toward him, and kissed her forehead. "I love you Reese Clayton."

"I love you, Emerson Lake. Now get the hell away from me. I need to get dressed in my Sunday best. My man is taking me to dinner," she exclaimed slapping him on the ass.

"Well," he said. "I never."

"Bullshit. If you behave, there is more where that came from," she winked at him as she slipped around the corner.

Reese and Emerson enjoyed a meal at their favorite Italian place.

"Let's take a walk Emerson," Reese suggested. "The park is so pretty this time of year and I could use a walk after that meal."

"Your wish is my command my dear." He gave her a little bow and wave of the arm for effect.

They wandered the park for about twenty minutes and headed back toward the restaurant.

"Emerson, is that car following us? It's turning the corners slowly, like they don't think we can see them."

"I see them," he said being cautious not to frighten her. He reached for his weapon. "Act normal. Flirt a little with me."

"Oh, really?" She laughed and leaned in, grabbing his arm lovingly.

A familiar male voice from across the street pierced the night air. "Hey coffee lady, it wasn't me. I didn't do it."

The car that was following sped around the corner and came to a screeching halt, just long enough for the man with the familiar voice to jump into the back seat before the car sped past them.

"Shit!" Lake drew his weapon, shouting license plate numbers and the direction of travel to Reese as she dialed for back-up. He had no shot.

"That was Tim Cole," Reese gasped. "I'll never forget that voice." They ran to Emerson's car, but by then, the other vehicle and its passengers were out of sight.

"What the hell did he mean, *I didn't do it*?" Reese tried to catch her breath. "He didn't do what? Geez Lake, he was right here watching us the whole time. He could have killed us both."

"But he didn't. I think he wanted you to know it wasn't him that tried to kill you. At least that's my theory. If he were going to kill you, it would have happened already, Reese. He could have taken us both out just now from across the street. But he didn't."

"You're right, but *why* didn't he? He wanted us to know it was him with that *coffee lady* remark. That was a nice touch, don't ya think? I should have boiled his coffee and poured it on his head when we had him in custody years ago, that asshole, instead of playing nice to get him to talk."

"I'm glad you *were* nice to him, or we might not be having

this conversation right now." Emerson did a quick check around the tires, under the hood and trunk, before he allowed his lady to get in his car. "I never thought we would have to deal with the likes of Timothy Cole again. That was probably the toughest case we ever had to deal with on this job, Reese. When the judge gave him the death penalty, I thought that was it."

"100%, but it's obviously not over yet. Someone is tying up loose ends, Lake. What loose ends, I don't know yet, but I will." As they drove off to the station, Reese continued to talk things through out loud. "Even before Carly hacked into the FBI computers, I knew there was some sort of corruption going on at the prison. I told the captain something was fishy, but why didn't she let us run with my suspicions? Do you suppose she *was* having an affair with Governor Cramer and is it possible she is the one that slit his throat?"

"Anything is possible, sweetheart," he said as they pulled into the precinct.

As soon as they entered the station, hoping for a miracle. Emerson asked, "Manning, what have we got on the getaway car?"

"They reported it stolen in Nevada two months ago." He typed his password into his computer and pulled up the details on his screen. "Uniforms found it just off the Reservation in a parking lot a mile from the Bur Oak Casino. No word yet, but I'm guessing it's wiped clean. Plates registered for a rental company. The person who rented the car was a vacationer in Las Vegas. I've got Nevada State Police checking on the guy who leased it."

"Nice work Manning. Brennen rubbing off on you?" Reese

smiled at the Deputy.

"Maybe, but I have skills of my own too, you know?"

Reese punched his arm. "I know you do, my friend. Any word about who planted the bomb in my car?"

"FBI is still working on that, thanks to your buddy Agent Wells. Got a feeling they will find something soon."

Lake jumped in. "I agree. Michael Wells does seem to have a bit of a crush on my lady. He won't let this act of violence against her go. He also has the means to do it quickly."

Reese opened her eyes wide in shock and shot Emerson a look.

"What's the problem Reese? You don't think everyone in this precinct already knows about us?"

Allen Manning gave Reese a pat on the shoulder. "We all know. For the love of God, you would have to be blind as a bat not to know. Now doesn't that feel good to clear the air? It felt great a couple of years ago when I found out everyone at the station already knew I was gay. It was like a tremendous weight being lifted. Reese, it will be for you as well. Embrace it."

CHAPTER 49

"Hi detective Clayton, Agent Olden here. How are you feeling?"
"I'm good. What have you got, Rob? Please tell me something good I can sink my teeth into."

"The explosives and the triggering device were both purchased in Jade County. The trigger was a burner phone, not traceable. Not yet, that is. They bought explosives online. We have the entrepreneur in custody now. He's just a kid, also sells illegal fireworks. Thought he was going to crap his pants when he saw the FBI show up at his house. Mommy and daddy weren't too happy with him either."
"I'll bet."
"My guys are questioning him now. It's possible he may know who bought the burner phone, too. Working on that angle."
"Rob, thanks for letting me know of the progress."
"You are welcome, Reese. Anything new on your end?"
Reese filled Agent Olden in on the brief appearance of Tim Cole and his stolen getaway car.
"Good work on your end. I'll continue to investigate and

keep you in the loop. Stay well Reese. Talk soon."

"Yes, we will, and again, thank you."

Reese filled Lake in on Olden's updates.

"Good. Looks like they have a handle on this, Reese. Now we need to find out what role Tim Cole played in all of this. If we can catch the guy, that is."

Carly had been listening to the conversation and added her own thoughts. "Sorry to eavesdrop, but I heard you talking and I think I may have an idea. It might sound a little out there, but it could work."

"Ok, we're listening," said Emerson.

"This guy seems to have a connection to you, detectives. He seems to have this need to engage with you. What if we create an event, something that might interest him or give him the opportunity to be in the same room with you, Detective Lake?"

"It's not Detective Lake that he wants Carly. It's me." *I know it is,* Reese thought.

"No, absolutely not! It's too dangerous." Lake shook his head.

"Carly has a point, though, Emerson. He obviously wants to make some sort of contact with me. I know it's risky and he could try to kill me again, but I think we have a connection. Remember, when we had him in custody, he said he appreciated I spoke to him like any other guy. I think I gave him a taste of humanity."

Lake let out a sigh. "You might be right, Reese, but this is insane. He's insane, that's for sure. Let's see what the captain has to say." Lake reached his arm around Reese and gently stroked her back.

"That's it!" Carly exclaimed. "Insane."

"Officer Brennen, you're on thin ice," Emerson got in her face. "What the hell is wrong with you?"

"Just hear me out. I remember seeing a benefit flyer online. If we could get the Captain an invitation to the event, it would tie in perfectly with the Captain's goals for the uniformed officers." Her fingers flew over the keyboard as she searched the internet. "She's been investing in more training to help officers handle mental health complaints more effectively. Got it." Carly spun her laptop around for the detectives to see the article in the South Dakota Times.

Mental Health Awareness Fundraising Gala

Doctor Jane Goldman Chief Executive Officer of The Jade Institute for Mental Health will host an evening of dinner and dancing along with a fine arts auction to raise funding and awareness for the hospital17

Special Guest Speaker: South Dakota Governor Willian S. Cramer

The event is by invitation only and will take place in the Benson Hotel Ballroom 11 East Main Avenue, Jade, South Dakota Friday, March 18

Dress attire is formal

"Great!" Lake said sarcastically. "Now all we have to do is get an invitation to this and then hope our escaped serial killer knows we are there."

"Long shot, Officer Brennen, but possible," Reese's mind was already considering ways to lure Cole into this little snare.

"Best case is to have the captain invited to represent the city of Cromwell. We can go along as her bodyguards, so to speak," Lake suggested. "Or, maybe we get our own invites as concerned Detectives trying to make a difference in our state."

"Nice touch, Emerson. Now do you believe that, or is it sugar coating on an already messed up world?"

"Possibly a bit of both Reese, but none the less it might get us the invitation. I'll send a note to this Doctor Goldman. My father was a buyer of Fine Art and History pieces for a museum in Sioux Falls years ago. They will know of his credentials there. That might help."

"Really?" this revelation impressed Carly. "Does he still have ties to the museum? That would be great publicity."

"No, he retired when I was in my early thirties, but I have no shame name dropping when I write to Jane Goldman to inquire about invites to her fundraiser."

The station phone rang interrupting their brainstorming session.

"Cromwell Police Department, Officer Brennen. Oh my god, what happened? Okay, yes, I'll send them right away. Thank you, Mr. Hollingsworth."

"What was that all about? Why is the captain's attorney calling?" Emerson was concerned.

"It's the captain. She's been admitted to Cromwell Medical Center."

CHAPTER 50

"Kimimela Brown. I'm here to see Denton Hollingsworth," she explained to the office assistant.

"Have a seat, Ms. Brown. I'll let him know you're here."

The captain scanned the waiting room. It was what you would expect of a high-priced attorney. Beautifully adorned, warm, and inviting. Probably purposefully decorated this way to take your mind off the hefty bill you could expect to receive after you retained his services.

"Captain Brown, thank you for coming. Right this way," Denton led her into his office. "Have a seat," he pointed to an overstuffed chair in front of his desk. "Are you comfortable?" he asked.

"Yes, I am."

"I wanted to meet with you for a reason."

"Yes, of course. What's going on? Why the formality?"

"The questions I am about to ask you are important to this case and in order to represent you, I need to know all there is to know about you, and your life as it is now, as well as your past."

"That's fine Denton, but you are aware, I haven't been

formally accused of anything so far. I am merely a person of interest. Correct? Unless you are telling me otherwise."

"Correct, you're still just a person of interest, but you asked me to be your counsel. I am more than happy to do so, but I need to know everything about you, past and present, in the event this case goes any further. As we both know, the Governor has an agenda, one that could enhance his career. This attempt on his life could go one of two ways. Shall we begin?"

"Okay."

"Kim, I'm going to start with a topic that has been controversial for quite some time. The Native American boarding schools and the accusations that the children forced into them were abused."

"I think the entire county must know about them by now," she remarked. "The schools were opened under the guise of government and religious leaders providing a good, free education to the children. But..." she stopped turning to stare at a photo hanging on the wall. She couldn't make eye contact with him. Her throat was feeling full.

"But..." Denton picked up where she left off. "Some of the children were forcibly taken from their families, removed from the Reservation and placed in these schools with the intent to civilize Native Americans and immerse them into European-American culture."

"Not only that, but they also forbade those children from speaking their indigenous languages and their tribal names were changed to English-language names."

Denton could see Kim was becoming agitated, but he urged her to continue. "You know more, don't you Kim? I can handle it.

Keep going."

She continued, "Yes, besides being forced to have their haircut and forced to wear American-style uniforms, the schools were not child friendly. Some did not survive the torture and abuse, especially the younger ones."

"And all of this," Denton continued, "was an effort to eradicate Native cultures purportedly by the government and Christian organizations. To this day, the tribes believe there are hundreds of Indigenous children yet to be found. Are you aware of bodies being found buried on the property of these schools?"

"Of course, I am aware of this. I'm Lakota, or did you forget? What does this have to do with anything?" she said, annoyed with Denton for bringing up such an emotional subject.

"I've been in contact with Reservation police Captain Jimmy Maka. I believe you know him?"

"I do. So what?"

"We have uncovered information," he continued, "that a child was taken from the Reservation and sent to one of these schools. The year was somewhere between 1978-1980. That would make this child approximately forty-two to forty-four years old. Captain Brown, how old are you?"

"Forty- two," she growled.

"You have an excellent education, wouldn't you say? Ms. Brown, you are the Captain of the Cromwell Police Department. Am I correct?"

"Yes, I am Captain of the Cromwell Police Department. What is the point of all of this Denton? Are you accusing me of something?"

"Please, be patient, I will get to the point. I didn't mean to imply you are guilty of anything. I was just making a statement. Where *did* you go to college?"

"Colorado, Mesa University. Majored in criminal justice. But I'm sure you are already aware of that."

"Are you sure you didn't, in your young life, attend and escape the rigors of a boarding school, possibly one on the Canadian border?"

"No, I did not! Unless you have proof, get the hell out of my way!" She stood to leave. "I need to eat something."

"Captain Brown, please sit down. I will have someone bring you something to eat. What would you like?"

"What I would like is to choke the shit out of you right about now."

"Please cut me a little slack here, Captain. Now, are you seriously hungry, or should we continue?"

"I need to eat something. I haven't had a meal in two days, just junk from the vending machines. I have a headache and feel nauseated."

Denton Hollingsworth stood up from his desk and moved closer to his client. "Actually, you look flushed, Kim. Do you think you might have a fever?"

"I don't think so."

Denton walked over to open a window for fresh air, but it was too late. Kim collapsed to the floor.

"Call 911!" Denton Hollingsworth yelled out his office door to his staff. "She needs an ambulance!" Denton got on the floor to check her pulse and breathing. Her skin was warm, but clammy. Her breathing was labored, but he did not need to administer mouth to mouth. "Captain, can you hear me?"

Paramedics arrived in what seemed like minutes. They placed oxygen over her mouth and nose. Checked her vitals and asked her attorney the usual questions.

"You're going to be fine," the paramedic reassured her. "We want to take you to Cromwell Medical to have you checked out. Is there someone we can contact for you, a relative, friend, co-worker?"

"No, I'll be fine," she said sitting up on her elbows.

"Captain Brown, you need to be checked out. I'm her attorney. I will follow you to the hospital."

Captain Brown reluctantly allowed the paramedics to place her on the stretcher and put her into the ambulance.

The well-trained emergency room team got her in right away and hooked her up to the proper monitors and asked the basic questions. "Are you a diabetic, Ms. Brown?" asked the nurse.

"No, not that I'm aware of. Why?"

"Your blood sugar counts were off."

The IV drip took effect, gradually bringing her back to nearly normal functions. The extremely high blood sugar spike exhausted her body.

"Captain, how are you feeling right now, other than tired?" asked the doctor.

"Weak," she responded. "I think I'll be fine now. I guess I need to pay closer attention to what I eat."

"Well, as soon as your lab results come back, we will get you up and walking and see how you do. For now, we want you to rest, and we'll have someone bring you something nutritious to eat. Any special requests?"

Before she could respond, Denton Hollingsworth warned her,

"Be nice, Ms. Brown."

Kimimela smiled at her attorney and nodded, "I get it. It's not the doctor that ticks me off."

He smiled back.

When the tray arrived, she took a couple of bites of her scrambled eggs, and a few spoonfuls of yogurt, washed down with a good cup of tea. "That's a lot of protein. I need a nap," she said. The high of her glucose numbers and blood pressure, plus the stress of everything going on, had taken a toll on her.

Detectives Lake and Clayton arrived at the medical center ER to find Hollingsworth and Manning in the waiting room, having coffee and hard rolls.

"Well, I see the gang is all here," Lake joked. "Any news?"

"Not yet. Just waiting for her doctor to release her. Appears to be a blood sugar event." Manning continued, "She's asleep right now. It's been nearly two hours."

"Well," said Hollingsworth, "we are lucky these people all know her. Pretty fast care, if you ask me. There are a lot of patients coming and going in this ER today."

The doctor approached the curtain of the bay where Captain Brown was asleep. Reese approached him for answers.

"I'm sorry, detective, but unless you are on her list, I cannot disclose, nor discuss any of her medical records with you. Now please excuse me."

Denton Hollingsworth approached. "I believe my name is currently on that list, Doctor."

He glanced at his chart and confirmed, "Yes, it is. Ok, but the rest of you will have to wait out here."

The captain started to come out of her slumber hearing the

voices around her.

"Ms. Brown, how are you feeling?" the doctor asked. "Still feeling light-headed and weak? You don't look as flushed as when you arrived."

"No, I feel rather good right now. Thanks for the help, doctor. May I leave now?"

"First, I have to go over your lab results with you. Is it okay to have Mr. Hollingsworth in the room?"

"Yes," she said. "Of course."

"We found out that you had an exceedingly high blood sugar event and you were also dehydrated. You were not aware of the diabetes?"

"No, I was not. I just thought I was hungry."

"Well, you really must pay attention to your diet and discuss all of this with your doctor. Diabetes is nothing to fool around with, especially gestational diabetes. You wouldn't want to harm your baby, Ms. Brown."

CHAPTER 51

The phone rang, jolting Reese. Her slippery hands finding the phone where she had left it, sitting on the floor next to the bathtub she was soaking in. "Clayton." She waited.

"Hello detective," the voice was eerily familiar. "I wanted you to know it wasn't my fault. I didn't know."

A shiver snaked its way down her spine and she jolted upright, sending beads of water splashing across the floor. Her free hand trembled as she pushed herself up and out of the tub, grasping for a towel, shaking from the sudden exit out of the bath water, or from the recognition of the voice on the other end of the phone. "Tim?"

"Yes."

"What wasn't your fault, Tim? You've always been able to talk to me." Reese kept her composure calling him by name to make him feel comfortable and safe. "What wasn't your fault, Tim?"

"I thought I was calling someone. They told me to dial the phone. I didn't know it was going to make your car explode like that."

"I understand Tim. Who told you to make that call?" Reese

kept her voice steady "Can you tell me who told you to do it? Please, Tim."

"My boss."

"Thank you, Tim. I'm glad it wasn't your fault. Does your boss have a name? Perhaps I know who he or she is, Tim?"

"Jack. I didn't know there was a bomb in your car, detective. I saw it explode, but I didn't mean to do it. I just dialed the phone."

"I know, Tim."

There was no response. The line went dead.

Emerson entered the apartment, all smiles, to find Reese still in her robe with wet hair cascading around her face. "Well, my dear, are you going to go to work or are you going to sit around in that get-up eating donuts all day? Got us coffee *and* donuts. What, no smart-ass remarks, Reese?"

"None. Listen to this, you're never going to believe it."

"What is it you want me to listen to? I've only been gone twenty minutes."

Reese took her phone out of her bathrobe pocket and played back the message she had just recorded.

"How the hell did he find your number, Reese?"

"That's what you're worried about? How the hell do I know? I believe him. I think they set him up to do this. Now, we have a name, only a first name, but it's a start."

"Well, Detective Reese Clayton, it is nice to have you back in the game. I haven't seen you this fired-up since before the explosion." He grinned. "Let's eat first and then make love before we get to work." He grabbed her around the waist and kissed her.

"In your dreams, Lake. We have work to do!" She shimmied

from his grip leaving him grasping the empty air looking dejected. "I'll get dressed. You set out our not so nourishing breakfast. FYI, that's going to change soon as well. Before we get married, we both need to get a grip on our lifestyle. I'm not walking down the aisle in something that looks like a maternity dress."

CHAPTER 52

Reese twirled side to side, admiring herself in the full-length mirror. "Rather stunning, even if I say so myself." Her gown was emerald green, satin and lace, and it brought out her beautiful green eyes that were sprinkled with hints of yellow specks. The dress was off the shoulder, full length, with a slit up her right leg just six inches from what her fiancé would call *the promise land.*

"I want to take you right now with that dress still on that beautiful body of yours." Emerson's hands were on her shoulders. "That slit in your dress is tempting me. It's saying *I dare you.*"

"Well, good things come to those who wait." she teased, but allowed him to reach through that slit and feel the warmth of her as she kissed him with all the passion she could muster. Without letting him have all of her, although the thought did enter her mind right there in the hall, waiting for the hotel elevator.

Emerson looked dapper in his tuxedo, ever so handsome. Before he made his way through the entrance to the ballroom, he did a mic test to be sure everyone was accessible.

The Benson Hotel Ballroom was decorated perfectly to showcase the art and artifacts on display. Emerson made the rounds through the crowds of elite, stopping whenever he spotted someone from his dad's old connections. All the while trying to keep a close eye on Reese and scanning the room for Timothy Cole.

The event was well-staffed with people in white gloves scattered around the ballroom ready to answer questions about each of the antiquities. All were displayed on velvet covered tables or hung on the walls draped in silk fabrics. Security was already tight because of the Governor's appearance, but Cromwell P. D. had their own on site, under the guise of guests, of course. Lake's Father had more power than his son ever thought.

Reese whispered into her hidden microphone. "Lake, are you seeing this? I've never seen so much hardware to protect a few statues and some artwork."

Emerson politely excused himself from a couple to answer Reese. "I know. It's like an arsenal in here. For good reason, these are expensive pieces, my dear. I've seen some of these in catalogues in my dad's office. Pretty spectacular. Anything you would like me to bid on, pretty lady?"

She didn't answer.

"Reese? Reese, where the hell are you? Shit!" he tapped the device in his ear. "Does anyone have eyes on Clayton?"

"No," Manning replied. "Last I saw her; she was talking with a woman near the lady's room door. Maybe that's where she is. Brennen can you check?"

"Already on it. Bathroom is clear," Carly responded. "She's not in there Lake. What do you want us to do?"

"Make your way around the ballroom. Check the coat room. I'll check the kitchen." Lake ordered.

"Got it."

"Wait, I see her." Lake was relieved. "She's near the staircase talking to...hold on...the crowds are blocking my view." Lake shifted from side to side. Peering over and around heads. "You've got to be kidding me!"

"Who is it?" Manning asked.

"My father. What the hell is he doing here?"

"Guess you'll have to ask him yourself, Lake. Maybe he has eyes on your girl. She looks beautiful tonight."

"Okay, Manning that's enough." Lake made his way over to his father.

Reese saw him coming and excused herself. "Oh, I must go over to say hello to our host. It was lovely seeing you Mr. Lake."

"Likewise, Ms. Clayton."

"Dad, what are you doing here?"

"I thought maybe I would try to get a good deal on that Remington over there. I believe you should, at the very least, shake your dear old dad's hand before giving him the third degree, don't you?"

"I'm sorry, dad," Lake apologized, extending his hand. "Remington?"

"Not the gun, son, the statue."

"I know what you meant, dad. No wonder there is so much security around."

"When the hell are you going to marry that beautiful girl, son? I'd like to see some grandbabies before I leave this world."

"I guess when she feels it's time. Right now, we have other matters to deal with, so please, no lectures."

"I understand son, be careful." He shook his son's hand as if he were a buyer for the auction and walked away.

"Well, here we go. Heads up everyone," Reese advised the team. "The Governor is entering. Looks like he has a bodyguard in tow."

Brennen straightened her fake press pass, ensuring it was visible around her neck.

"Carly, get a photo if you can of the guard," Reese ordered. "I've seen him before. Send it to agents Wells and Olden. We need facial rec, A.S.A.P. Lake. Can you see the guy I'm talking about?"

"Got him. Shit. He's the guy from the State Prison. The one that was overseeing the injections for the execution. Reese, I'm guessing he's not a physician."

"Yes, that's exactly who it is! I knew I recognized him. Stay just far enough away, Emerson. We don't want him to recognize you."

"Detective Clayton," Carly interjected, "Agent Olden is telling me the bodyguard is Jack Roman. It's possible he was the hit man hired to kill Judge John Orrick."

"Thanks Brennen."

"Detective Clayton, Agent Olden said he wants to meet with me. Any idea what that's about?"

"Not now, Brennen. You need to focus."

"Detective, you should know the FBI is also here. Agent Wells is in the Art room with the host of this event. Doesn't sound so happy we are here."

"Copy."

Reese gradually made her way to a piece by Renoir. She came up behind him. "Lovely painting. I've always admired his work."

"Yes, it is. While I am not a genuine fan of Renoir, I must admit, he draws a crowd." Wells turned toward Reese. "Wow! Could you possibly look more beautiful? If I were your fiancé, I would have you on a beach. No, maybe on an island somewhere safe. Somewhere where I could make love to you in that dress and then again without it. It's taking all my willpower not to grab you and kiss you."

"Mine too," Lake appeared in the doorway. "Reese, is everything okay in here?"

"Yes, I'm fine. I'll be out in a minute."

"Lake, I can't say I'm sorry, Pal. I just can't."

Emerson didn't respond. He just walked out of the room, hoping he still had a fiancé.

"Agent Wells," she whispered. "I am truly flattered, but we are on the job, all of us. So, let's move on. Please. What are you doing here?"

"Searching for the person who tried to take the governor's life. Reese, seriously, I want you. I would love for you to give me a chance. I can't help myself. I've never been so smitten with someone in my life."

"Michael, it will not happen. I love Emerson with all my heart. We are engaged to be married. You need to get hold of yourself if we are to remain friends. Are we clear?"

"Yes ma'am, clear. Not happy, but clear."

Emerson heard every word she said. He smiled, knowing his lady loved him.

"Michael, we want to draw Timothy Cole out of hiding. We have a feeling he might show his face, knowing Emerson and I are here. I guess you could say I'm bait."

"Great, now how do we stay the hell out of each other's way?"

"See that lady in a blue gown over by that portrait? she said. "You go out first. I'll strike up a conversation with her, and then try to walk out with her."

"Perfect. By the way, I'm not sorry," he smirked as he turned and walked away.

Reese approached the lady in blue, but as she got closer, she stopped short. She couldn't believe her eyes.

"Emerson," she whispered, "get in here now. We have an unexpected guest." No response. "Emerson?" she repeated. Nothing. "Manning, are you near the arts room?"

"On my way. What's up?

"Shit, it's a trap."

"Isn't there already security in there?"

Reese didn't have time to respond. She never questioned why there was no security in the room that held some of the most valuable art in the world. She would somehow have to protect the woman in blue on her own. Reese slid next to her. "Beautiful, isn't it?"

The lady turned toward Reese. "Why yes, it is lovely."

Reese whispered, "What are you doing here?"

Before she could reply, Jack Roman approached both women. "Excuse me, Kim, would you come with me, please? The governor would like a word with you."

"Enjoy your evening," she nodded to Reese, as Jack Roman escorted her away. Leaving Reese stunned.

Lake and Manning entered, circling the arts room. "What's going on Reese? What's the trap?" Emerson asked finding nothing.

Wells entered the scene. He followed close behind when he saw Manning and Lake make a sudden move toward the Arts room.

Manning and Wells continued to search every nook and cranny, but nothing. "Find out where that door leads," she ordered.

"What the hell happened?" Emerson asked, holding onto Reese's elbow.

She turned toward Agent Wells. "Michael, that lady in the blue gown."

"Yeah."

"It was Captain Brown."

"So, where is she?"

"She left with Jack Roman. He told her the governor wanted a word with her."

"What?" Emerson exclaimed. "And you just let her leave?"

"She acted like she didn't know me. I figured she didn't want me to blow her cover. She never said she was coming to this event. But she did say it was our job to clear her name. That guy could break her in half. I'm worried about her. What the hell is she doing?"

"Why wouldn't she tell us about this? I don't get it." Emerson shook his head.

Brennen broke in. "Guys, I just saw the captain get in a limo with Jack Roman. What's she doing here?"

"Tell me you got a plate number," Emerson was hoping for

the best.

"Already sent it in and it's coming back now. It's registered to Black Tie Events. Vehicle was picked up late this afternoon. Name on the license, Jack Roman."

"You and Manning get a location on where that limo is now. They have GPS tracking devices in these rentals. Hopefully, you can tail them. Stay far enough back they don't see you, but close enough to keep the captain safe."

"Copy that," Manning replied.

"Detective Lake, we'll take it from here. Agent Olden and I have got this. I suggest you stay at the Gala and keep your eyes peeled for Timothy Cole. He must be close by. The odds are he either heard or was told the two of you were on the guest list. Keep Manning and Brennen on the limo, until we catch up. I will let you know when we find out what the hell is going on with the governor and your captain."

Before Emerson could respond, Reese jumped in. "You listen to me, if you let anything happen to Captain Brown under your watch, I swear I will find you and rip you apart piece by piece. Understood?"

Michael Wells winked at Reese. "I promise, let's get to work."

CHAPTER 53

"May I have your attention, please?" The voice was familiar to Emerson Lake. It was his dad. "It gives me great pleasure to introduce you to our host for this extraordinary event. Please give a warm welcome to Doctor Jane Goldman, Chief Executive Officer at The Jade Institute for Mental Health.

The room burst into applause.

"Thank You for such a warm welcome. I would like to express my gratitude to all of you for coming out tonight and for supporting those who work tirelessly at our hospital every day to provide exemplary care, compassion and understanding to our residents in need of support with their mental health and well-being. It's challenging, but important work."

"Gun!" Reese's voice boomed over the hushed crowd.

It was too late. The 44-magnum fired toward the podium, directly at Doctor Goldman. The bullet pierced her neck. She grabbed at her throat. Her arm hitting the microphone, causing an awful shrill screech. Blood ran down her arm from her neck to her gown. Her eyes held steady at the crowd as she fell to the floor. Complete chaos erupted on the ballroom floor. Lake's father dropped to the ground and ripped apart his white shirt to bandage the wound of his friend Jane Goldman and yelled for someone to call 911.

"You have eyes on him Reese?" Lake yelled into the coms.

"No", she shouted back, "but I saw who it was. It was Cole, but I couldn't get through the crowd to stop him."

"Which way did he go?"

"He's headed to the patio," she said bursting through the exit door. "I'm close. Can't see him, but he must be out here. No cars nearby. They're valeted to the back of the hotel. He must be on foot."

"I'm right behind you, Reese. Which way are you headed? Reese? Reese? Talk to me," Emerson pleaded. There was only silence.

"Brennen, Manning, where the hell are you?"

"Wells took over the tail on the Governor and the Captain. We're about two minutes out from the hotel," Manning responded.

"Make it 30 seconds. I need you both here now! Cole is on the property. He may have Reese."

Emerson burst out the same door Reese exited. The sounds of sirens approaching permeated the quiet of the outdoors. Emerson's eyes adjusting to the darkness. The hotel was taken over by EMT's, fire apparatus, and state and local police. Ambulances were dispatched from all surrounding areas.

Emerson proceeded ahead with caution, sliding along the brick wall as he rounded the corner of the building, still not seeing Timothy Cole or Reese. He passed a gazebo that was lit up for the occasion and people gawking at all that was going on. He ordered them to get down and pointed them in a safe direction. That didn't work. He heard heavy foots steps coming toward him. He spun around and saw it was Carly. "Get those fucking morons away from here, Brennen!" he yelled. "Someone is going to get killed." With that, he took off sprinting into the darkness.

Reese didn't see the man approach her from behind. She did, however, feel the butt of a pistol hit her in the head, knocking her off balance. "You're coming with me."

"Tim?" she asked, wincing. "I'm not here to hurt you. I want to help you. Please believe me. I've always been honest with you, Tim. Remember?"

"Walk," he demanded, pushing her toward the tree line, his gun held against her rib cage.

"Why did you shoot that woman, Tim?" Her question met with silence as he squeezed her arm tighter. "Tim, please let me help you."

"Shut up! I don't want to talk anymore."

"Okay, Tim, what do you want to do?" Reese caught a glimpse of what she hoped was Emerson out of the corner of her right eye. She halted and faced Tim.

"Tim, would you like to go with me somewhere we can talk? Maybe Hannigan's Diner? It's near here and we could get something to eat. I'm starving. What do you say, Tim?" It bought her just enough time for Emerson to reach them.

"Cole, hold it right there," Emerson's gun aimed in his direction.

Cole made a swift move, with Reese in tow, grabbing her around the neck.

"Hello Tim, it's me, Detective Emerson Lake. Long time, no see. What are you doing with my girl, Tim?"

Cole's gun was pressed against Reese's head, his arm tightly wrapped around her throat. He could snap her neck in a split second. That power excited him in the past, but for now he had to focus his attention on Lake. Timothy Cole slowly raised his gun and aimed it at Emerson.

"You fire detective, and she's dead," Tim was sweating, yet his voice was alarmingly calm.

Emerson didn't have a clear shot and was afraid to lose the love of his life. "Let her go. If you want a hostage, take me. I won't cause any trouble. You and I both know how much trouble it is to have a woman tag along. We can get out of here right now, just you and me, get a cup of coffee. Tim, I got you buddy. Look at me, look at me, Tim, let her go."

Tim put his mouth close to Reese's ear and whispered. "I am ready to die now, just not surrounded by gray walls. Don't trust Jane, or the system, Reese."

"Do you know Jane, Tim?"

"No, but those places are all bad. They hurt people. I don't like any of them. Please aim high. Do you understand?"

"Yes, Tim, yes I do."

Tim shoved Reese to the ground and fired his gun toward Emerson, missing him on purpose. Reese rolled, drawing her gun from the holster under her gown. She and Emerson unloaded their weapons, Emerson aiming center mass, Reese firing at Timothy Cole's head and neck. Aiming high just like he asked. It was suicide by cop. The only way it would happen.

CHAPTER 54

Reese lay silent in the grass, tears escaping her eyes, wondering why this had to go down the way it did. Knowing it was the only way, but also wondering...was it the only way?

Emerson made sure Cole was dead before attending to his partner. "He's dead, Reese. He can't hurt anyone ever again." He helped her up. "Are you okay? Did he hurt you?"

"I'm fine." She brushed herself off. This was not the time for Emerson to be hugging or consoling his fiancé. They both knew the conduct code.

"This was a suicide, Emerson. He could have snapped my neck like a pencil, but he didn't. He told me he was ready to die and asked me to aim high just before he shoved me to the ground."

"I couldn't take the chance of him turning the gun on you Reese, so I just unloaded on him."

"I know. He didn't want to be caged any longer. He wanted to die, on his terms."

Jade Police began securing the crime scene, roping it off with yellow tape. The M.E. was already dispatched.

"You've got yourself a well-oiled machine," Emerson said, complimenting their old friend, Jade Police Officer Clark.

"Thank you, sir. Just doing our jobs. It's a pleasure to collaborate with you again, detectives. Sorry it has to be under these circumstances."

"Likewise, but no need to call me sir," Emerson said.

"You definitely do not need to call him sir," Reese laughed, giving Lake a shove.

All were grateful for a bit of levity.

"We'll meet you at the Jade station when we finish up here, officer Clark," Reese said. "Tons of paperwork and we still have the auction/ball to tend to. At least what's left of it?"

"Not to worry," Clark reassured. "The museum's curator and your father have removed all the valuables from the ballroom. We loaded them into the van to be taken back to their places of honor. All accounted for before leaving my sight. Here are the papers your father said to give to you, Emerson."

"Thank you, Officer Clark. You saved us a tremendous amount of work." Reese and Emerson shook his hand and headed back toward the ballroom.

"He may have taken one thing off our list, Reese, but it's going to be one long night ahead."

"You can say that again. Jane Goldman was sent to Jade Medical Hospital. Hopefully, she pulls through, so we can ask her some questions. Not to mention our missing captain. No sleep for us tonight."

They reached the entrance to the ballroom, assessing the mess left behind. Half empty glasses of red wine, some tipped over, stained the white linen tablecloths. Food and broken dishes scattered around the floor. Emerson shook his head, "what a difference compared to how elegant it all was at the beginning of the evening."

"Detectives, have you heard from the FBI agents since they left to tail our captain?" Carly was worried. "What do you suppose the Governor wants with her?"

"Well, Reese and I think that if the governor really believes she is the one that took a knife to his throat, the outcome looks bleak. What we don't understand is why she came to this event without telling us and with no back-up. It's totally out of character. What could she prove by making herself vulnerable to a mafia hitman? That guy is no joke."

Reese agreed, "Something just doesn't add up. I don't believe under any circumstance that Captain Brown is involved with any of this."

"I understand how you feel, Detective," Carly replied, "but how can you be so sure? You saw the videos for yourself. All roads are leading to our captain."

"Why would the Governor jeopardize his position by going after the captain on his own?" Manning questioned.

"Great question," Emerson said. "The Governor knows the feds are already investigating. If anyone caught wind that he was taking matters into his own hands, his career would be over. Shit, come to think of it, Reese, did you ever actually see the hitman escort the captain to the Governor?"

"No, the last I saw the Governor he was at the side entrance to the ballroom, probably waiting for Doctor Goldman to introduce him to the podium."

"Maybe the Governor isn't involved and this hitman Jack

Roman has her. Try Wells again."

"I've pinged his phone at least five times already. If something goes down, he'll be in touch."

"We can't wait, Reese, just make the call."

Reese dialed and put it on speaker.

"Wells here."

"Michael, I'm with Emerson, Brennen, and Manning," Reese said. "Do you have eyes on the captain?"

"We do, Reese. She's with our hitman Jack Roman. We saw them entering a residence on Pineview Road, about 18 miles outside of Jade headed west."

"No sign of the governor?" she asked.

"Not so far, it's pretty quiet in there. We can see the captain walking around. She doesn't appear to be in distress. Why? What have you got?"

"None of us has seen the governor since the shooting. We assumed he was with his bodyguard."

"We'll send a team to the Governor's residence," Wells replied.

Olden entered the conversation on radio. "Eyes open people, a large white van just passed us. Pulling into the driveway of an old barn a few hundred feet from the house. Cutter, Adams, you see this? It's the van from the Benson Hotel.

"Yes, boss. We see it."

"Cutter, you keep eyes on the house."

"Adams, you're with me," Olden said screeching to a halt to let Adams in the car.

"Lake here. Wells, what's happening?"

"Go, go, go!" The FBI agents blasted orders to their team.

The Cromwell team could only sit back and listen to the

commotion through Agent Wells' phone.

"Get your hands in the air, now! Both of you." The agents had the van surrounded. "Make one move and I'll blow your fucking heads off, got it? Get out of the vehicle, hands in the air. You, yeah, you. Put your weapon on the dash. Adams, you got him?"

"Yes, boss." Adams took the passenger's wallet with ID and weapons. Two Glocks.

Olden slammed the driver against the door, patted him down, took his wallet then dragged him to the back of the van. "Open it, Adams," Wells ordered the rookie.

"Shit, now who the hell are these two?" Olden removed the blindfolds and restraints from the two people lying in the back of the van.

The gentleman gasped. "My name is Emerson Lake. This young lady is Alyssa Bryant. She is the curator for the Jade Museum of Fine Arts. We were at the Benson Hotel for a charity auction. We were supervising the loading of these antiquities that are on loan from the museum. I think you will find a couple of security guards tied up somewhere near the hotel, officer. These thugs tied us up and kidnapped us."

"I'm Agent Olden. We're with the FBI. Are you all right, Miss?" Olden asked the shaken curator.

"I am now. Thank you, agent. I need to get these items back to the museum, thoroughly inspected, and catalogued in. These are priceless and irreplaceable works of art."

"Do you have ID on you, miss?" Wells asked.

"Yes, of course." She reached to her side. "Oh no, it's in my purse which got left behind. Hopefully it's still back at the hotel.

I have my museum security badge on me though." She pulled it up on a lanyard from her hip. "Here it is."

"And you Mr. Lake? ID, please."

He reached into his jacket pocket and retrieved his museum badge and his driver's license.

"Interesting," Wells remarked. "Do you know a detective from Cromwell named Emerson Lake?"

"Yes, of course, he's my son. I was with him this evening at the Gala. But I assume you already knew this?"

"Yes," he chuckled. "I've got him in my other ear on my cell. He's screaming obscenities at me as we speak. I am guessing you do not have a phone on you, sir?"

"No idea where it is at the moment, agent."

Wells tapped his ear bud. "You want to take the conversation from here, Lake? We'll meet up later to go over everything. Right now, we still have work to do. Your dad and Ms. Bryant will be driven back to the Benson Hotel after we get their statements."

"Thanks Mike. I owe you...again."

The agent handed Emerson Lake Sr his cell phone and left them to talk to his son.

After clearing up what happened, Emerson hung up the phone, knowing he was in excellent hands and would see him later.

"Reese, you and I need to change out of these clothes. Manning, you and Brennen gather what info we have from the hotel Gala. We will meet all of you in the hotel lobby in twenty. Tell Officer Clark we will meet him at his precinct within the hour. Wells and Olden are on the captain. That's out of our hands for now, anyway. Let's go."

CHAPTER 55

Emerson and Reese got off the elevator and entered the room, which had been booked for Reese, but contained the clothing for both.

"Let me look at you," he said with passion. He turned her to face him, grabbing her around the waist. "Are you sure you are alright? You're not hurt anywhere? Cole shoved you hard. He also had you in a choke hold for quite a while, babe. I thought I was going to lose you." He tilted her chin and gently kissed her.

"Not exactly the conclusion any of us wanted for Cole, but this was probably best for him."

"I guess," he said.

"We had better get moving. What a waste of this gorgeous gown." She looked down at the tattered hem.

"Indeed," he replied. "I had big plans for that dress this evening, on and off you. So did Mike Wells, I think."

She laughed. "Oh, you did, did you?" She whipped it over her head and landed it on the floor. She stepped on it with her bare feet and ordered him. "Get changed. We have work to do."

"Yes, boss," he quipped. He grabbed her once again and

kissed her forehead, her cheek and then her lips. Feeling himself becoming more aroused by the look and feel of her naked body.

"Stop! Not now," she said. But as she pulled away, she made sure he had a full-frontal view. She slowly turned and performed her sexiest strut knowing the empty holster strapped to her thigh would drive him crazy as she slipped away into the bathroom.

CHAPTER 56

Jade P.D. had been modernized since the last time Reese and Emerson visited the station. "Nice job," commented Lake. "Looks great in here. Ours had a recent makeover as well. I never thought I'd see the day, but the powers that be came through."

"Looks like they came through for all of us," the desk sergeant said.

Reese asked, "All the shell casings accounted for?"

"I believe they are, detective. I'll get the paperwork ready for your signatures. Then you should be able to go down to the cages to retrieve your weapons from holding."

"Officer Clark back yet?" asked Lake. "Any word from Olden and Wells on the stake out?"

"You know the FBI; they are a closed mouth group, Detective. They show up just when you think you are rid of them. There are a couple of chairs and a desk over there for you both. If you need to, just plug in your laptops, and have at it. Copy machine behind that wall over there for whatever you need. I'm sure you want to get started on your reports."

"Thanks," Lake and Reese both nodded.

Officer Clark arrived about forty-five minutes later. "Detectives, have everything you need?"

"Absolutely, Calvin," Reese looked up from her laptop.

"The two perps that stole the antiquities van from the hotel had to be processed. They're here waiting for transport to FBI headquarters. What I can't figure out is how these two could be part of a mob group from New York City? Seems they would have had better cover and not so easily caught. And by the FBI no less. From what I know about organized crime, they left out one thing."

"What's that?" Reese asked.

"Organized," he chuckled. "Plus, why wouldn't they get rid of the curator and that other guy? Why keep witnesses alive?"

"While I agree, Officer Clark, that *other* guy is my father. So, I am quite glad they are alive."

"Oh, my apologies, Detective. I had no idea he was your dad. Didn't mean to sound so callous."

"No sweat, Calvin. You know, it was funny when I spoke with my father earlier. He was all hyped up on adrenaline from the entire ordeal. He sounded like a young man again. Funny how that happens with age. Instead of feeling like their lives are in danger in a crisis, they embrace the rush. Like it's a game. He scared the hell out of me though."

"I'll bet he did, but remember," Clark reminded Lake, "you will be him before you know it." He let out a belly laugh. "I know, because I'm close to retirement myself. My wife tells me all the time; I do stupid shit."

"Sorry to interrupt gentlemen," Reese said, "but Calvin do you have the names of the two van drivers?"

"Yeah, Kyle and Frank Gerard. Brothers. Last known address, the low-income apartments on the edge of Jade City Park. Appear to be locals. Not New Yorkers. Just kids, really. My guess is, they took the job for a few bucks and were never to be heard from again."

"What do you think the odds are that we could have a word with these guys?" Lake asked. "We have to go down to the cages anyway, to retrieve our firearms."

"I'm off duty as of now. I see nothing, I know nothing. Good night, detectives."

"Good night, Officer Clark."

Once they retrieved their weapons, Lake asked the officer in the cage. "Could you point us in the direction of the holding cell? We haven't been here since we arrested Timothy Cole a few years back, and that was before the renovations. Looks good. We want to see what you've done with the place. Get some ideas for our own station."

"Sure, detectives," the officer replied not realizing he was being played. "Down this hall, take a right at the end. It will be right in front of you. We are all glad Tim Cole is gone now."

"We are too," Reese replied. "Thank you, officer."

As they walked down the corridor, Reese whispered to Emerson, "I'll take the lead. They might be more willing to talk to a female, especially if they're scared."

Emerson just nodded.

"Gentlemen," she began. "I'm Detective Clayton, this is my partner Detective Lake. We would like to ask you a few questions, if you don't mind? Are you okay? Do you need anything? Water?" The boys shook their heads no.

Lake took over. "Were you read your Miranda rights? Do you understand them?" The boys looked at each other blankly. *These kids don't have a clue about anything*, Lake thought. "Do you know what Miranda rights are?"

They shook their heads no.

"Let me explain them to you," Reese said softly. They listened intently not taking their eyes from her. "Do you understand your rights now, boys?"

In unison they replied, "Yes, Ma'am."

Reese continued. "What are your names? And where do you live?" They answered honestly matching what Officer Clark had shared. "Are you still in school?"

"I quit school about three weeks ago," Kyle replied. "Frank said I could make more money working for him."

"And how is that working out for you, Kyle?"

"We were going to make a thousand dollars each for picking up these pictures and these statues." Frank said. "The boss told us to bring them back to this barn. But those two people tried to stop us, so we tied them up and put them in the back."

Lake pulled Reese away from the holding cells. "Calvin was right. These kids have no clue. They were out to make a quick buck. They have no idea they were driving around with millions of dollars in art for a lousy two grand payoff, which they probably would never have received. They have no idea that by getting caught, they probably saved their own lives. Unfortunately, I'm guessing a prosecutor will not care how naïve they are."

Reese nodded and they stepped back to the cell. "Frank, who told you to pick up these items? Does your boss have a name?"

"Kim. That's all we know, I swear!"

Reese shot a concerned look at Emerson.

"Kyle didn't want to do it. It's my fault," tears streamed down Frank's face while Kyle just stared blankly at the detectives.

"Could you give us a description of this Kim person?" Reese asked.

Frank's description was eerily close to the description of the *Kim* identified at the Bur Oak Casino the night the Governor was attacked. Close enough to implicate their captain, yet vague enough that it could match a million others.

"Would you recognize her from a photo?"

"Yeah, I guess," Frank shrugged wiping his wet cheek.

Reese pulled her phone out and showed the young teens a photo of Captain Brown.

"Hell, no! She ain't no cop. The Kim I dealt with has long hair, pretty make-up, and long, long legs. She even told me I could feel her legs if we did what she wanted." Frank blushed and giggled like a typical clueless teen. Kyle remained oblivious to it all, still staring into space.

Reese didn't bother telling them to look at the photo with fresh eyes. To visualize the captain with her hair down and make-up. She turned to Lake and said, "I think we are just about done here."

"Now, can we go home?" Frank jumped up from the bench seat.

"I'm afraid not," Lake said, bursting his bubble. "You boys are in some deep trouble. Did you get to make a call to your parents or an attorney?"

"I can't call my ole man," Frank said. "He will kill me. He

ain't exactly father of the year."

Kyle remained lost in his own thoughts a million miles away.

"Let's go Reese."

CHAPTER 57

Reese and Emerson made one more stop at the Benson Hotel to pack up their belongings and any leftover paperwork before heading back to Cromwell.

"Reese. We haven't heard a word about what's going on with the Captain and Jack Roman."

"I know. Thought we would hear from Wells or Olden by now. I'll see if I can reach one of them again." She dialed Mike Wells' number, amazed to have him pick up on the first ring.

"Agent Wells, what happened to our captain? Are you still on the stake-out? Any word on the Governor and where he might be?" Reese pelted questions at him.

"Whoa, slow down Reese."

She came clean about talking to their two young prisoners. "You know your van drivers were just kids looking to make a few bucks. We don't think they were involved in anything other than an attempted art heist, arranged by someone else."

"They informed us of your little escapade at the Jade precinct. Not much gets past us, Reese. As far as your captain is concerned, we watched all evening. Neither her nor Jack Roman left the house, and no one entered either. We have nothing to hold either of them on. She didn't appear to be in distress at all, so we pulled the team. We have witnesses confirming they saw the governor leaving from the Gala in a limo. We had a tail on him all the way back to the Bur Oak Casino. Nothing since. Where are you and Lake headed now?"

"We are at the Benson," Lake said. "Packing up, and then headed back to Cromwell. Any word on Dr. Goldman? She looked in bad shape."

"Unfortunately, she didn't make it through surgery. I already notified her family," Olden replied. "Glad you got Cole though. Nice job!"

Reese got back on. "I'm not convinced Cole was the brains behind my car bomb, or Jane Goldman's demise, Robert."

"Probably not, Reese, but right now we will have to wait on what our teams find."

"Send us your paperwork before you head back to Cromwell," Michael requested. "We will do the same when we finish up here."

"Will do." Lake knew full well the FBI was not about to do that.

CHAPTER 58

Reese walked over to the end of the bed, where her beautiful green gown lay in a heap on the floor. "Well, this was a waste of a paycheck. And the shoes another."

"Come here," Emerson grabbed her hands. "May I kiss you? I have that vision of you in my head and it won't go away."

"Oh, really Mr. Lake, and what *vision* might that be?" She kissed him, holding his hands by her side.

"The one where I see that gorgeous body of yours in emerald green, all shiny. And then you whip it off over your head, toss it on the floor. The one where all you are wearing is the holster on your thigh and I am on top of you for hours making love to you. The vision I want to finish right now."

"Well, detective, I do not recall that vision," she replied coyly. "Can you show me? So what if we get charged another day for the room?" She kissed him hard, wrapping his arms around her waist. "Hold me, Emerson. Kiss me. Make love to me forever."

"I'm here to oblige, my sweet Reese. Your wish is my command." He walked her to the bed, tossed the blankets and sheets aside and guided her gently to the position he wanted. Kissing her from her forehead to her navel, telling her, "I love you Reese with every inch of my soul, please marry me, so we can be one forever and a day." He moved on top of her, no longer able to stop himself. He entered her, and they both surrendered to the passion and release.

Afterwards, still feeling the glow, Reese said, "Emerson Lake, I love you too and will marry you today if you like."

He propped himself up on his elbow. "Where can we get a marriage license in a day? I'll work on it."

They laughed, kissed, and held each other for a few moments longer before agreeing it was time to head home.

CHAPTER 59

"I'm sure our crew is back in Cromwell by now, Emerson. I'll check in with our hotshot Officer Brennen and have her do a background check on those two kids who stole the museum van. She knows her way around that computer."

"Good idea. While you're at it, check in with Manning. See if we have any updates on Jennifer Orrick and the breaking and entering charges against her. I wonder if she got her new counsel?"

"I'll check in with him later, I think he had an appointment this morning."

"Ok, just as long as Brennen doesn't go rogue and start digging into it herself. Could ruin the entire case. Conflict of interest."

"Agreed."

"Okay, I'll jump in the shower while you call Carly. Unless, of course, you would rather join me?"

"Emerson Lake, love of my life, you are impossible! The answer is no."

Reese spent most of the ride back to Cromwell in silence

rewinding in her mind what happened with Timothy Cole.

"You know Emerson, I have to admit, in all my days as a detective, I have never felt bad about an arrest, a conviction, or a sentencing. But, for some reason, Timothy Cole is one that I won't easily, if ever, get over. I know all the reasons they sentenced him to die, but I felt bad for him. I don't understand why his family left him in that awful facility. They claimed it was a place to help him with his mental illness, but they just used him as an experiment. It's sickening."

"Sweetheart, we will never know what that family went through, including Cole himself. They didn't have the means to care for their son at home. They probably thought they were doing what was best for him and didn't know what was really going on inside the institution. Back then they didn't have the kind of care that's available now. Even today, there is so much more work to be done to help people struggling with their mental wellbeing."

"I guess."

"I have an idea, Reese. Suppose you and I find time after we get married to volunteer somewhere that helps people like Tim and their families. Maybe we could be part of the solution to prevent another tragedy. I believe that is the only way you will ever feel at peace about what we just had to do to this man. What do you say? Are you with me?"

Reese Clayton, a fierce woman that could take someone down like a ninja. A woman tougher than most men, also had a heart, began to sob. Emerson Lake pulled to the side of the road and held her until she cried it out.

"Thank you, Emerson, for really listening to me. And yes," she sniffled, "let's do it. I'm in."

CHAPTER 60

Arriving at Cromwell P.D. around four thirty in the afternoon, Reese and Lake spotted Allen Manning leaving the precinct. "Hey wait up. Are you trying to avoid me, deputy?" Reese joked. "What did you find out about the judge's daughter?"

"Hey guys, welcome back," he smiled. "Jennifer Orrick has another lawyer, poor bastard," Manning shook his head. "She has a court date for tomorrow morning. The judge is asking that one of you be present for the hearing. So, I'm guessing you know how that's going to go."

"It will be interesting, Allen," Emerson commented. "Got anything else for us? Any word on the captain?"

"Yeah, she called and said she would be in tomorrow. Said she was feeling better and wanted to get back to work."

"Wait, what?" both detectives exclaimed in unison. "Did she mention anything about her sudden appearance at the Gala?"

"Nope. And I knew better than to ask. Good luck with that, you two. I would not want the job of asking her questions. I'm off duty. I'll see you both in the morning."

Emerson looked at Reese as they walked toward the door.

"Shit, I don't blame Manning for side stepping this land mine. Should we flip a coin or double up on her when she gets here in the morning?"

"We need to be in court tomorrow morning," Reese reminded him. "I say we wait and approach the captain after the hearing. That will give her some time to get settled in."

"Sounds like a good plan."

They entered the precinct, greeted by officer Brennen. "Hey, you two, what took so long getting back here? Never mind, none of my business," Carly immediately regretted she asked.

"Uh, traffic," Lake said as he turned and winked at Reese.

"Sure, whatever. Listen, I found some information about the kids that stole the van from the hotel. You were correct, Detective Clayton; they are just Jade locals. First offenses for both, well other than stealing fruit from a grocery store once. I'm working on finding more on these two, but either way, these guys are looking at some major time, first offense or not. Damn sure they can't afford excellent attorneys."

CHAPTER 61

Captain Brown tried to stay in control as she entered the Reservation Police Department.

"Captain Maka please, he's expecting me."

"And you are?" the desk clerk asked.

"I think you already know that," she glared at the officer.

"I'll let him know you're here."

She waited for 15 minutes before going to the desk again, her patience running thin. "Excuse me, how long will he be?"

"Not long at all," Jimmy Maka appeared in the doorway. "Come in Kim, it's nice to see you again. Sorry, I had to take a call," he led her into his office. "Have a seat," he gestured toward a chair in front of his desk and closed the door.

"I need to talk to you about this whole governor thing. I wasn't there, Jimmy. It wasn't me."

"Well, you could have fooled me, Kim. What the hell were you thinking? The Governor no less; that sleazy piece of shit? I thought we had something special between us. How long have we been friends? I've known you nearly my whole life. How could you do this?"

"Please," she pleaded, "trust what I say."

"No. I don't have to do anything of the sort. You hurt me, Kim. Remember, you're the one who left the Reservation in pursuit of a new life. A life that took you away from here and into a whole new world. One that didn't include your heritage. And now it seems like one that didn't include me either. I don't know you at all."

"I need help to gain access to the Bur Oak Casino, Jimmy. I need to speak to the employees. Jimmy, I need you more than ever. Please?" she begged.

"Kim, I have spoken to your detectives and told them what I know. All that I know. You understand, I can no longer speak with you, but will continue to inform detectives Clayton and Lake of any updates in the case, as a courtesy to you." He stood up from his desk and hovered over her. "I think that is all I have time for today, Captain Brown." He touched her face gently, cupping her chin and lifted her mouth toward his, pausing just before their lips touched. "I will always love you, Kim. I am just at a loss here." He led her to the exit and said his goodbyes. Kim got in her car and beat the steering wheel with her fists swearing as loud as she could before she eventually left the Reservation. Never having the chance to tell him what she needed to say.

CHAPTER 62

"Captain Brown is requesting you and Reese meet at the precinct by 7am," Carly notified Lake. "Manning as well. I'll call him now. Can you tell Reese for me?"

"Jesus Brennen," Lake was pissed she interrupted his morning shower. "We have court this morning with Jennifer Orrick. The captain knows this. That doesn't give us much time to hash all of this out."

"I hear you," Carly replied.

"Yes, I'll contact Reese," he confirmed knowing she was just steps away in the next room.

"Sorry, Detective, just following orders."

"Thanks Carly," he huffed and hung up.

Once the detectives arrived, Carly headed for Captain Brown's office, "Captain, they are ready to update you on the trip to Jade."

"Have them meet me in the conference room. I want you to attend as well. Put someone else on the desk."

"Yes, Captain."

They gathered around the conference table, just like before.

Paperwork and videos ready to roll.

"Captain Brown," Emerson was the first to speak. "With all due respect, what were you thinking? We can't protect you if you don't tell us what is going on."

"Exactly," Reese agreed. "Why didn't you tell us you would be at the Gala undercover? You put all of us in a very difficult situation. The Governor's bodyguard is a hitman for the Rossi family. His name is Jack Roman. We suspect he killed Judge Orrick. He could have killed you too. Matter of fact, why didn't he kill you?"

"Yea, Agents Olden and Wells said you didn't appear to be in distress when they left the stake-out," Lake added. "What went down in that house? We haven't heard a word from you this whole time. Do you know where Roman is now?"

The captain stood up, "Is there anyone else that has something to say to me?"

Carly Brennen raised her hand, "Captain, I believed we were a team. Work together, not apart. Isn't that what you always say?"

"Manning, how about you?" the captain jabbed. "Do you have any comments on my behavior?"

"No, ma'am."

The captain paced around twice before planting herself at the head of the table. "I need," she paused, "no better yet, *you* need to listen to me. All of you. I am being set-up. There is someone out there impersonating me. For what reason, I do not know. I was here in town while you were in Jade. I never left Cromwell."

"Pardon me, Captain," Reese wrinkled her brow. "I saw you myself at the Gala. You spoke to me like you were undercover and didn't want me to blow it. You had on a blue gown and were admiring a painting when Jack Roman approached us and told you the governor wanted a word with you. He called you Kim. Like he knew you." Reese went on to explain that the FBI followed her and Jack to a house outside town.

"What time was this?" the captain inquired.

"Around eight maybe," Reese replied.

The captain reached over and dialed the conference phone. "May I speak with Denton Hollingsworth, please? This is Captain Brown of the Cromwell P.D."

Denton Hollingsworth joined the call.

"Mr. Hollingsworth, you are on speaker with my team. They have some questions about my whereabouts last night."

"Lake here. Denton, do you know where Captain Brown was last night between the hours of 8pm and midnight?"

"Well, for starters, we ate at the Rock on Veterans Way. Had reservations for 8pm. You can contact the restaurant if you wish. The bartender can verify as well as the chef. What's this about?"

"Counselor," Captain Brown continued, "it appears someone is trying to impersonate me."

"And why would they do that?"

"I believe," the captain responded, "that's what we need to find out."

"Captain, be sure to keep me apprised of what is taking place, understand?"

"Yes, I will, Denton, and thank you."

The conference phone beeped as the call ended.

"Now, do you believe me?" The captain stood in front of them with her hands on her hips. "Get the FBI on the phone,

Brennen. Tell them we need them in on this."

"Captain, I hate to interrupt this meeting, but Reese, Brennan and I are expected to be in court in fifteen minutes. Jennifer Orrick's hearing," he reminded her.

"Right. Ok, I will contact the Agents myself and update you later with a time to meet back here at the station."

• • •

Emerson and Reese entered the courthouse and found the room quickly. Sitting front and center was Jennifer Orrick, along with her new attorney. This one had a few bucks, like the others, but had better control over her client.

Carly Brennen entered the courtroom with her lawyer. Her counsel was older, but sharp.

"Your honor, we are here to determine the severity of the charges against my client Jennifer Orrick. Daughter of the recently murdered Judge John Orrick."

"I am well aware of who Miss Orrick is, Counselor."

"I apologize, your honor."

"Continue," he said with a motion of his hand.

"The charges against my client are for breaking and entering an apartment currently rented by Officer Carly Brennen, of the Cromwell P.D. My client wishes to plead guilty to the charge of entering the said apartment, but denies breaking in. She claims the door was open, and she knocked, but no one answered. She did, however, let herself in, to look for a passport her fiancée left for her."

Lake leaned into Reese. "Smart lawyer. Making her look

totally innocent while pleading guilty."

"Could you explain that further, please?" the judge asked. Jennifer's attorney went into detail about the fire, and Miss Orrick's distrust of her now deceased fiancé Alessandro Rossi.

"Your honor, if I may," Carly's attorney stood to address the judge. "My client understands the emotional impact on Miss Orrick due to the loss of her father. No one denies that. But it does not give her the right to enter someone's home without permission. That is still unlawful entry. Officer Brennen didn't even know Miss Orrick until all of this happened."

"Counselor, would you like to take my place behind this desk?" the judge snapped peering at her over the top of his glasses.

"No, Your Honor. I apologize. What I meant was..."

"I know what you meant," the judge said in a firm tone. "I have the files in front of me. Please take a seat."

"This is a troublesome case," the judge began. "I have looked at both files. We will set bail at five thousand dollars. Ms. Orrick, you will remain in Cromwell until you return for sentencing. You will be required to wear an ankle monitor until such time. I will set a court date for three weeks from today. Court dismissed." The judge's gavel landed like a thud on its target.

Carly's attorney had no issue with the judge's decision.

As they headed to the parking lot of the courthouse, Lake said, "Carly, don't get upset about the judge letting her out on such a small amount of bail. Reese and I both figured this would happen."

"I did too," Carly responded. "The daddy thing."

"When we return to the station, Carly, we need your computer skills," Reese advised. "Let's get the Bur Oak Casino videos from the night of the governor's attack. We need to use facial recognition to compare against the video footage the night of the Gala. If there is someone impersonating the captain, she is damn good. I would have bet the farm it was Captain Brown I was speaking with that night. She has a solid alibi, but stranger things have happened. Oh, and Carly, this time try not to roam around the FBI files. Let us know what you need and Lake or I will contact Michael or Robert for you. Do you understand what I'm saying?"

Carly looked at both detectives with deep concern. "They know?"

"Yes, they know," Lake confirmed. "And if it wasn't for Reese, you might be in a jail cell right now and I don't mean one of our own. We will discuss this at a future date. So, behave or I'll send you to your room without dinner and take away your phone for a month, young lady," he joked trying to lighten the mood. He gave her a reassuring pat on the shoulder as she got into her car and headed back to the precinct.

"I hope she is smart enough to heed the warning, Reese," Lake shook his head as they drove back to the station. "She is a smart girl; very smart. It wouldn't surprise me in the least if our FBI friends decide to recruit her for their agency."

"I had the same thought."

CHAPTER 63

In her pursuit to positively ID the captain, Carly Brennen reached out to some of her friends. Gearhead friends, proficient in the latest in modern technology. She could not risk getting caught in a similar situation as before. The FBI was off limits, for now anyway.

"Detectives, and you too, Deputy Manning, come here and take a look at this."

They all huddled around Carly's desk staring at her monitor.

"I pulled the footage from the Bur Oak, the Gala, and I sourced a photo of Captain Brown from a formal event held after Captain Brown's swearing in ceremony. The Governor held the event as a publicity campaign of sorts. To promote himself as the candidate that pushed for change. First female, and first Lakota to hold the position. The date in the photo was a couple of years ago, but she still looks the same. I'm attempting to run a new program as we speak. It goes deeper into her facial structure, skin tone, eyes, and even the posture. It's going to take a while to load the software onto my computer and get it to process, but it's not illegal," she reassured them.

"Where did you find all this?" Manning asked. "Sounds pretty deep, if you ask me."

"The photo came from the news story on the captain. Well, more like the story on the Governor, I should say. The captain didn't come close to being the lead in that story. It was all about him."

"And the program itself?" asked Emerson.

"I believe all of you in the field have secret informants, correct? Well, if I'm going to become the officer that I want to be, then I need to have my own sources of, let's say, intelligence."

"Nicely played Brennen," Manning leaned over and gave her a high five.

"Officer Brennen," Reese cautioned. "Keep in mind the legal aspect of your actions, understand?"

"Yes, I will. And I'll notify you when I have results if it works."

Emerson added, "Remember Officer Brennen, you called in this tech group to assist you. Be aware of how much information you give them. If things go wrong, and they most often do, their careers and their lives could be at stake. As well as your own. That is your responsibility, and yours alone."

"I understand Detective."

"Okay, where do we want to start?" Manning rubbed his hands together. "I say, let's get the FBI agents on the phone and find out more about the residence where Jack Roman took our Captain Brown imposter. The captain wanted us to get on that right way. Find out who lives there. Show up at the door and ask questions."

"We also need to pay another visit to the Reservation Police," Reese added. "Manning you contact Reservation Sheriff Jimmy

Maka. See if he has time to meet with us. Carly, is there anything you need from us right now to help with your search?"

"No, not that I can see, anyway."

"Good. Let's get busy team!" Lake cheered as if he was a coach for a ball team. "We have our work cut out for us."

"One more thing, do we know when they are going to release Cole's body?" Reese asked. "I know he'll be cremated, but I want to scatter his cremains on the top of the hill in the cemetery where we first arrested him. I'll take on the cost."

"I can look into that for you, Detective," Carly offered. She wasn't sure why the detective wanted to do it, but knew this was not the time to ask.

CHAPTER 64

"What's going on, Reese?" Manning asked as the three of them headed to the car. "Why do you want to bury Cole? I know it's none of my business, but this seems odd after all he has done. Would you have buried him if they had executed him? The lunatic tried to kill you, Reese."

"No, he didn't, Allen. That was never his intention. This was suicide by cop. He told me he was ready to die. He told me a lot of things that we now have to investigate."

"Ok, I'll shut up now," Manning threw up his hands. "None of my business."

"No, it's okay," Reese assured him. "We need your help. Please, I'll explain all of it later. Right now, we need to head to that house. It's on Pineview Road. Did the agents get back to you yet with the house number?"

"Not yet. Guessing they won't either."

"Well, let's follow the breadcrumbs," Lake suggested. "When we get on Pineview, we'll look for a barn with a residence nearby."

'Wow! That's a genius plan, Lake," Manning teased. "I believe most barns have a house nearby."

"Bite me, Manning," Lake laughed, shaking his head. "It was misting a little last night. Maybe the Agent's cars left tire tracks in the mud. Geez, I amaze myself at my brilliant plans sometimes."

"Yeah, Lake, old-fashioned investigating, unlike our little miss webpage whiz. I'm impressed." Manning laughed in the back seat.

As they approached the Jade city limits, "The Agents mentioned the road was eighteen miles west of Jade," Emerson recalled. At least we have the direction. Keep your eyes peeled."

Eventually, they located where the FBI had set up the night before. Manning was the first to see a barn. The house was nearly a quarter mile away. They turned around and saw nothing going on at the residence. Circling back in the opposite direction, still nothing.

"Pull into where the barn is, Reese."

She slowly edged the car onto the muddy drive, "What do you think is there, Emerson?"

"Not sure yet, gut feeling perhaps."

"Well, one thing is for sure," Manning said peering out the window, "there are a lot of footprints around. Probably from the van episode."

"I want to see what is in that barn. Reese, you stay in the car. Manning, you and I will have a look around."

They opened a small door on the side of the barn. Emerson looked down at his feet. "Two sets of footprints leading into this barn. One, set of high heels." He cautiously entered, calling out. "Is anyone here?" No answer. Emerson nodded to

Manning, continued inside, guns drawn.

"Lake, over there. Someone left their wardrobe behind. A blue ball gown and high-heeled shoes."

They continued to search the barn, finding nothing else.

Once back at the car, they filled Reese in on what they found. "Why didn't the FBI Agents search the barn? Got to be a lot of DNA on that dress. Shoes too. They were right here. It makes no sense," Manning speculated.

"Okay, this is not our jurisdiction, but I have an idea." Reese picked up her phone and dialed her friend, Officer Calvin Clark, Jade P.D.

"Officer Clark, can you meet with us? Here in Jade? We need a favor."

"I'm listening."

"The barn and van episode last night. You weren't there, correct?"

"No, the agents sent those two kids that stole the van back here. That's when I heard about it."

"Did anyone mention going into the barn on the property?" Reese was being careful to not put this officer in a compromising position.

"No, but I'm guessing that's because they caught the guys before they got to the barn."

"What's this about, detective?"

"We were just on the property, Calvin. My partner and one of our deputies. We found a ball gown in the barn. Shoes too. They looked exactly like the outfit worn by a woman I spoke with at the Gala. We believe she might be impersonating our Captain. We can't take the clothing in as evidence without jeopardizing the case, but you can. Can you take care of this? Maybe say you had a hunch about the barn? Bring the evidence to your labs or turn them over to the FBI?"

"Detective Clayton, are you stepping on FBI toes? I don't know about this; I could lose my job."

"I doubt it, Officer," Lake reassured. "But we could lose ours. And there is evidence in that barn that could clear our captain. Or, it could convict her. Either way, we have to find out."

"I hear you, detective. I'll see what I can do. I can't imagine why the FBI agents didn't go into the barn, doesn't make much sense," Clark mumbled. "I'll grab another officer for back up. We need to protect whatever else is in there. They could have used it as a stash house for many things, drugs, money. Who the hell knows?"

"Thanks Officer Clark," Reese said. "Lake and I owe you one. We'll head out. Contact one of us when you have some info, please. Or the FBI."

CHAPTER 65

"This is officer Clark, Jade P.D. Would you connect me to Agent Wells or Agent Olden please? We are working a case together."

"Wells. What can I do for you, officer?"

"Did your team find anything at the barn last night? Another officer and I were curious to know if they could have used it for other stolen items from around town. Maybe stolen tv's, electronics, firearms, ammo? We are here now, but thought we should ask you first, before we head in."

"We found nothing in there, Clark. Why?"

"Gut feeling, I guess, sir."

"Those are usually the best clues. Bodycam on Clark?"

"Yes, sir."

"Take it slow," Wells cautioned.

Before Clark could hang up, he heard a noise from the loft, a rustling sound above his head. He pulled his weapon. "Jade Police! Who's there?" he shouted. No answer. The smell of old hay filled his nostrils. He signaled the other officer to go around to the other side of the loft to cover him before he climbed the ladder.

The shots pierced Wells' ears on the other end of the phone. "Clark? What the fuck is going on?"

He heard the other officer yelling. "Shots fired." Then silence.

"Jade P.D. What's your emergency?"

"This is FBI Agent Wells. We need all units in the vicinity of Pineview Road. Barn near a residence at 2173 Pineview. Shots fired. Officer Clark and another officer on scene in need of backup. Proceed with caution. We are on our way. About 15 minutes out."

Reese, Manning, and Lake weren't far when they heard the dispatch for all units to assist. "Shit!" Lake shot a concerned glance at Reese. "Something is going down. Step on it! Go, go, go!"

Reese whipped the car around, turned on the flashing red lights and siren, stepped on the gas eventually joining the Jade police cars, ambulance, and fire rigs en route.

"Lake, look," Reese pointed. "The barn is on fire."

"Holy shit!" Emerson Lake jumped out of the car before it even came to a stop. "We need to get in there! Officer Clark may be inside." He raced toward the barn.

"No!" the fire chief jumped in front of Emerson. "It's way too dangerous. The whole thing could collapse."

"Hose me down. That will give me a few minutes. Now, damn it!"

"You are fucking crazy!" a firefighter exclaimed as he doused Emerson with the fire hose.

Emerson shot a quick glance back at Reese before running inside. A firefighter handed him a full facemask and a helmet.

"Hello, anybody in here?" The intense heat of the flames

stung his bare hands. The crackling sound deafening. And yet eerily quiet at the same time somehow. He kept hoping for someone to answer him.

Fire crews surrounded the barn, fighting the flames.

Emerson yelled again. Still no answer. He could feel the intense heat and smoke take over his lungs, even with the mask. He yelled again. "Anyone in here?"

This time, he heard a cough.

Emerson yelled to the firefighters, "Over here!"

Again, Emerson heard coughing and gagging.

The sight of the hose through the smoke and the feeling of cold water gave the victim hope.

"I've got you," Emerson dragged the limp body toward what he hoped was the door. Stumbling, he lost his footing and landed on top of something. It was another body. He yelled to the firefighter that was with him. "You take Clark! You got him?"

The firefighter grabbed Clark and threw him over his shoulder. "Yeah, I got him!"

Lake waved the firefighter toward the exit. "Go! I got her!"

CHAPTER 66

Wells and Olden arrived on the scene to see one side of the barn collapsed.

"Anyone hurt?" Olden yelled out.

"We don't know yet." Reese ran toward the agents. "Lake is in there. If he lives, I'm going to kill him!"

"What?" Wells shouted over the noise. "What the hell is he doing?"

"Playing the fucking hero." She was angry, but tears streamed down her face.

The firefighter came out of the blazing barn first with Officer Clark. The lower half of his body was burned, but EMT's quickly noticed what appeared to be a gunshot to his right shoulder.

Not far behind was Emerson Lake, carrying a female in jeans and a gray hoodie. She had burns on the right side of her body. The door that had collapsed on top of her protected the left side. The flames extinguished by Emerson's wet clothes on top of her.

Helicopters were on the ground in minutes, ready to transport the victims to the burn unit at Jade Medical.

"Hey, we have another body over here!" a young firefighter shouted. "He's a cop!"

Reese and Olden ran to help. "Who is this guy?" asked Olden.

"I recognize him from the Jade precinct," Reese confirmed. "Is he alive?"

"Barely," a paramedic had rushed over. "His burns appear to be superficial, but it looks like he's been shot multiple times."

"Get him in the chopper," Olden directed. "We'll meet you at Jade Medical."

"Wait!" shouted another firefighter. "I have a little boy. He was crouching in the tall grass over there, crying for mommy."

"Is he hurt?" Manning yelled over the whir of the helicopter's blades.

"No, just scared!"

"Give him to me." Reese scooped him up trying to cover his ears. "I'll take him in our car."

There was no more room on the helicopter for Emerson to accompany the burn victims. He reached for Reese carrying the little boy who appeared to be maybe five or six years old.

"Here, let me take him."

"I got him," Reese snapped. "Are you okay? Because I am going to beat the crap out of you later. I hope you know that. Manning you drive with Lake up front, I'll get in the back seat with our little friend here."

"Yes, ma'am," Manning replied.

Safely inside away from all the commotion, Reese spoke to their tiny passenger. "Let me look at you sweetheart, are you hurt anywhere?"

The little boy shook his head no.

"It's going to be okay."

The little boy was still crying.

"My name is Reese. I'm a police officer. I'm here to help you. What's your name?"

He didn't answer.

Reese couldn't see any signs of injury. "Can you tell me your mommy's name?" She found some tissues in her pocket and helped him blow his nose. She took another tissue and dried the tears. Reese held him tight, rocking him back and forth, humming a tune. Hoping to relax him.

It worked for a while, until the little boy saw the commotion at the hospital, and heard the sirens and the helicopter on the rooftop. Reese placed him on a gurney. "Everything will be fine, sweet boy. This nice nurse is going to make sure you are not hurt. Okay?"

He did not want to let her go. He pulled at her arm, wailing. Reese tried to re-assure him. "I'll be right here when you come out. Is that all right with you? You're a big boy, right?"

He nodded yes as the nurse pushed the gurney into a curtained emergency room bay.

Emerson grabbed Reese, elbow and led her to an empty corner, and held her for a few moments.

"Emerson, what did we just do? This is all our fault. If we hadn't sent Clark out there, none of this would have happened."

"You don't know that," but he knew it was true.

"Any idea who the woman you carried out of the fire might be?"

"Reese, I would have bet my life it was Captain Brown."

CHAPTER 67

"Lake, why don't you check in on officer Clark. I'm going back to the little boy. See if I can get a name out of him, possibly find out his mother's name. I'll text you with any info on my end. You do the same."

"Okay, sounds like a plan." He turned to head down the hallway.

"Emerson," Reese snatched his hand and pulled him back. "I'm so glad you are okay." She kissed him on the cheek.

"Hey, you two," Wells interrupted their tender moment. "We are going to need a statement from you both. What the hell were you doing there anyway? Why do I have a nagging feeling that you put Clark up to this? Care to elaborate?"

Lake let out a sigh. "This was totally our doing. We thought the barn may have been a stash house. We thought there could be evidence in there that was overlooked. When we got close, we realized it wasn't our jurisdiction, but walked in anyway. The only thing we saw was a blue gown and shoes sitting in a pile." "The same blue gown the lady I thought was Captain Brown was wearing at the Gala."

"Reese, what do you mean *you thought was Captain Brown?*" he wrinkled his brow.

"Exactly what it sounds like. It was the same dress and shoes that woman was wearing. So, we notified Clark. We asked if he would be interested in checking it out and grabbing the clothes for the lab, see if we could collect some DNA. He's a good man, Wells. I hope to hell he is going to be okay. The other officer as well."

"I hope so too," Wells paused, "for all our sakes. Clark called us and said he had a *gut feeling* about the barn. We were on the phone with him when we heard the gunshots."

"I'd like to go check on the little boy, if that's okay with you?"

"Of course, I'll go with Lake to check on the others. Let's keep your involvement between the three of us for now. Deal?"

"Sounds good to me," Lake nodded.

"Me too," Reese agreed, walking away.

Lake and Wells entered the burn unit and approached the staff, credentials in hand.

"What's the prognosis on our female burn victim, Doctor?"

"She has some major burns on the right side of her body, from just under her left breast to above her knee. Will need extensive surgery to repair. She has a rather good lump on her head, but nothing that won't heal. We are keeping her heavily sedated for the pain. She didn't have any ID on her, Agent. Do we have a name?"

"No, but we think the young boy in the ER may be her son. There is a detective with him now to see if she can get him to answer a few questions."

"Good, let us know what you find out."

"Doctor, what about Calvin Clark and the other Jade officer that was with him?" Lake inquired.

"Let me pull the charts. It looks like Officer Clark is in surgery now to have a bullet removed from his shoulder. He has burns on his legs and feet. We will let you know when he comes out of surgery."

"Officer Patrick Nolan had multiple gunshot wounds; it doesn't look good right now. His family is on their way. He's also in surgery. We're doing the best we can for him. That's all I can say for now."

"Thank you, Doctor," Emerson patted his arm. "Wells, let's head to the ER and see how Reese is doing with the little boy."

Lake was the first to enter the ER bay and saw Reese holding the frightened little man tightly in her lap. His thumb in his mouth, face red from crying and a little drip dangling from his nose that seemed to be there no matter how many times Reese wiped it away.

"Detective Lake, Agent Wells; I'd like you to meet Kevin," she said when they pulled the curtain back.

"Hello, Kevin," Lake greeted him moving a little closer. "Do you know that the young lady holding you is a police officer? She carries a badge and everything. She helps people like you and me all the time. She once helped me find my mom. I was afraid, just like you."

Reese, impressed with her fiancée, agreed. "That's true Kevin. Hey, would you like to be a police officer when you grow up? Detective, do you have an extra badge with you?"

"I do." Emerson reached into his pocket and pulled out a child-sized gold colored shield.

He reached over and pinned it on the boy's dirty blue, and almost white, long sleeve striped shirt. "Can you raise your right hand, young man?"

Kevin nodded, raising his left hand keeping his right thumb in his mouth.

"Do you, officer Kevin, promise to help other kids find their mommies if they get lost?"

The little boy removed his thumb and wiped his nose on his sleeve, "Yes!" He smiled wide and reached out and grabbed the badge as though it was his best gift ever on a Christmas day.

Michael Wells couldn't believe the lengths Clayton and Lake were going to make this little boy feel comfortable and safe so he would open up and bare his soul.

Reese and Emerson saluted the tiny tot and said, "Welcome to the Cromwell Police Department Officer Kevin... uh...what's your last name, Kevin?" Lake asked. "We need to make this official."

"Brown. I'm officer Kevin Brown," he slid himself off Reese's lap and saluted back to Lake.

Reese and Emerson stared at each other, shock on their faces, mouths open.

Mike Wells also snapped to attention and said, "Welcome to the force, officer Brown."

Little Kevin Brown saluted back. Once again wiping his nose on his sleeve.

CHAPTER 68

"Reese, could I have a word with you?" Lake asked. "As long as that's okay with you, officer? Oops, I mean, Officer Brown?"

Kevin smiled, nodded and went back to looking at his brand-new badge.

Reese and Emerson stepped out into the hallway of the ER. "Reese, how the hell is this possible? This little guy has the same last name as our captain. This can't be a coincidence, can it?"

"I'm as baffled as you are. We need to pay a visit to the young lady we brought in from the fire."

"I agree. Hopefully, the pain meds are wearing down so we can talk to her. Our impersonator has some serious burns, but not life threatening. Hopefully, they let us in. We need to be there when she wakes up."

"I agree," Reese said. "Give me a few minutes to talk to this little guy to reassure him I'm not leaving the building."

"Okay, I'll wait out here."

Reese re-entered the ER bay with a smile on her face. "Kevin, the detectives and I have to leave your room for a few minutes, but I promise I will be back in just a little while. We have a police officer right outside this curtain. Will you be okay until I get back? Can you take care of things here like an outstanding police officer and do what the nurses ask you to do while I'm gone? Are you strong enough?"

Kevin raised his arm in the air and bent his elbow to show Reese he had muscles.

"Good job!" Wells praised the little boy as he peeked inside. "We'll be back before you know it." Wells once again saluted the little guy.

Wells, Lake, and Clayton met Olden in the burn unit. It had been a few hours since the victims were first brought in. "May we see the female Jane Doe from the fire? We need to ask her a few questions. It won't take long," Emerson asked the desk nurse.

"Right this way, but only two of you. I'm not choosing. I'm too tired to get into a pissing contest with any of you."

"Understood. Wells, you and Reese go in. Olden and I can grab a coffee."

They entered the room to see the woman whimpering. It still shook Reese to see just how much she looked like Captain Brown.

Wells took the lead.

"He introduced Reese and himself. "Could you tell us your name, please? he asked. "We need to know who you are and if there is anyone we can contact for you, relatives, friends."

"Where's my son?" she yelled wincing from the pain of the burns. "I need to find my baby."

"Ma'am, we will find your son," Wells said, trying to calm her down. "But first we need to know your name."

"It's Kim. Please, I need to find my son," she pleaded.

"Your full name?" Reese asked the now frantic woman.

"Kimimela Brown."

CHAPTER 69

"It's a unique and beautiful name. Your son, what is his name and how old is he?" Wells asked.

"Kevin and he's five. Black hair. He is part Lakota."

"Is he in school yet?" Wells asked.

"Don't you dare!" she exploded with pure anger in her voice. Terror in her eyes. "I say when and where my son goes to school!" She had tried to sit up, but the pain was too much and she fell back in a heap. "I will kill you, cut your heart out and place it on a telephone pole for the birds to eat if you make any attempt to take my son away. You got that?"

Reese stepped in between Wells and Kim. Not to protect him, but to reassure this mother her son was safe. "Kim, I believe we have your son downstairs. The nurses are checking him over to make sure he doesn't have any injuries, but we believe he is perfectly fine. A firefighter found him hiding in the field near the barn that caught fire. Can you tell us what happened in the barn, Kim? I promise, as soon as we get your statement, we will bring your son in to see you."

Kim looked away, not knowing whether to trust this woman

tossing questions at her.

"Look at me, Ms. Brown, I wouldn't lie to you. He is a beautiful little boy. No one will hurt him. No one will take him away from you."

"I went to the barn to get the dress I had on last night. I was meeting someone at a Gala, at the Benson Hotel in Jade, and had to dress appropriately." She suddenly realized she recognized Reese. "Oh Shit, that was you I saw there! We spoke about the painting, right? Wait, what is going on? Were you following me?"

"Why would you need to get changed in a barn? Why not in the house? FBI Agents saw you in the house after the Gala?" Wells was pushing hard to get answers before Kim lawyered up.

"I bought the dress, but knew I couldn't afford it. I was going to return it and get my money back. You *were* following me. Both of you."

"No, I was not," Reese assured her. "I thought you were someone else when I saw you in the Arts room. That's until that big guy whisked you away to speak to the Governor. Do you care to explain why the governor would want to see you? And why that thug called you Kim? Who was he anyway?"

"I told you my name *is* Kim. And that guy you call a thug is my son's father. His name is Jack Roman. I never saw the governor that night. Jack and I got into an argument about putting my son up for adoption. He wanted no part of being a father. Never did." She softened her tone. Her pain from the burns was now more obvious than before. "I told Jack I would never give him up. Never."

"Would you like some water, Kim?" Wells asked.

"I need something for the pain more than water."

"We know, and we can get that for you, after we hear the rest of your story."

"So, what happened next?" Reese continued. "You know you do not have to tell us anything Kim. You have a right to legal counsel."

Wells was furious. Reese had just caused Kim's entire statement to be tossed out.

"I am not stupid," she continued, "but I am tired of all of this. Tired of running."

"Running from what, Kim? Please, let us help you."

"You know what, Reese, I think it's time we bring our newest officer up here. What do you think?"

"I think that's a great idea," she smiled.

"I'll be back in a few Kim," Michael Wells said with a grin.

It didn't take longer than ten minutes before there was a tap on the door of Kim's room. Agent Wells had told the little boy what to say.

"Open this door!" he said with as much authority as a five-year-old could muster. "I'm looking for my mommy!"

Wells clicked the door latch and Kevin shoved it open with all his might. He saw her and his face lit up.

"Mommy, Mommy, I found you!" He turned toward Agent Wells and detective Clayton. "I told you I would find her. I did it just like you said I could. I am a good officer, right?"

Reese patted his little head. "I knew you could do it. Great job, Officer Brown." She also knew she had to be cautious with her emotions after seeing this mother/son reunion. "I'm going to get the nurse to give you something to help you rest

Kim," Reese said. "We will come back tomorrow for the rest of your statement. In the meantime, Kevin will get great care. The nurses will not let him out of their sight. Do you trust me, Kim?"

Kevin climbed into the bed with his mommy, giving her the biggest hug, not knowing the pain his mom felt from the burns. But mom didn't care. She could manage any pain if she had her little boy.

Kim looked at the badge on her son's shirt, tears flowing down her cheeks. "Thank you for this. Kevin, you will go with this lady while I take a nap. I want you to be a good boy. She will bring you back in a little while. Mommy loves you and thank you for finding me, officer." She smiled. "Now give me a big hug and kiss."

As Reese and Wells led Kevin out of the room, Kim mouthed the words thank you.

Wells nodded and whispered, "You're welcome."

CHAPTER 70

Carly Brennen was in the Cromwell Police Department break-room getting some water when Lake and Clayton walked in.

"Oooh, Detectives, I'm glad you're back. You're not going to believe what I found out. Hold on one sec." She leaned out the doorway and called for Manning to join them, waving her hands for him to hurry.

"All right, all right, I'm coming. Don't get your knickers in a knot. Is my dinner ready, dear?"

"Shut up Manning. No, I have some pretty big news about my research into Captain Brown." Carly lowered her voice. "Kimimela Brown was born on the Lakota Reservation back in 1980. Her parents had five children."

"Really? She's never talked about any siblings before. I wonder why?"

They suddenly heard someone clear their throat. "I'm right here. Why don't you ask me yourself?"

They turned to see the captain standing in the doorway. Her face reddening with each passing second.

"In the conference room. All of you. NOW! And Reese, get

our FBI friends over here. I want them both to hear this conversation too. Understood?"

"Yes, Captain." Reese and the others sheepishly filed out of the break room. They felt bad the captain thought they were speaking about her behind her back.

Reese made the call from her desk.

"Hey Reese. You're on speaker. Olden is here too."

"Hi guys. We need your help."

"Again? Can't you and that Lake guy do anything by yourselves?" Wells teased.

'Well, I can think of a few important things, but that's none of your business," she laughed.

"Seriously though, are you and Robert able to come to the station? We have new information, and the captain is insisting everyone meet together."

"What kind of information?" Olden asked. "Can't you just conference us in?"

"It would be better if you were here in person. As a favor to us."

"If we say yes, does this mean you'll go to dinner with *me*, Reese?" Robert chuckled. "I mean, I knew Mike here wasn't right for you all along."

"The two of you are impossible, and the answer is still no. Flattered though."

"Sure, we can be there," Wells elbowed his partner in the ribs. "When do we meet?"

"As soon as you can get here. Thank you both."

As the FBI agents approached the entrance to the Cromwell station, Denton Hollingsworth joined them. "Well, this can't be a good thing," Hollingsworth commented.

All three entered the conference room where the captain, the detectives, Brennen and Manning sat silently.

"Boy, you could cut the tension in here with a knife," Olden joked.

No one laughed.

"Officer Brennen," Captain Brown addressed her, "start over, please. From the beginning."

"Yes, Captain." Carly swallowed hard while trying to clear her throat and coughed. "Sorry." She took a drink from her stainless-steel water bottle and began again.

"I have new information on Captain Brown and her doppelgänger." She took a deep breath. "Back in 1980, the Brown family lived on the Lakota Reservation. They had five children, three boys and *two* girls. Our Captain Kimimela has a sister. Her name is Zitkala."

Allen and Reese's mouths fell open. In the few years they had known Captain Brown, none of them had ever seen her shed a tear. Until now.

"Captain, I'm sorry if it sounded like I was gossiping in the break room earlier." Carly was waiting for the captain to either fire her on the spot or throw a right hook at her; she knew she deserved both.

The captain wiped her cheek. "Make yourselves comfortable. This could take a while. Grab some coffee, soda, whatever you need. No one leaves until I say so. Understood?"

"Understood, Captain," they all replied in unison.

"Manning, see to it the desk is covered and shifts are all full. You will manage any problems on the street tonight if necessary."

"Absolutely, Captain. Can I get you something? Water?"

"I'd like a bottle of scotch, but water will be fine. And grab me a bottle of juice and a protein bar, just in case."

When they all returned and settled in, she began. "Officer Brennen is correct; I have four siblings. Three older brothers and a sister. I was just five years old when men in suits came to the reservation. They told my parents some of their children would have to be placed in a boarding school nearby. They reassured my father the children would live at the school and be provided an excellent education all for free. My mother did not want her children to leave, but she had no choice. They took my oldest brother, Mato. He was ten. I remember he was kicking and screaming when the men tried to escort him out of the house. My sister Zitkala ran up to the man holding my brother and started yelling *they couldn't take her brother away.* She started punching the man in the stomach and he grabbed her. I was hiding behind a blanket that divided the room. The man told my father he was taking the girl too. The men didn't know there were two girls in the household. When the men asked her name, my father replied Kimimela. I didn't understand why he told them her name was Kim. My mother told him later that day about his mistake. Years went by. We had no contact with my brother or sister until one day, my parents were informed that my siblings had died at the school." Her voice wavered. "They never said what happened to them. My parents were informed the children would be buried on school property at the expense of the government." Kim paused and sipped on her water, trying to regain her composure, and then continued. "What I didn't know back then, but now know, is that these boarding schools were an abomination. The government and church officials used them to indoctrinate Native American children into the white man's way of life under the guise of free education. The children were forced to abandon their traditions, their heritage and culture. If that wasn't bad enough, the atrocities committed at these schools were unforgivable. Some children were physically abused and others sexually assaulted. Those that did not survive were buried on grounds. Their souls were never at peace. To this day, humanitarians continue to search for and identify the bodies of these kids using the latest in modern technology. Both my parents are deceased now. They never knew what really happened to their two children. And I'm certain my mother died of a broken heart."

"Oh my god Captain, I'm so sorry your family had to endure that." Reese was visibly shaken.

"When I saw the photos and videos from the Bur Oak Casino. I was in shock. I didn't want to believe it, but there she was. My sister was alive. I had so many questions running through my head. How had she escaped? What had she endured at school? Why didn't she ever come home? And why was she involved with the Governor?"

"Speaking of the Governor," agent Olden interrupted, "don't forget, you're still under investigation for the attempt on his life."

"Actually, I think I can shed some light on that agent," Carly said.

"Is that so?"

"Yes, I have a team of friends who have been researching the latest methods of reconnecting families."

"You mean like one of those .com sites?" Manning asked.

"No. It's much more sophisticated. It's called Forensic Genetic Genealogy, or Investigative Genetic Genealogy. More intense research on DNA and the SNP's in genetics."

"Should I even ask what SNPs are?" Manning raised his eyebrow.

"It means single nucleotide polymorphism. They are the most common type of variation among people. Each one represents a difference in a single DNA building block, called a nucleotide."

"She's right," Denton Hollingsworth explained. "They used the technique to find the Golden State Killer back in 2018, I believe. Since then, the process has improved. New advances every day."

"Wow, Brennen." Manning was impressed. "Where the heck did you come from and why aren't you in some underground lab doing research and making boatloads of money? I told you guys she is a whiz at this stuff." Manning gave her the thumbs up.

"Believe me," she replied, "there is an amazing amount of research going on in this field. I don't understand a lot of what my friends do. They are at genius level. I don't have the time to dive into it like they do. I'm not even sure if I can discuss how all of this landed in my lap. There is one request that I have. I do not want them implicated in any of this. I need to protect them at any cost."

"Even if it means you lose your job or go to jail?" Denton asked.

"Yes, even if it means all of that."

Lake interrupted, "This is fascinating and all, but what does this have to do with the attack on the Governor, Brennen?"

"Oh, right, that's the reason the body fluids on the mattress in the governor's suite matched yours, Captain, but the fingerprints didn't. Twins share the same DNA, but not the same fingerprints. Zitkala is the captain's *twin* sister."

CHAPTER 71

"Kimimela." Denton knelt down next to her and placed his arm around her shoulders. "I'm so sorry. Why wouldn't you tell me any of this?"

The captain just hung her head not making eye contact.

"We need to find your sister and help her."

Wells, Lake, and Manning shot each other a glance. They knew exactly where she was.

Denton turned to the room. "Listen to me, all of you, do whatever you have to do to find Zitkala. Find her, bring her back. I promise, she will not go to jail for anything. We are going to see to it, isn't that correct Agents?"

Wells and Olden wanted to nod in agreement, but knew they couldn't make that kind of promise.

"I'll handle the courts," Denton continued. "The rest of you, dig up every piece of evidence you have. Carly, I heard about your technical savvy, get it done."

"I will," she replied, "but I have to be in court in the morning. Jennifer Orrick's sentencing."

"That's right, shit, I forgot about it myself," Lake said.

"Shouldn't take long. Reese and I will be there as well."

Denton turned back to Captain Brown, "Whatever happened to your other two brothers?"

"One is living in Arizona; he worked many jobs to educate himself. His name is Chatan. He now owns a hotel near the entrance to the canyon. My oldest brother, Chaska, also worked his way through school to learn all he could about agriculture and farming. He owns a cattle farm in Montana. I haven't seen them in years. They both blamed the family for losing our siblings, especially me, for hiding. In my defense, I was five years old. And yes, I too blamed myself. Besides finding Zitkala, I have to know what happened to my brother Mato. I have to find out if he really did die at that hell hole, or did he escape like Zitkala?"

"Well, said Lake, "I think it's time we updated you on our trip to Jade, Captain."

"Yes, please, go ahead."

Wells spoke first. "Captain Brown, we have new updates on the victims of the barn fire in Jade." "Officer Clark is out of surgery. They removed a bullet from his shoulder. He will be off duty for some time, but otherwise, he's expected to be okay."

"That's great news," she replied. "And his partner?"

"Out of surgery, but in critical condition. And the other victims," he paused. "Captain, I think you should take a deep breath."

Captain Brown wasn't sure why Wells was so hesitant to share. "Just tell me what else you found. It's the girl that Detective Lake pulled from the barn, right? Did she die? Or is it about the little boy? Either way, Agent, I don't have time for drama. What have you got?"

"Reese, do you want to take it from here?" Wells asked.

"The little boy is fine, Captain. He is the son of the woman Lake saved. His name is Kevin. Cute little guy." She smiled thinking of his sweet face. "We got a statement from the woman, at least a partial statement. She is in a lot of pain, second-degree burns. We will go back later today for her full statement, if the doctors agree."

"I'm sure you have guards on her, correct?"

"Yes, of course," Reese replied. "Captain, we believe this woman," her voice trailed off.

"You believe what, Detective?"

"This woman calls herself Kim. We think she might be your identical twin Zitkala, which would make little Kevin your nephew."

The captain raised her hand to her mouth and gasped. "You found her."

The room fell silent as the news sunk in.

Agent Olden broke the silence, "Your sister, if she is indeed your sister, is in major trouble Captain. She tried to murder the governor of South Dakota, for Christ's sake. She may also be involved with grand theft of several major art pieces and artifacts worth millions. Then to top it off, she's connected to the Rossi crime family. As much as I appreciate Mr. Hollingsworth's desire to clear her name after all she lived through, we just can't look the other way and make all of those charges go away. We like you, Captain Brown, and have a great deal of respect for you, but we have a job to do as agents for the Bureau."

"Does my client," asked Hollingsworth, "need to keep quiet

here, Agent Olden? Because I thought we were fighting for the same results. If not, I need to know now, and this conversation never happened. Detectives, officers, Captain Brown. You didn't hear anything, did you?"

"Knock it off with your lawyer bullshit," Olden fired back. "For probably the first time in the history of South Dakota, the police and FBI are working together. Captain Brown, first we need to speak with your sister and get her side of the story and we need to get her someplace safe. I'm sure she has others searching for her. The Rossi crime family has been low level, but in recent months has picked up momentum. We need to be sure the kid is safe too, or they will use him for leverage. Trust is the optimal word among us. Can we achieve that level together?"

"I agree with my partner," said Wells. "We have to approach this professionally, not just a mushy heart. Although I could cry thinking of what those bastards did to those boarding school kids. Are we in agreement?"

"Captain Brown, Hollingsworth, we are leaving the decision to you," Lake said. "We are with you one hundred percent, whatever you decide."

Denton looked at Captain Brown, "Never thought I'd say this, but I'm in."

"Okay then," the captain replied. "When can I see my sister?"

"Well, before we figure out that detail, there's one more thing you should probably know Captain," Reese said. "Your nephew's father is Jack Roman. The governor's bodyguard."

"Are you fucking kidding me?"

The detectives had never heard their captain use that kind of language. She looked at Denton. "What else could go wrong?

And this has been verified?"

"That's what your sister told us. She also said he wants nothing to do with the kid. He wanted Kevin to be put up for adoption. She claims she absolutely refused. The fear now is what lengths will he go to get rid of the child. He's ruthless. I'm guessing he wants Zitkala out of the picture as well." Reese now wished she hadn't been the one to break that news.

"Captain, I think the agents need to get Zitkala's full statement," Deputy Manning suggested. "From here on out, we need to do this by the book. Albeit a different rule book."

"He's right," Lake paced the room. "She will need to be placed under arrest. At least until Hollingsworth gets her out on bail."

"I doubt any judge will allow her out on bail for attempting to slice and dice the Governor," Denton surmised. "Believe me, the governor's attorneys are not going to go for that. Unless she didn't do it, but we need some serious evidence to prove otherwise. Maybe Miss tech whiz over here can come up with something?"

"Only thing we have other than DNA is fingerprints. We need hers and I'm pretty certain they will match Zitkala's. Captain, I'm sorry."

"It's okay Brennen. You know, it actually might be better if she's placed in our jail. We can keep a close watch."

"Won't work," Reese said. "She is under Jade and FBI jurisdiction."

"But," Lake chimed in, "they can place her under arrest at the hospital. She is still under a doctor's care for some major burns. The hospital and her room are under 24-hour surveillance. Am I correct Olden?"

"Yes, that's right. She should probably have an attorney there to represent her. That's where you come into the picture, Hollingsworth. Are you up for an attempted murder case?"

Denton looked at Kimimela, "You won't be needing me anymore, Captain. The courts frown on having the same attorney represent more than one suspect in the same case, and you are no longer a suspect. Right Agents?"

"As far as we know, there is no warrant pending for the captain," Wells confirmed.

"Let's wait to see if Zitkala's prints do in fact match the ones secured from the governor's suite," Reese suggested.

"Okay, sounds good to me," Denton agreed. "Okay with you, Kimimela?"

She nodded yes. "So, we agree? We wait for the fingerprint match before I can see her?"

"Yes, ma'am," Wells said. "Meeting in person after all these years will be a shock for both of you, I'm sure. We better give the doctors a heads up about this unique situation so they can be available for your reunion."

"Speaking of doctors," Reese said. "I'm going to see if Officer Clark is up for a visitor. Get his statement on the barn shooting. If that's okay with the agents?"

"That would save time," Olden agreed. "Just send us your report when you get back."

"Of course," Reese replied. "While I'm there, I will check on the status of his partner. I also told little Kevin I would be back to see him."

"If it's okay with you Captain, I'll go with Reese," Lake said.

"That's fine with me, but you can't say a word to my sister."

"She's right," Denton said. "Avoid that topic at all costs. Right now, her life may depend on it."

"Copy that," Reese nodded.

Early the next morning, Reese, Emerson, and Carly made their way to the courthouse. "This will be a nightmare," Lake announced. "I can hear the woes of Jennifer Orrick already."

The judge began the proceedings. "A name or a title does not release you from guilt, even if your father's name is Judge John Orrick. Having a lifestyle that affords you privilege is a gift, Ms. Orrick. How sad you didn't think that was enough. Your father spoke of you often praising your accomplishments. However, I never heard him say what those accomplishments were. Sometimes, as parents, we don't think of the consequences of giving our children so much for so little in return. That is our fault. Jennifer Orrick, I sentence you to Cromwell women's prison for five years. Possibility of parole in two years. I also order you to pay a $10,000 dollar fine. The money will go to a charity of Ms. Brennen's choice. I hope this teaches you the value of others property and privacy. Court adjourned."

Jennifer Orrick didn't tantrum. She didn't talk back. She just hung her head in silence as the bailiff escorted her out of the courtroom.

The detectives were shocked. Carly smiled the whole ride back to the precinct.

CHAPTER 72

"Agent Wells, the captain of the Jade Fire Department is on the line."

"Put him through. I am so sick of this phone. I'd like to toss it in the nearest dumpster."

"Agent Wells, I have the final report on the incident at the barn. Appears the fire started due to the gunfire and dry hay. Found no chemicals or igniter fluid around the area. The entire barn, although not a complete loss, will still need to be torn down. Too much damage to repair. Your forensic team is there now looking for evidence."

"Is it cordoned off, Captain?"

"Just the police tape right now, proper fencing will be installed so no one wanders in and gets hurt. I will notify the county and let them know it's cleared to be torn down as soon as they can hire the right people to do it safely."

Agent Olden contacted the lead on the forensics team. "What did you find?"

"Shell casings," the team member replied, "blood and the blue dress, which was partially burned, and one high heel shoe."

"Okay, good. Now, get your team out of there before the place either collapses or the county throws you out."

"Got it," the head tech said. "Someone will let you know the results once we get them back to the lab."

"Thanks. Put a rush on any prints you find."

CHAPTER 73

"Emerson, what's your take on all of this? I'm not sure how the captain is going to handle seeing her sister. I don't think it's going to be as easy as she thinks."

"I was thinking the same thing Reese. That had to be torture living with all that guilt her family laid on her shoulders all these years. For God's sake, she was five years old. What did they expect her to do?"

"I agree. How in hell are we going to keep Zitkala out of prison?"

"I don't know," Lake shook his head. "But if anyone can pull this off, it's Hollingsworth."

They pulled into the Jade Medical Center parking lot, sharing a quick kiss before exiting the car.

"What do you think about this fall, Emerson?"

"What about it? Great season. Love the colors," he smirked.

"No, you goofball! What do you think of us getting married this fall?"

Halfway to the door of the hospital, Emerson grabbed Reese around the waist, lifted her in the air, swung her around in a circle and planted a kiss on her beautiful, lightly tinted lips. "Yes, yes!" he yelled.

She giggled like a child. "I love you Emerson Lake, and I don't want to wait any longer to be your wife. Now let me down. People are staring."

"I don't care. I love you, Reese. I would love to be anywhere but here right now, but we have work to do." He kissed her one more time before letting her down. "I am so happy you chose a date, or almost a date. This fall sounds perfect."

CHAPTER 74

Emerson and Reese entered Calvin Clark's room cautiously, not knowing what to expect. He was awake, hooked to all kinds of apparatuses, and tubes going in and out of his burned body.

"Calvin, how are you feeling?" Reese asked gently.

"I'm going to be fine. Thanks for coming."

"Of course. We had to make sure you were ok," Emerson replied.

"My shoulder will heal. I should be out in about a week. The paperwork will take longer, I'm sure," he scooted himself upright in the bed.

"Here, let us help you get comfortable. Lake, can you grab the middle sheet and pull with me to sit him up a little? That's it." Reese arranged more pillows around him for support. "Can I refill your glass of water?"

"No, I'm good for now."

"We'd like to get a statement from you if we could," Emerson said.

"Detectives, it's not going to be the statement you want."

"Really?" Reese cocked her head. "Ok, then let's start from

the beginning."

"My partner, Patrick Nolan, and I entered the barn. There was movement, we heard a shuffling sound. I sent Nolan around to the other side so we could cover who or what was in there." Officer Clark took a deep breath. "You know, I think I would like a drink of water after all."

"Not a problem." Reese refilled the pink hospital pitcher with fresh water from the bathroom tap and poured Calvin a glass.

Calvin took a long swig and then continued. "I saw a woman carrying a blue dress. You won't like this next part. It was your captain. Captain Brown.

"Yes, we were aware there was a woman in the barn with you. Emerson saved her."

"Suddenly, shots were fired. It was my partner, Nolan. He was firing in the direction of the woman but missed. I yelled for him to cease fire, but he just kept shooting. I fired a warning shot in the air to get his attention, but he fired back and hit me. I stumbled backwards from the force and noticed the flames. The gunfire must have ignited the hay. As I was regaining my balance, I saw the woman grab a gun, from where I don't know, and fire back in Nolan's direction. It was definitely self-defense for her detectives. Everything after that became a haze. I really don't remember much more. None of it makes sense. I don't understand why Nolan would fire his service weapon at this woman. She wasn't a threat. She only pulled the gun after he fired at her first."

"So, you're saying it was Officer Nolan that shot you?" Lake asked.

"As much as I hate to say it, yes. I'm sure the bullet from my shoulder will match his gun.

CHAPTER 75

Reese and Emerson went back to the nurse's station and asked if they could visit Officer Nolan.

"Yes, Detective, but please be quick," the nurse urged. "He is not in great shape, as you know."

They entered his room, not expecting so many machines to be hooked up to him.

"Officer Nolan, I'm Detective Lake. This is my partner Detective Clayton Cromwell P.D."

Reese continued, "We'd like to ask you a few questions about what happened at the barn before it caught fire."

Nolan reached for his oxygen mask and pulled it under his chin. "I don't have much time, detectives," his voice was weak. "I know that. Please turn on your phone to record what I have to say."

Emerson did just that, "We're ready Officer Nolan."

"I want you to know I had no choice."

"What do you mean by that?" Emerson asked.

"When Clark ordered me to move to the other side of the barn for cover, a man came out of nowhere and confronted me.

He said he worked for Governor Cramer and if I didn't follow his every instruction, my family would die." Nolan seemed to run out of air as he spoke and grabbed for the oxygen mask. Once he caught his breath, he continued. "I pulled my service weapon on him and told him he was under arrest. He laughed for a moment and then suddenly stopped and locked his steely eyes with mine. He swung a crowbar at me and knocked the gun out of my hand momentarily. When I knelt down to grab it, he got me in a chokehold and forced me to look at photos on his phone. Pictures of my wife and kids." He struggled to catch his breath. "I'm sorry, I can't breathe," he rasped.

"Patrick, if it's too painful to talk right now, we can come back," Reese said.

Nolan once again grasped for his mask and inhaled deeply wailing from the excruciating pain that rippled across his burns as his lungs expanded. He stared at the ceiling, tears falling from his eyes. "No, I have to get this out! Please, my almighty God in heaven, please give me enough time." A droplet of blood leaked from his nostril.

"I'm getting the nurse," Reese said.

"No, I have to finish, please."

"Ok, what did he tell you to do, Officer Nolan?" Lake asked.

"He told me to kill the woman and her son in the barn. Are they all right?"

"They're ok," Reese held his hand.

"I didn't want to do it. How do you deal with someone that has that kind of power?"

"Who officer Nolan? Who had the power?" Emerson was terrified this poor guy would not have time to finish his statement.

"He showed me photos of my little girl at her day care center. The governor was standing next to her with his arm on my baby's shoulder. I'm sorry. I didn't mean to hurt anyone. I'm begging you Detectives. Please see to it my family is safe."

"We will take care of it," Reese assured him. "I promise."

Nolan coughed as he struggled for air. Every shallow breath rattled deep in his chest. His eyes bulged with fear as a trickle of blood snaked its way down the corner of his mouth.

"I don't want to die," he sobbed. His whole body shuddered, setting off the alarms. His last words on the recording, a whisper. "Pray for my soul and my family." Then nothing more than the dreaded long, single toned squeal of Officer Nolan's heart monitor.

CHAPTER 76

The detectives immediately exited Nolan's room to let the hospital's crash team do their job.

"Emerson," Reese whispered, "Nolan's family might still be in danger if the Governor's thug knows he didn't finish the job. We need to contact the FBI. They need to find that daycare center."

"I know. This is some serious shit, Reese. The Governor and his hired guns are willing to hurt little kids now. How low can he go?"

At that moment, the doctor emerged.

"Mrs. Nolan, I'm Doctor Kelly. I'm so sorry. We did all we could for your husband. His injuries were just too severe. I'm sorry, he's gone."

"No, no," she cried, "not my Patrick."

"Give us a few minutes to clean him up and then you may see him. Is there anyone you would like me to contact for you?" The doctor was trying to be as sympathetic as possible.

Mrs. Nolan dropped her face into her hands and screamed, "WHY?" Her knees buckled underneath her as Emerson caught her and eased her back into a chair. He let her cry into his shoulder for a few moments.

"I don't understand how this could happen." She sobbed wiping her nose with tissues Reese handed her.

"Mrs. Nolan, I'm Detective Lake and this is my partner, Detective Clayton. We're from the Cromwell Police. We would like to ask you a few questions. Are your children with other relatives?"

"Yes," she sniffled. "They are staying with my sister. This would be too much for them."

"All of them, Mrs. Nolan?"

"Yes. Why?"

"Your husband wanted us to make sure you and your children were okay."

"Yes, they are fine. They are at my house. My sister is looking after them. Please don't tell them anything. I want to be the one to tell them what happened to their daddy."

"Of course." Emerson rubbed her shoulder.

Reese walked out of earshot and called Agent Wells. "Patrick Nolan just passed away, but not before giving us a video statement. We need to meet, but first you need to get a security watch on her house."

"Why?"

"Trust me Wells. I'll explain later."

"Got it. I'll send someone right over. Text later when you are clear."

Reese hung up the phone and sat down to console the officer's wife. "Mrs. Nolan, what daycare does your little girl attend? Your husband spoke of her going to a daycare center."

"It's called Rush for More Daycare on Main Street in Jade.

Why? Is something wrong with it?"

"No, I was just wondering. It sounds lovely. What a cute take on a historic monument."

"Mrs. Nolan," a nurse interrupted, "you may see your husband now."

"Would you like one of us to go in with you?" Reese asked.

"No, the nurse will be with me. Thank you."

"Someone from the Jade Police Department is on their way here and will escort you back to your home," Lake informed the grieving widow.

"Thank you both." She grabbed the nurse's arm as she entered her husband's hospital room.

Emerson and Reese had pits in their stomachs as she disappeared. They knew all too well how devastating the loss was for her.

Reese composed herself. "Emerson, let's make a quick stop to see Kevin and Zitkala while we're here."

They left the waiting room and entered the secure wing.

"Hi there." Emerson saluted Officer Kevin who was guarding the doorway. Kevin had on different clothes. Emerson was glad to see the little boy clean and happy. "How is everything going, big guy? We would like to see your mom if that's okay with you."

Kevin glanced at the security guard and said, "These people are okay. They're with us."

The guard nodded and asked to see the detectives' identification. "You're right, Officer Kevin, they're okay." He winked at Emerson.

Kim was still in a lot of pain from the burns. They would require lots of time and many skin grafts to heal.

Emerson asked, "How do you feel today Ms. Brown?"

"Worse today. I guess the adrenaline rush is wearing off. Thanks for allowing my son to be with me, Detectives. That makes this a lot easier to deal with."

"We just wanted to stop by to say hello to your son and check in on you. There will be other law enforcement stopping by for your statement. Agent Wells and Agent Olden. If you need anything," Lake said, "here's my card. You can also ask the guard outside your door to contact us if needed."

Reese looked down at Kevin and smiled. "The taller guard would probably be the best source of information."

Kim started to laugh, but a jolt of pain shot down her side. "Thank You officers."

On their way out of the hospital Emerson texted a copy of Nolan's video statement to agent Wells and then called him to make sure he received it.

"Thanks for passing this along Emerson."

"Is Nolan's home secured?" Reese asked.

"Yes," Michael confirmed. "There's an unmarked out front. You and Lake can tell the family why the house is being watched. Tell them it's just protocol after an arson or something."

"Olden and I are on our way to the Medical Center to make the formal arrest. Hollingsworth is right behind us."

"Ok, just keep in mind her son is outside her hospital room door," Reese reminded him. "You should probably send him back to the daycare wing under full security. I don't think it's a good idea to have him witness the arrest of his mother. It could traumatize him. Ms. Brown will certainly not react well."

"Good call, we'll take care of it."

CHAPTER 77

"Ms. Kim Brown?"

"Yes?"

"I'm FBI Agent Olden and this is Agent Wells.

"Nice to meet you. And who's this guy?" She gestured to the suit.

"I'm Denton Hollingsworth." He handed her his business card.

She looked at his card, perplexed.

"Ms. Brown," Olden continued. "We are placing you under arrest for the attempted murder of Governor William Cramer and the murder of Officer Patrick Nolan, Jade P.D. You have the right to remain silent. You have the right to an attorney." Olden proceeded reading her the Miranda rights.

"I am counsel for Ms. Brown and my client has nothing to say to you."

"What do you mean you're my attorney? I can't afford you. I'm guessing your fees are steep by the look of that Italian suit and silk tie. Your haircut probably cost more than my apartment."

Wells choked back a laugh. She was probably right.

"No need to worry about my fees," Denton replied. "That has been taken care of."

"By who?" she barked. "By that fucked up Cramer. If so, no thank you!" she tossed his business card toward the end of the bed.

"Ms. Brown," Agent Olden said, "video footage from the Bur Oak Casino places you at the governor's hotel suite on the night he was attacked. Your fingerprints are a match for those found in his room, and the bodily fluid on his mattress matches your DNA. In addition, you are accused of stealing artwork from the Charity Gala at the Benson Hotel. What do you have to say about these accusations?"

"I am your attorney, Ms. Brown. I am advising you, do not answer any of these questions."

She looked back and forth at all of them and folded her arms across her body in defiance.

"Fine, Ms. Brown," Agent Olden continued, "You will remain at the hospital under surveillance while you need medical care. You will be required to wear an ankle monitor during this time."

"Your son will have visitation rights," Wells advised. "He will remain here at the hospital under adult supervision until your release at which time other arrangements for his care will need to be made."

She turned to her new attorney. "Please have a guard on Kevin. I fear for his life."

"Already done," Denton reassured her.

"I still don't understand why you're representing me. What is going on?"

"I will explain when the agents finish here," Denton replied.

"Ms. Brown, can you explain what happened at the barn?" Wells asked.

Hollingsworth nodded for her reply. Her account matched that of officers Clark and Nolan.

"Ms. Brown, one more question. Do you have a permit for the gun you used to shoot officer Nolan?"

"What do you think?" she sneered.

CHAPTER 78

The agents left the hospital to meet with Clayton and Lake at a nearby diner. Denton Hollingsworth remained behind to speak with his new client.

"Ms. Brown," he began, "what I am about to tell you is of the utmost importance. If you are to have any chance at all, I need you to be honest with me. I also need you to trust that I am here to help you in every way possible. Your life and your son's future depend on it. Do you understand?"

"Yes, I understand you are here to help me and my son. I just don't know why. Who hired you? No one I know could afford you. And please don't lie to me either."

"I'm sorry. I can't tell you who hired me. I am doing this for a friend and they asked me not to divulge their identity. But soon. I promise you, soon. Do you think you can find a way to trust me?"

She stared at him intently for quite some time, knowing the eyes were the window to someone's soul. Finally, she spoke. "Okay, I will trust you, Mr. Hollingsworth, but if something happens to my son, I will be your last case. Do you trust me on that?"

That, he thought to himself, is the love of a mother. Not a smart one, but none the less a loving mother. "I trust you, Ms. Brown."

"What is it you want to know?" she asked.

"Where did you first meet the Governor?"

"He wasn't a governor when I met him in New York."

"Did you live in New York at some point?"

"Yes. I was thirteen years old, but I wasn't born there. As you probably can guess by my looks, I am Native American, Lakota Sioux. I was taken from my family and placed in a boarding school when I was five years old. Believe me, I didn't go peacefully, and neither did my brother Mato. He was ten years old. That was around 1985, I believe."

"Where was this school?"

"It was in Minnesota near the South Dakota border. I fought like hell, but they ripped me away. Anyway, I escaped in 1993. I didn't know where I was going. All I knew was I wasn't going back to that hell hole. I hitched rides from anyone that would pick me up. It cost me for those rides, but nothing that I hadn't already paid in that school. When I made it to New York, I was alone with no money, nothing. I met a man who said he knew a couple that was looking to hire a live-in housekeeper. I agreed."

"Do you remember the names of this couple?"

"William Cramer, but like I said, he wasn't governor then. I don't remember her name and didn't care. She knew what that prick was doing to me and never once tried to stop him. I wasn't even fourteen years old. I kept their house clean, cooked, and kept him out of her bed. That's all she cared about."

"Why did you stay after everything you had been through?"

"I needed the money, but eventually I couldn't take the abuse any longer and I left in the middle of the night with what little savings I had. I bounced around a lot between New Jersey and New York. That's around the time I met this guy. He was very charming and he made me feel safe. Things were good, that is, until I got pregnant. Jack got spooked and took off. So, there I was, alone and on my own again, but I was determined to be the best mother I could be. I took any job I could get to make ends meet. While I was waiting tables, I met a woman who said she could help someone in my situation. She connected me with a community program for young women in unplanned pregnancies. The program connected me to resources that helped me prepare for little Kevin's arrival. I will never understand why this woman helped me, a complete stranger, but she did and I was grateful."

"Do you remember her name?"

"Her first name was Jane. To be honest, I think she may be the same Jane Goldman that was shot at the Benson hotel gala. I heard her name and saw her photo on the news. It could have been her. Just a much better dressed version."

"Why did you come back to South Dakota?"

"Jack Roman. He found me and said he wanted to get back together; start fresh as a family. Like I said, he was very charming and talked me into giving it another shot."

"Wait a minute, so Kevin's father is Jack Roman?"

"Unfortunately, yes. I didn't know he was connected to the Rossi crime family until Kevin and I moved here. It turned out his family dream was all just a lie. He just wanted to use me for my connection to Cramer. He threatened me. Told me to cozy up to the governor; shake him down for a shipment of guns, rifles actually, for the Rossi family and in return, my son would not be harmed. So, what choice did I have? I got close to Cramer again. I'm not proud of myself, but in exchange for the guns, I slept with him…" Her eyes welled up and she wiped them with her hospital gown sleeve. "It was torture. In the end, he refused to help me with the weapons, anyway. Called me his little Indian princess and told me to see myself out. I was so mad that I pulled my knife on him, just to scare him. I never touched him! The asshole actually got stitches and called it his Lakota war wound." She gripped the waffled blanket on her bed, clenching both hands into fists. "If I ever see…"

"Stop right there!" Denton advised. "I never want to hear what you were just about to say. Got it?"

"Yeah, fine." She relaxed her hands and leaned back against her pillow.

"Back to this Roman guy. Why not just leave him? Have him relinquish all ties to your son?"

"I can't afford to support my son, any more than I can afford you. Jack wasn't about to pay child support. That's something you have to report to the state. Which would mean his name would be on the radar. He hasn't exactly been an ideal citizen. I was hoping the art heist would work and maybe Jack would give me a share so Kevin and I could leave him once and for all. Now, I think he was trying to have us murdered in that barn."

"Is there anything else or any other reason you came back to South Dakota?"

"While I was here, I wanted to find my brother Mato. They

forced him into that same shitty boarding school at the same time they took me away. The word was that he died there. I just don't know. I was hoping to find someone on the Reservation that may have heard what happened to him." She began to cry and reached for a tissue from her tray, cringing with every movement.

"Let me get that for you." Denton handed her the tissue box. "Do you need a break? I can have the nurse get you a cup of tea or something. I know this is difficult, but please don't leave anything out."

"I'm okay," she blew her nose.

"I need to know what happened to you at that school. What did they do to you and your brother?"

"Mr. Hollingsworth, what I went through at that boarding school is not something I can tell you in a short sentence or two. I am exhausted and my whole side hurts. Would you mind if I take a nap?"

"Of course not. I just have one more question. Do you know if you have any other brothers or sisters, besides your brother Mato?"

"I'm not sure, maybe. I was so young; everything back then is fuzzy. Not even sure if I lived on the Reservation. I don't remember a lot about me," tears welled up in her eyes again and she turned on her side, moaning in pain.

"I will be back to see you tomorrow," Denton took her hand in his. "I'm so sorry you had to go through all of this. If you need me for anything, tell the security guard or a nurse, they will contact me. Get some rest."

Denton was on his phone with the Detectives before he reached his car. "Where are you meeting the FBI. I need to speak to you."

"Dexter's on Hawthorne," Reese said. "We are all here now."

"Okay, on my way."

The vintage diner was what one would expect a fifties-style diner would look like. Shiny silver bullet exterior. A throwback to a different era, but a little larger than most, with an addition built on at some point. Long bar with round red barstools. It was obvious someone cared enough to have it renovated. There were not only red leather booths, but rows of tables for larger parties. All exceptionally clean and the staff well trained in manners. Of course, a Wall O Matic Juke Box in every booth.

Reese motioned Denton over to the tables near the back for privacy.

A server took his order. Ice water and a Belgian waffle with a side of corned beef hash.

"What is the verdict on Zitkala?" Reese asked.

"I am going to represent her; I think I've convinced her to trust me. She is an angry woman, but there is a soft side to her as well. Now, which side of her appears in court will be a challenge. I believe what she has told me so far, anyway. We need the Governor to drop the charges against her. That won't be easy, but if I can have a conversation with him, I'm sure his reputation will outweigh his decision to press charges."

"Let us handle the Governor." Lake tapped the end of knife on the table.

"Speaking of knives," Denton said, "she claims she never sliced the governor's throat. Just pulled a knife to scare him.

That's still considered menacing, but certainly a much lesser charge than attempted murder. Do we know if the governor ever even got stitches?"

"Only one way to find out," Lake said. "But getting close enough will be an issue."

"One other thing, she doesn't remember if she has other siblings besides the brother taken to the boarding school with her."

"I say we bring the captain in tomorrow," Wells suggested. "Rip the band-aid off."

"Tomorrow is probably as good as any other day," Denton agreed. "We definitely need a professional counselor in the room for the introduction. Seeing her reflection standing right in front of her will be incomprehensible."

CHAPTER 79

"Ms. Brown, I'm Dr. Chang. I work here at the hospital. I specialize in mental health."

"And who, may I ask, is going to pay your fees? Certainly not me, so you can leave right now." Zitkala waved her hand toward the door dismissively.

"Give her a chance," the nurse urged.

"Ms. Brown, I am only here to observe while the FBI continues their questioning. My fees are of no concern. I assure you."

"This is crazy," Kim grumbled as she struggled to maneuver herself into a more comfortable position in the hospital bed.

"Perhaps you would be more comfortable in the recliner?"

Zitkala nodded in agreement.

The nurse steadied her as she eased into the chair next to the bed. The nurse propped the pillows around her, adjusted her no slip socks and then covered her with a lightweight sheet. "There, how's that? Here, take a sip of water and a little more of your yogurt. You need some protein. It will make you feel better. A little more of the toast too will help. Carbs will give you a little boost," the nurse smiled.

Zitkala did as she was told and took a few bites and drank half of her water.

"Better?" the nurse asked.

"Yes, thank you," Kim softened.

The guard tapped on the door before opening and announced, "The agents are here."

"Are you ready Ms. Brown?" the psychiatrist asked.

"Ready for what, I don't know, but I yea, I guess I'm ready."

"Good morning, Ms. Brown," Wells introduced himself and his partner, Olden.

"I remember who you are," she said.

"Ms. Brown, we'd like to bring someone in who is eager to see you," Wells said. "Is that okay with you?"

"My son?" Zitkala's eyes brightened. "Of course, I'll see him."

"No, Ms. Brown, not your son," Wells answered.

Zitkala wrinkled her brow, confused.

Dr. Chang observed her reaction carefully.

Zitkala didn't know what to say. She peered toward the door, part in fear, part anticipation.

Wells nodded to the guard. The door slowly swung open and Captain Brown walked into the room. She was wearing street clothes. Her hair, no longer pinned behind her head, was now cascading, just below her shoulders. As she locked eyes with her sister, tears immediately flooded to the surface, running down her cheeks. Denton Hollingsworth was right by her side, holding her by the crook of her elbow.

Denton began, "Ms. Brown, your real name is not Kim, it's Zitkala."

Zitkala froze, staring at Kimimela, not saying a word. Her

eyes inquisitively focused on the face, identical to her own.

Denton tried to hold on to Kimimela, but she dropped to her knees in front of her sister, the tears flowing.

Zitkala lowered the footrest, reaching her hand out to touch the face of her mirror image.

She studied Kimimela intently for a moment, her inner core shuddering from the shock. Then suddenly her eyes brightened and she embraced the woman at her feet.

It seemed an eternity before they released one another, but still their hands remained clasped together as one. And then they finally spoke.

> *"Zitkala, Zitkala, how can I find you?" the captain sniffled.*
>
> *"Oh, my sissy, just look in the mirror. In your eyes, I will be there."*
>
> *"Kimimela, Kimimela, where can I find you?" Zitkala continued the refrain.*
>
> *"Oh, dear sissy, find me in the reflection of your eyes. I am there."*
>
> *Zitkala's voice cracked as she uttered the last line of their secret verse, "No longer the mirror, my image of you. I see you with my eyes. I too am right here."*

The captain smiled through the tears. "Zitkala, you remember me!"

"I remember you. I do."

CHAPTER 80

Their foreheads touched. Kim holding onto her sister's hands, kissing them. "I have missed you so much. I thought you died at that school. That's what we were told. But I somehow could feel you. We were just five years old when we made up that little ditty. In case we were ever scared or alone. I can't believe you remembered it, Zitkala."

"I remembered it because I was alone and scared for more days and nights than you would want to know. I have so much to tell you, Kimimela, so much."

Dr. Chang interrupted, "Zitkala, may I ask why you used your sister's name instead of your own?"

"It made me feel close to her and gave me hope that one day I would see her again," she gave Kim a loving glance.

"Zitkala, I hate to break up this reunion," Wells interrupted, "but we still have a lot of questions to ask. Your attorney will stay, but I am going to ask Kimimela to step out of the room."

"I understand," she responded. "Please Kimimela, don't be far away. We have a lot to say to each other."

"I will be right outside the door with the guard." Kim kissed her sister's hands and gave her a delicate hug. Denton escorted her out.

"I'll be back in a minute, Zitkala. Don't answer anything until I am in the room, understand?"

She nodded yes.

"I want the nurse to remain in the room as well."

In the hallway, Denton advised Kimimela to get something nutritional to eat while he stayed back with her sister. "You will need all the strength you can muster right now. I'll come to get you when we are through."

"You're right," she nodded. "I'll run to the cafeteria, but then I'm coming right back."

Denton had barely opened the door when Olden fired off the first question.

"Zitkala Brown did you attempt to murder the governor of South Dakota, William Cramer?"

"Seriously, agent? Right out of the gate, that's what you ask my client? Don't answer that Zitkala."

"That's okay," she responded. "No, I did not attempt to murder the Governor, I just wanted to scare him. He lied to me to get what he wanted. I didn't leave a scratch on him. And if he does have an injury, he did it himself to set me up. Believe me, if I wanted him dead, he would have been years ago."

"Meaning?" Olden asked.

"Meaning, your pure as the driven snow governor raped me when I was thirteen years old!"

The agents exchanged a troubled glance.

"So if that is true, why would you willingly visit him now as an adult?" Olden asked.

"I had no choice. My son's father blackmailed me. Said if I didn't get the Governor to supply him with high-powered rifles, he'd kill our son."

"Who is your husband, Zitkala? Why would he threaten your son?"

"Jack Roman and we are not married. He wants nothing to do with Kevin. I told Mr. Hollingsworth earlier; I only learned about Jack's connection to the Rossi crime family after we moved back to South Dakota with him. My son is my top priority, I would do anything to protect him!"

"Ms. Brown," Wells asked, "did you shoot the police officer in the barn?"

"One of them, yes, but he shot at me first. That's what started the fire."

"And what about the other officer?" Wells continued. "Did you shoot him too?"

"No, I did not. As I told my attorney, the other officer shot his own partner. I don't think he meant to do it, though. He was a terrible shot for a cop. I think it was just a mistake. He was aiming in my direction." Zitkala choked up knowing how close she had been to leaving her son all alone, but fought back the tears.

"What about the art heist at Benson Hotel?" Olden asked. "What part did you play in that?"

Denton jumped in. "Have you formally accused my client of theft?"

"We are now," Wells responded.

"I didn't take anything, not a fucking thing!" Her voice raised a few octaves higher.

Denton placed a calming hand on her arm and she took a deep breath.

"I was hoping the heist would help me."

"What kind of help are you referring to, Ms. Brown?" Olden asked.

"I knew I needed to get Kevin away from Jack. It wasn't safe, for either of us, but I didn't have enough money. I thought if I helped Jack get what he wanted, he would cut me in on the deal. He needed a driver for the heist, so I hired the boys to drive the van for him." Zitkala lowered her head in shame. "I paid them by letting them feel me up. It makes me sick; my life has always been about using my body for someone else's gain. But, I would do it again to protect my son's life."

"Zitkala!" Denton reprimanded her and she began to cry.

"I believe my client is tired and could use some rest agents. It's been a trying few hours for Ms. Brown."

"When can I see my sister?" Zitkala asked.

The nurse helped her up from the recliner. "I think you need some rest before you see her again my dear. How about in, let's say, an hour? Some lunch and your meds. We will redress your wounds."

Captain Brown was eager to see her twin again after returning from the cafeteria. "What do you mean I can't go in? I can sit quietly while she rests."

"You know the answer, don't you?" Denton asked as he sat with Kim outside Zitkala's room.

Kimimela did not want to wait, but Denton convinced her it was the right choice.

"Fine, I will abide by your wishes Denton, but I am not

leaving this hospital without seeing her again."

"I hear you; I'll be right here with you after I see the agents out."

He patted her on the hand and walked away with the agents. Once out of earshot he asked "So, what do you think?"

"I think we have our work cut out for us," Olden replied. "She has been through a great deal in her lifetime."

"True," Wells agreed, "but that doesn't absolve her from the crimes she may have committed, nor her involvement with the Rossi crime family. I think *you* counselor have your work cut out for you."

"Look Hollingsworth," Olden said, "we like you and we agreed to help as much as possible, but she's making some serious allegations against an elected official. We're federal agents with a job to do. None of us need to be accused of having a conflict of interest in this case."

CHAPTER 81

"This is Detective Emerson Lake of the Cromwell Police Department. I would like to speak with Governor Cramer. Is he available?"

"One moment, please," the voice on the other end sounded more mature than Emerson had expected. "I'm sorry, detective, but the governor is not accepting calls. May I take a message?"

"Yes, you may. Tell the governor I wish to speak to him or his attorney now. Whichever is best for him. Or, if he needs more time, I can always speak with the News 7 team that is hovering over the Capitol building."

There was a moment of silence before the assistant responded. "One moment, please."

"This is Governor Cramer. What can I do for you, Detective?"

"My partner and I would like to meet with you today. Invite your attorney if you wish. You may choose where and what time."

"Fine. How about my lawyer's office, Detective? He can answer any questions you may have. I cannot be there. I have other appointments scheduled for the rest of the day."

"Are you sure about that, Governor? What we have to discuss involves the murder of two little girls in New York."

There was a slight pause, "I'll call you back on my private line." And then the line went dead.

Reese smiled as she imagined ringlets of smoke spiraling out of the governor's ears.

Emerson's phone rang. He never got to say hello.

"Listen to me you little prick, don't you ever call my office again! Do you hear me?"

"Why Governor, is that any way to speak to law enforcement?"

"Lake, you have no idea what I'm capable of; I'll have your job, your badge, your entire career on a platter!"

"Now, now Cramer, you need to calm down. Reese and I need to speak to you privately. We have information about your daughter. Yes, we know all about her and the warden's little girl as well. Do I have your attention now? We need to meet in person. This is for your protection and that of another small child."

"I'm listening."

"Contact your lawyer and we will meet you at his office. Send us his address."

"I will be there in 20 minutes; I'm texting the address to you now. Lake, I'm warning you, don't fuck with me!"

"Actually, I could say the same to you, Governor. See you in twenty."

Reese pulled up the name and address of his attorney.

"We don't need any surprises upon our arrival," Lake noted.

"You're right. I don't trust this guy. I'll have Manning and Brennen on back-up in an unmarked vehicle."

"Smart thinking Clayton. Have Carly run a background check on his attorney. Photos, whatever she can find. We wouldn't know if we were speaking to a real lawyer or one of Cramer's thugs before he got the chance to blow our heads off."

The address was on the upper east side of town. The building looked newer than the others on the street. Lots of offices occupied the space, but the large exterior windows allowed plenty of natural light to filter in making it feel light and airy.

They saw the governor's detail pull up in a black SUV with government plates. A big burly looking guy got out of the driver's seat and opened the back door for Cramer. He looked around first before he nodded to Cramer. "All clear."

Reese and Emerson approached the SUV. "Governor, I'm..."

"I know who the fuck you are," he hissed. The governor briskly walked past Emerson, ignoring his extended hand.

Carly was in Reese's ear. "All good Reese, attorney's legit sending you a photo now. Address is legit as well."

Reese gave a nod to Emerson as they walked into the building and entered the elevator, leaving the bodyguard at the car.

"Top floor. Must be a magnificent view from up there." Reese tried to make small talk. "Look, we know you're pissed, and that's understandable."

"Pissed, really detective? You don't know what pissed is." He glared at her.

The elevator doors opened directly into the suite of Attorney Alton Kane. Panoramic view. A mahogany desk, Reese thought would fill her entire living room. Furniture was top of the line, with fabrics to enhance the beauty of both the inside of the office and the outside view as well.

"Let's get on with it," Cramer snapped. "I haven't got all day." The governor made introductions, his voice calming down a bit.

"Mr. Kane," Reese began, "we have evidence connecting your client to the New York City Rossi crime family."

"One member of that crime family is Benito Rossi," Emerson continued. "Cramer accused Benito of murdering his daughter and her friend at a sleepover many years ago. Long before William Cramer became Governor. The other little girl murdered was the daughter of Warden Steven Daniels."

"Where are you going with this, Detectives?" Kane asked trying to get a handle on the situation.

"I'm getting to that," Emerson assured him. "Unfortunately, Benito Rossi was never convicted. In fact, the case was thrown out and Benito walked free due to a rather colossal mistake made by Cramer's legal counsel at the time, John Orrick."

Reese took over. "The same John Orrick, who somehow became the sitting judge for Jade, South Dakota. The same Judge that was murdered recently at his daughter's wedding."

"While the death of Judge Orrick is tragic, I don't understand how that has anything to do with my client, detectives."

Reese continued, "Judge Orrick's daughter was about to marry Alessandro Rossi. A short time after the death of the Judge, Alessandro's body was found along highway 102. He was also murdered."

"I'm still not seeing why you are here, Ma'am." Kane leaned back in his chair.

"We believe," Emerson continued, "that Governor Cramer persuaded Steven Daniels to move to South Dakota and eventually appointed him as the warden at the State prison."

"Detectives," Kane said in a calm voice, "there is no law against my client hiring an old friend for a job."

"No, you're right," Emerson agreed, "but this wasn't just a case of giving his old buddy a leg up in his career. We believe this was a conspiracy to seek revenge on John Orrick and the Rossi family for their roles in their daughters' unresolved murders. Revenge is a powerful motive, wouldn't you say?"

Alton Kane leaned back in his big leather chair.

"We have evidence to back up our theory," Emerson continued. "The governor's fingerprints were found in an abandoned limousine at Sioux Falls Regional Airport. There were two other sets of prints pulled from that vehicle, those of Alessandro Rossi and Timothy Cole."

"I have ridden in many rental cars for events and official engagements," Governor Cramer interjected. "There could be thousands of other passengers in that car besides me."

"Don't say another word," Kane shot his client an annoyed glance. "Unless I tell you to."

The governor scowled, but heeded his counsel's advice.

Kane continued, "Who is Timothy Cole and what does he have to do with any of these allegations?"

"Timothy Cole was a serial killer on death row at Warden Daniels' prison," Reese replied. "He conveniently escaped the night of his execution. We believe Cramer and Daniels hired him to do their dirty work and get rid of the people that hurt their families."

"And what about this Benito Rossi that was accused of killing the little girls? Where is he now?"

"No one knows," Emerson shrugged. "He was next in line to

take over the Rossi family business, but now he's in the wind." Emerson turned to the Governor. "You recently made some serious accusations against our captain. Something about her assaulting you, right?"

"Don't answer that," Kane warned his client.

"The governor may want to reconsider his accusations against Captain Brown," Reese said. "Governor, can you please remove that bandage from your neck? We'd like to see your wound."

"Absolutely not! I don't have to show you anything."

"If you don't, we'll just subpoena your doctors and ask the courts to have the bandages removed. It's up to you how you want to handle this Governor," Reese taunted him.

"What exactly are you accusing my client of detectives?"

"We suspect that the Governor does not have an injury on his neck, or if he does, it was self-inflicted," Reese said.

"This is ridiculous!" Cramer yelled.

Kane put his hand up to quiet his client. "Detectives, do you have a warrant for my client's arrest?"

"No, we do not have a warrant, Mr. Kane, but I'm sure Mr. Cramer would agree he does not want one presented. Am I correct Governor?" Reese was loving every minute watching him squirm.

"I think we're done here detectives. Come back when you have a warrant," Kane waved them toward the exit.

The detectives stood to leave.

"Oh, Cramer, by the way," Lake said, "it wasn't Captain Brown that you were with the night of your alleged slice and dice incident. It was her twin sister. Her *identical* twin." Governor Cramer's eyes widened in disbelief.

"The one you raped when she was 13 years old while she was working for you and your wife. Got a thing for young girls, do you, Governor?"

CHAPTER 82

"Reese," Agent Wells said, "we just left the lab. About your car exploding, we have new info."

"Great, what have you got?"

"Is Lake with you? Just thought I should ask. I'm still feeling lucky."

"Knock it off," Olden rolled his eyes. "Don't pay any attention to him Reese."

"I usually don't Rob. What's up?"

"We found out where the burner phone was sold. Kid identified Jack Roman as the purchaser."

"So, Timothy Cole was telling the truth. He didn't know that by dialing that phone, he was detonating the bomb planted under my car. It's all adding up. Cole told me his boss' name was Jack. We know Jack Roman is the governor's bodyguard, so I'm guessing the governor is the one that wanted me out of the picture." She looked toward the sky, her hands in prayer formation, "Thank you, Tim."

"I believe," Lake said, "you should look toward hell, Reese. Don't you think?"

"What's that supposed to mean?" asked Wells.

"Nothing, Michael. Emerson is just being an ass." Reese glared at Emerson. "Thanks for the update, guys."

"Now that Cole is dead," Wells said, "we can't prove it was Jack Roman or the Governor that ordered him to do this. Tim was the only witness. They found nothing else in the car."

"Understood," Reese nodded. "Thanks again guys. It is what it is."

• • •

Emerson pulled the car into the parking lot of a coffee shop around the corner from his apartment.

"Are you okay Reese? Can I get you something?"

Reese sat silently staring out the window.

"I'm sorry about that hell comment. You feel very differently about Timothy Cole than the rest of us. I should know better."

"It's alright, Emerson. I know you were just trying to make light of the situation. There is just so much shit going on with this case."

"I know, babe," he squeezed her hand lovingly.

"Now go get me a nice big cup of coffee and I'll have a rather large cinnamon bun to go with it. Do you want the money for it?" she asked.

"Do you think I want my balls cut off during the night?"

They laughed as he got out of the car and headed into the coffee shop.

CHAPTER 83

"How the hell did you get mixed up with the mob, Bill?" Attorney Alton Kane was now re-thinking his decision to take on this case.

"Do you have kids?" The Governor choked back tears, but it was a losing battle as he continued. "Do you know what it's like to lose a child? To have them murdered and not be able to do a damn thing about it?"

"No, I don't, Governor. But I highly doubt murder would be my first choice at rectifying the situation."

"Well, I tried the legal way. That didn't work! Those two detectives are a thorn in my side, but they are right about Benito Rossi. The courts set my daughter's murderer free. It has taken years to avenge her death, but now I realize it hasn't helped anything. My life is a mess. My career will be over if this gets out. I've lost my wife. That can never be repaired. I'm not strong enough to fight my way out of this. I'm tired and miss what might have been with my little girl." His voice cracked; tears began streaming down his face. "What now?"

Kane went to the mahogany cabinet that graced the wall

of his exquisite office and pulled out a bottle of 21-year-old Glenlivet Scotch and two glasses. "First, we need to discuss the bandage on your neck." He poured the scotch, took a sip himself and asked the question. "Did Captain Brown, well I guess if the detectives are correct, I mean did Captain Brown's sister actually slice your throat? Did you require stitches? I need the truth if I'm going to represent you."

After taking a sip of the scotch, he set the glass down on the coffee table. "Alton, I am embarrassed to admit that she did cut me, look I have the stitches to prove it." The Governor removed the bandage from his neck, "See for yourself."

Kane peered closer at the wound on the Governor's neck. "I thought you said she used a knife? That doesn't look like the type of injury a knife would leave behind," Kane surmised as he snapped a photo with his cell phone.

"How would you know?" The governor snapped, pushing the attorney's phone away. "She did it. End of story!"

"Fine. I will contact the detectives to find out exactly what it is they want from you. And, if there will be charges pending. The other hornet in the nest is, did you actually rape that woman as a child while she was employed by you?"

"No, I did not! Look, I have an important meeting that I'm already late for. Can we finish this later this evening or in the morning?"

"Governor, your own life is at stake here. Isn't that more important than what is on your desk today? I need the truth, all of it, if I have any shot of helping you keep your job and out of prison. Do you see where I'm heading here, Bill?"

The conversation lasted for another half hour.

"I think I have enough to take to the detectives. I'll notify you when I hear back. Be prepared. This might require you pay damages for the trauma you caused Captain Brown's sister. The one thing we have going for us, in the event we do have to go to trial, is your public denouncement of the boarding schools during your campaign."

The governor left the building and returned to his limo.

"How did it go, sir?" Roman asked opening the car door for him.

"I need you to take care of him."

"Who?"

"Alton Kane. He knows too much. And make sure you get his phone when you're done."

"Your attorney? Whatever he knows, he can't divulge it because of attorney client privilege. You know that, right? Shit, even I know that much."

"Unless the communications are to cover up a crime. As a high-society attorney, he will protect his reputation first. I've seen his type before. Too ethical to be a competent fixer. I don't trust him anymore."

"So, what next? Who else has the smarts and lack of ethics to represent you?"

"I don't know yet. But I'm not going to prison. Now let's go."

CHAPTER 84

"When do you think they will release my sister from the hospital?"

"I really don't know," the head nurse replied. "Her burns will heal, but the trauma of what she endured before the fire and now finding out she has you back in her life can take a tremendous toll on anyone. The mental stress, well, that will be determined by her doctors. I wish I could be of more help. I highly doubt you will learn anything unless your sister grants permission. It probably wouldn't hurt for you to speak to someone about this traumatic experience yourself, Captain Brown."

"Thank you. I appreciate your help and advice."

"Oh, one more thing Captain, I know she is your sister, but remember she is under arrest and has an ankle monitor."

"I understand," she replied. But deep down, the captain wanted to throw caution to the wind and take her sister away somewhere no one would ever find them. Leave everything she worked so hard to achieve to make up for all that Zitkala had been denied in life. "Maybe I do need help getting a better grasp of this situation."

"Captain, I can refer you to someone if you wish. I know this has to be unnerving." The nurse compassionately reached for her hand, giving it a gentle squeeze.

"Thank you, I will think about it."

Kimimela returned to the waiting area and curled up on the sofa, not feeling any more confident about her sister's life outcome. She closed her eyes and fell into a deep sleep. Something she had not expected.

"Hi, mommy! I'm here, mommy! Wake up!" Kimimela felt a tugging on her sweater. Then a weight that landed on her chest. I'm dreaming, she thought, but the movement across her torso told her otherwise.

"Wake up!" the voice kept urging. "I'm here. Officer Kevin Brown at your service mommy."

Kim opened her eyes, wiping off the spot of drool seeping from her lip. "What?" she asked, still groggy.

The guard that was with the little boy took his hand. "I'm sorry. I thought I was supposed to bring him up here to see you. It's 3 pm." The guard scooped Kevin off of Kim's lap. "Let's let your mommy sleep."

"No, wait," Kim said as she came out of her slumber fog. It came rushing to her all at once. "Oh, my goodness, you're Kevin."

The little guy turned to the guard. "What's wrong with my mommy?"

"Sweetheart," Kim said softly, "nothing is wrong. I was asleep. I didn't know it was you."

The guard suddenly realized his mistake. "What do I do now?" he asked.

The head nurse and Zitkala's psychiatrist proceeded toward the three of them. "We will handle this," the nurse said, but Kevin was too scared to let go of the guard.

"It's okay, officer Kevin, I'm right here with you. For back-up."

Kevin put his thumb in his mouth, letting go of the guard's hand.

The nurse approached Zitkala's room. "I'll be out to get you in a few minutes, Kevin." She opened the door and Kevin could see the woman in the bed. He ran toward the door, pushing his way past the head nurse. "Mommy!" he yelled. Then turned back to see the other woman at the entrance to the room. He cocked his head confused. "Mommy?" Tears started welling up in his eyes. "Who's my mommy? Where are you, mommy?" His gaze moving swiftly back and forth between both women. "What happened to you, mommy? Why are there two of you?" He ran back through the doorway, finding the guard right outside the room. He grabbed his hand and then wrapped his body around the guard's leg, holding on for dear life.

"It's okay, you're okay," the guard reassured him. "I'm right here to protect you, remember?"

Through his tears, Kevin looked up never releasing his bear hug on the guard's leg. "I see two mommies and I don't know why," he cried.

Zitkala and Kim watched all of this unfold, neither knowing what to do. Kim took a step toward the door to go console the boy, but Dr. Chang stopped her.

"Let's just wait a moment. I think the guard may have the answers your son needs. Listen," she whispered.

The guard gently pulled his little arms away from his leg and picked Kevin up. He walked to the empty chair in Zitkala's room and took a seat, placing Kevin on his lap. "Okay Kevin, I want you to listen carefully, because that's what outstanding police officers do, right?"

Kevin didn't answer.

"Right, Kevin?"

"Right, cause I'm officer Kevin," he finally replied through the tears. He sniffled and wiped his nose with his shirt.

Zitkala wanted to scold him. Instead, she just smiled and wiped away her own tears with the sleeve of her robe.

"Which one of these people, Kevin, do you think is your mommy? Just point."

Kevin didn't hesitate and pointed to the lady sitting on the bed in the robe.

"That's right. Now before I let you give her a hug; I want you to meet someone. Is that okay with you?" Kevin nodded yes, no longer crying.

"Did you know your mommy has a sister that looks just like her?"

"No," he said, ready to put his thumb back in his mouth.

The guard gently pulled Kevin's hand away from his mouth.

"Well, she does, and that lady over there is your mom's sister. And that makes her your aunt."

Kevin looked at Kimimela and smiled.

"Do you know what the word 'identical twin' means, Kevin?" Dr. Chang asked.

Kevin shook his head, "No."

"Come here, baby," Zitkala said. "Come, give mommy a hug."

Kevin jumped off the guard's lap and ran to his mom. "I got it right," he exclaimed, saluting his fellow officer.

CHAPTER 85

Jack Roman made eye contact in the rear-view mirror with the governor, now seated in the back of the Limo. "Sir. I don't think it's a good idea to have your attorney murdered. There is far too much press on you as it is Governor. You can bet that would bring every national news outlet here to cover the story. Eventually, they are going to connect the dots back to your daughter's murder. Aren't we supposed to quiet things down, not ramp things up?"

The governor sat in silence.

"If I may suggest, sir? I say you pay off the girl. Drop the charges. Let her have her freedom. The public will think you have a kind heart by letting her be with her son. As far as sleeping with her, tell everyone you made a mistake. A lot of other politicians have been caught cheating on their wives and come out unscathed. No one needs to know about your relationship with her when she was a kid."

Governor Cramer didn't respond to anything Jack Roman had to say during the ride back to one of his private residences. Not once answering his bodyguard. As Jack opened the door for the governor to exit, all he said was, "I need time to think."

"Yes, sir."

Jack parked the Limousine and returned to the street in his own SUV. It was late, and he decided on Olio Vito for dinner. Nice Italian restaurant. He knew most everyone there, and they also knew him. They knew he would protect them at any cost. The owners were like family.

"Jack, what brings you out so late?" the owner greeted him.

"Need some of your pasta, my friend. Can I get it to go?"

There were only two other diners sitting at a table.

"Absolutely," the owner snapped his fingers toward a dark-haired server.

"Is she new?" Jack asked admiring her beauty.

"Been here for a while. You are looking for dessert too? Hey Carmella," he yelled without waiting for a response from Jack.

"No, not tonight, my friend. Some other time."

Jack took a seat at the bar and had a beer while waiting for his food, pondering what to do about the governor. Hoping some sleep might clear that stubborn head of his. He re-positioned on the stool, trying to remove the thoughts of the last few hours and was now disappointed in himself for turning down dessert.

His food arrived, and the scent of perfect Italian cuisine floated to his nostrils. "Ah, this is just what I need tonight. Thank you, Carmella. I'm sure it's delicious." He handed the server the money for his takeout and added a generous tip. Only one other person remained at the far end of the bar, fin-ishing his beer.

"Having a bad day?" the server asked Roman, leaning over to

wipe down the table so he could see her long, bare legs, and the edge of her black lace panties.

"Could be worse, I suppose." He fidgeted on his bar stool. "But I'll be fine. Hey, Carmella, when do you get off work? Maybe you'd like to share this dinner with me at my place?"

She smiled, walking over to the bar, "We don't even know each other. Why would I do that?"

"My name is Jack Roman. I'm with the governor's detail, but I think you already know that don't you?"

"And you feel it's okay to just approach me with your dinner plans and then what, Mr. Jack Roman?" Her accent was heavy and broken, but sexy. She stood, hands on her hips, awfully close to him.

Jack placed his container of food on the bar, stood up, placing his hand in her jet-black hair. His fingers caressing the skin between her neck and ear. It felt like silk. Then he leaned in and kissed her, at first very gentle, releasing his lips from hers. He stared into her beautiful eyes for a moment before kissing her again, this time with more passion and need. "I believe beautiful Carmella; you know the answer to that as well."

"What's in it for me?" she asked.

"I knew you would spoil the moment. How much?" He slammed his bottle of beer on the bar and reached for his food to leave.

"No, wait. She placed her body between him and his food. Please listen to me for a moment. I don't want your money." She looked around the room to make sure everyone had left the restaurant. Only the owner remained in the kitchen. "I need you to get me in to see the governor. I will do whatever you want me to."

"What the hell is this?" he gave her a shove out of his way.

"Immigration. If I don't get the right papers in the next two weeks, they will deport me. Can you help me?"

"And your boss knows about this? Are you related to him?"

"I work for him, do what I am asked to do. You understand, no?"

Jack was losing his mood and the warm feeling he had for his favorite restaurant. "All right. I will see what I can do. No promises though."

She gave him a hug as she rubbed her body against his trousers. "Thank you," she said. "Thank you."

Now he had to have her. He picked up the food, but wasn't planning on having dinner with Carmella, anyway. His primary goal; take her to bed. They left the restaurant and headed for his apartment.

"Yes boss," he said, answering a call from the governor. "Yes sir, on it, sir."

"Change in plans Carmella. Your wish to stay in the country may be closer than you think," he stepped on the gas as he made a quick U-turn, nearly hitting the curb.

"I don't understand," she grabbed the door handle as he quickly changed direction.

"That was the governor. He's looking to get laid tonight and you're all I have right now."

"The governor? He wants me? Oh Jack, I don't know about this," she cried.

He reached over the center console and slapped her in the face. "Listen to me. I don't like this myself, and I certainly don't like sloppy seconds. You will do as you are told. And if you want to remain here, this is your best bet. I suggest you be extra nice to him. Are we clear?"

She sat in silence the rest of the way to Governor Cramer's residence.

"Jack, she's a beauty. What do I owe you for getting her here so quickly?" Cramer eyed her up and down, reaching under her uniform, touching her inner thigh. "Oh, she is good, Jack."

"It's not me you owe, sir; the young lady has a request of her own. She wants you to help her stay in the country."

"Well, I think I can arrange that. You are a pretty little thing. Let's see what you've got for me," he said as he pulled down his pants before Jack could leave the room.

Jack shook his head at the sleazy bastard. As he opened the door to leave, a gun met his face. "Hold it right there, Roman. Hands up. Inside!"

"What the fuck do you think you are doing?" the governor hastily pulled up his trousers. "This is my home. Do you know who I am?"

"I certainly do Governor William Cramer." Carmella reached into her restaurant uniform pocket and pulled out a badge. "FBI. You are under arrest for soliciting prostitution and human trafficking." One of the other two agents at the door tossed handcuffs to her. "Turn around. You have the right to remain silent…"

"I know my rights, you little whore!" he growled.

"Oh, is that a nice thing to say to me? I'll bet you aren't used to the woman handcuffing you, are you dirtbag? Take him in," she ordered the agents. "Right behind you."

She grabbed Roman by the arm, his hands cuffed behind his back. "Too bad you didn't see the com in my ear when you kissed me. Might have been an interesting night if you hadn't traded me to Cramer." She reached between his legs and squeezed. Pausing for effect. "The next time you feel someone between your legs, it will be some big beefy dude in your prison cell. Let's go!"

CHAPTER 86

"I want my attorney present; do you hear me?" the Governor, furious for being arrested and dragged out into the open for anyone on the street to see. "I have a reputation to uphold as an elected official of this state. I demand some respect here!"

Agents Olden and Wells were waiting next to their vehicle.

"We'll take it from here." Olden placed the governor in the back seat. "Thanks, *Carmella*, for the help." He did not want to expose her real identity. Carmella nodded her head and got into a black SUV with the other agents.

They headed back to FBI headquarters.

"Would you care to explain yourself, governor?" Wells asked. "I mean really, governor, you haven't had enough press on your sexual habits of late? How many bottles of little blue pills do you carry around with you?"

"Fuck you!"

Arriving at the FBI field office, they placed Jack Roman and Governor Cramer in separate rooms. Wells interrogated Roman and Olden interrogated the Governor.

Jack Roman sat at a table handcuffed to the top rail, waiting for all hell to break loose. Not even knowing an attorney in the state he could call. Alton Kane wouldn't be an option.

"Jack Roman," Wells sauntered into the brightly lit room with the proverbial wall of mirrors. "Can I get you a bottle of water? Or perhaps a pen and paper for your statement?"

"I'm fine, just like I am."

"Is there anything you'd like to say, Jack? About the charges against you?"

"I don't remember charges being brought to my attention, Agent Wells. As far as I knew, I was just bringing a friend over to visit with the governor. Doesn't really seem like I'm guilty of anything. Besides all that, they did not give me the opportunity to contact an attorney, so I really would like my phone call."

There was a knock on the door. Wells opened it. "What?" he barked at the agent.

"Alton Kane is here to see the Governor."

"I'll be right in. Make sure Mr. Roman gets his phone call."

"I'm sorry," the recorded voice began, "the number you have reached is no longer in service."

Jack Roman hung up the phone and dialed again. Same recording. "What the fuck is going on?" he banged the phone on the edge of the desk. He dialed another number. Again, a complete disconnect. Jack was nervous, but had no one else to call. He tried a New Jersey number, one that he was only to use in the event of an emergency.

"Hello," the sweet voice of a young woman answered.

"This is Jack Roman. Would you tell Mr. Rossi I need to speak with him A.S.A.P?"

After a brief pause, the young lady returned to the phone.

"I'm sorry, Mr. Roman, but Mr. Rossi says he has never heard of you. Have a nice day Mr. Roman."

CHAPTER 87

"You are not a smart man, Governor," Alton scolded his client. "You weren't gone from my office less than two hours, and you had to have another woman at your residence."

"It's no one's business who I have at my home," he replied angrily.

"It is if you're buying that person. Damn it, Governor, what were you thinking? The agents are going to want a statement. The charges are serious governor. This will be a field day for the press. The public will put you on their own trial. Either way, the outlook is grim."

"I'm not going to go to prison. Do you fucking hear me? Do you know what would happen to me in there? Do you have any idea?" He pounded the table. Sweat beads formed on his forehead, his eyes wide with fear.

"My suggestion to you, Governor, is to find out exactly what these agents want from you as a tradeoff for resuming your life. I know it has something to do with that young Native American girl. You had better listen. At this moment, I have no defense for you. I'm good at my job, but there is only so much a judge will listen to."

Olden and Wells entered the interrogation room together.

"I am Governor Cramer's attorney. Alton Kane." He handed the agents his card. "Why is my client here?"

"Do you know why we are here, Governor?" Wells asked, smirking.

"Do not answer that, Governor." Alton hoped his client was smart enough to keep his mouth shut.

"I believe you have met with Detectives Clayton and Lake, Governor. From the Cromwell P.D. Am I correct?" Wells continued.

"So, what if he has? What does that have to do with why my client being arrested? Cut the bullshit, Agent. What is it you want from my client? Governor Cramer is a busy man. He has no time for theatrics."

"Oh, Mr. Kane, theatrics are the least of your client's worries. How does rape of a minor sound to start?"

"That little bitch!" the Governor snarled.

"Her name is Zitkala Brown, Governor. I don't think calling her a bitch is genuinely nice."

The governor leapt to his feet, ready to fly at the agents. "How dare you! I'm the Governor of this fine state of South Dakota. You can't talk to me like that!" he clenched his fists as well as his teeth.

"Governor!" Alton Kane wrapped his arms around Cramer's torso and jammed him back down in his seat. "Sit down! Let me handle this. You'll be out of here within the hour. Agents, I repeat, what is it you want from my client?"

"Governor Cramer," Agent Olden said sternly, "we believe

you should drop all charges against Zitkala Brown."

"I will not have her ruin my reputation!" he slammed his fists on the table. His face reddening with each passing minute.

"Your reputation, *your* reputation?" Wells repeated. "Seriously Governor? If this series of events gets to the press, your reputation is shot. You ruined this girl's life by raping her as a child. By the way, we are searching for your wife. She, too, will face charges if she knowingly let you assault this young girl and kept it silent."

"You leef mi wiif..." the Governor's speech slurred. He appeared confused and began to wobble losing his balance. His face began to droop as he reached for the table to steady himself, but missed and fell straight to the floor with a thud.

CHAPTER 88

We interrupt your regularly scheduled programming with breaking news.

Governor William S. Cramer has died.

State officials confirmed the governor passed away late this morning of a stroke.

The Governor is best known for denouncing the now infamous Native American boarding schools and his unyielding efforts to lift up indigenous people in our community.

More recently the Governor also advocated to raise awareness about mental health and wellness.

Stay tuned right here for the latest updates.

This is Keith Riverton, News 7.

CHAPTER 89

"Captain, Alton Kane is requesting a meeting with you, the detectives, and the FBI agents."

"Where is this meeting taking place, Officer Brennen?"

"He has requested at his office. I'm sure he will agree to wherever you wish."

"Would you notify him I will speak with him later today and we can discuss a convenient time and place then. I am not leaving this hospital without seeing my sister again and not until I secure her safety."

"Of course, Captain."

"Anything new on the governor's bodyguard?"

"Last I heard, he has a public defender. Doesn't appear he has the deep pockets for someone like Kane. Guess his *family* back east doesn't feel he is worth it."

"Have Clayton or Lake notify me with the latest."

"Yes, Captain."

As Kimimela hit the end button on the call, she heard a voice.

"Captain Brown," the nurse peeked around the corner to the waiting room. "Your sister is asking to see you."

"Thank you," she replied. Nervous about going back into the room, she noticed her reflection in the glass from a piece of art on the wall. *I look like hell,* she thought, running her fingers through her hair to make some sense of where it should be. She massaged her forehead and rubbed the bags under her eyes. *That's the best I can do, for now anyway.* She quietly opened the door.

"Zitkala, how do you feel? Can I get you something to drink?" Kimimela was happy to see a light in her twin sister's eyes that she had long forgotten.

"No, I'm fine, my sister," she paused and repeated, "my sister. I can't believe you are here."

"I know. I can't believe it either. I never thought I would see you again." The captain fought off the tears. "I have so much to tell you. First, Zitkala, I love you."

"I love you too," Zitkala grabbed for her sister's hand.

"You have more family," Kimimela continued. "We have brothers. We have informed them you are alive. They all have families of their own now and when you are ready, I will arrange for us to meet with them. Kevin will have cousins to play with and grow up together," she smiled.

"What about our brother, Mato? Is he alive? Did he escape? They separated us immediately when we arrived."

"I don't know, Zitkala. I am praying he is alive but remaining realistic. The government has been working on locating and identifying the remains of children buried on school grounds. I'm working another angle. One of my officers is very resourceful. I have her searching for Mato."

"Wait, what do you mean one of your *officers*? Does that

mean? Are you a cop?”

"Yes, my sister. I'm the Captain of the Cromwell Police Department. But please trust me.”

"How is it possible?” she panicked. “You're going to take my son away and put me in jail. How could I be so stupid to think you cared?” Her fear and mistrust were getting the best of her. “You said you loved me. Get out!” she screamed. “If you touch my son, I will kill you.”

"Zitkala, listen to me. I would never do anything to hurt you or Kevin. I'm hiring all the best people to help find a way to get you and Kevin out of this mess. I want you to have everything you missed growing up. My sister, I adore you.”

Zitkala softened, “Won't you lose your job, if you help me?”

"Look into my eyes. You are me. I am you. Forever, I promise.”

The two embraced and once again shared tears. “May I tell you a secret, Zitkala?”

Zitkala nodded in anticipation.

"I'm pregnant.”

Zitkala's eyes lit up with joy. “Kimimela you are going to be a mom?”

Kim blushed. “Yes. I can't believe it. I am so excited, but a little scared as well.”

"You're going to make a great mother, Kimimela, my little Butterfly.”

"If it's a girl, I want to name her after you. Zitkala, my little Bird.”

"Oh, my goodness.” Zitkala held her hands close to her heart flattered at the thought. Then, in the blink of an eye, she yelled, “Why on earth would you saddle that poor baby with my name?

It's not very feminine."

There was a pause before they both broke into laughter. "You're right, Zitkala. We will find a better way to honor you."

"Who's the father?"

CHAPTER 90

"Jack Roman, as your court-appointed attorney, I am here to advise you the charge against you is soliciting prostitution. I believe you should plead guilty to this charge."

"Are you out of your fucking mind?"

"Hear me out. You can get the sentence reduced because the Governor forced you to find him a woman."

"I'm not sure about this idea."

"The other option is cooperating with the FBI. They may be willing to work out a deal in exchange for information to support their case against the governor. Maybe they'll even drop the charges against you or at least reduce it down to a misdemeanor."

Jack thought for a moment. "What do I have to tell the FBI?"

"Let me have a conversation with them to see what it is they are looking for."

Jack got the feeling his mob boss and the Governor had both hung him out to dry. And he knew he still had loose ends dealing with that bitch and his son. "Hey, is there a possibility I can get out of here on bail?"

"I highly doubt it, but I will recommend it at the hearing."

"Let me think about this. I'm not sure of anything yet."

"Very well. I'll speak with the agents and check the court docket, find out the day and time for the bail hearing. Don't say anything to anyone unless I am in the room. Do you understand?"

"Got it."

Jack knew the Rossi family would never allow him to live. He knew too much. When he called the emergency number, he sealed his fate. He had to find a different way out now.

CHAPTER 91

Officer Carly Brennen nearly choked on her granola bar as she watched the large TV on the wall of the precinct. Headlines scrolled across the bottom of the screen.

***The FBI is running a full investigation into
The South Dakota State Prison.***

"Manning, come look at this," she coaxed him over to the TV. "Aw shit, now you have to wait a minute till the scroll runs by again."

"Do you always talk with your mouth full, Brennen? Not very attractive," Manning joked.

"Shut up. There it is."

"Wow, it's about time they did something about that place. Does the Captain know about this?"

"I do not know; this is the first I'm seeing it."

"I'll call her now," Manning wanted to see how she was doing with her sister, anyway.

The call went straight to voice mail. He dialed Detective

Clayton.

"Hey Allen, what's up?" Reese answered. "You're on speaker, so don't say anything bad about Lake. Got it?" she teased.

"I wouldn't dream of it! Hey, did you guys see there is a full investigation into the South Dakota State Prison?"

"No, we did not. It's about time." Reese was relieved. "I'm surprised the agents didn't let us know about it."

"I'm sure they have their hands full, Reese," Emerson said. "I'm sure if they need our help, they'll ask. Thanks, Deputy, for the heads -up."

"One more thing, Detectives. Have you heard from Captain Brown? I tried to call her, but it went to voice mail. That's not like her. She's never *not* taken my calls."

"Hmm, I'll try to reach her and call you back," Reese said.

Reese dialed the number. "You have reached Captain Kimimela Brown..." She hung up. "That's odd. I'll call Jade Medical to see if someone there could relay a message that we are trying to reach her."

"Go ahead," Emerson said, "but don't be shocked if she gets pissed because you interrupted her visit with Zitkala."

"You're probably right, but I'll feel better knowing everything's okay."

"Yes, my name is Detective Reese Clayton, Cromwell P.D. Would you mind sending someone to Zitkala Brown's room? I've been trying to contact, her sister, Captain Kimimela Brown. Yes, I'll hold."

It was at least a ten-minute wait. "Yes. I'm here," Reese said politely, but thinking what the fuck took you so long.

"I'm going to connect you with the hospital administrator.

Please hold."

Reese looked at Emerson, mouthing the words, *What the fuck is wrong now?*

Emerson shrugged, "Beats me."

"Detective Clayton, I'm sorry, but you need to contact the FBI. I'm not allowed to give you any information."

Lake jumped on his own phone and called Agent Olden on speaker.

"Hey Lake, I was expecting your call. We are aware of the situation."

"What situation?" Reese questioned.

"Detectives, we got word from Jade Medical. It seems our sisters have left the building."

"What?" Reese exclaimed.

"You heard me correctly, detective. Zitkala's ankle monitor was found under the bed. Guard says that Captain Brown told him to take a break while she brought Zitkala down to the hospital daycare to see Kevin. A witness places both of them at the daycare, but when we looked at the exterior video footage of the hospital, Kevin was not with them when they left. Detectives, I'm afraid it looks like Kevin may have been kidnapped and your captain has decided she and her sister can handle going after him by themselves."

"How long ago was this?" Lake asked.

"Just about a 45minutes ago. They left in your captain's vehicle. Believe me, the entire state of South Dakota is looking for them. Your Captain should know this is not protocol," he scolded.

"I'm afraid our Captain is no longer thinking like law

enforcement," Lake responded. "She's thinking like an aunt, doing what she can to save her sister's son. How the hell did someone get into the daycare?"

"We have a team at the hospital conducting interviews and Wells and I are on the way to the last known location of her vehicle," Olden said.

"Robert, stay on the line. I'm calling Manning on my phone." Reese was panicking. "Allen, the Captain and her sister are in trouble. We need to track them down before they get hurt. They are going to need back up."

"Tell him to put Brennen on the phone," Emerson urged.

"She is right here with me Lake."

"Yes, detectives, how can I help?" Carly asked. Her fingers were already flying over the keyboard, contacting her sources just in case they were necessary.

"We need you to use your skills to find the captain. Ping her phone or do whatever is necessary and I mean *anything* else you can. We need to find them fast. This is life or death, do you understand?" Emerson ordered.

"I'm aware of the urgency, detective."

"Reese and I are headed toward Jade, so just point us in the right direction."

"Got it!" she exclaimed. "I have located a cell tower in the general vicinity of the last ping from the captain's cell phone. There's no time, detectives. You need to contact the FBI. Her phone is pinging near the Old Bay Cell tower about 30 minutes from the hospital. Address coming to you ...right...now!"

The agents were still on speakerphone with the FBI.

"Old Bay Cell tower, got it." Wells didn't want to piss off

Reese, but he and Olden already had that info. They knew the captain's phone would be within a 25-foot radius of its pinged location and were already in route. "Hopefully, the captain is with her phone when we get there."

"We're on our way, Michael, just *too* far away," Reese advised.

"We will keep the lines open," he promised.

Officer Brennen called Clayton again. "I've got more information and not the good kind. I have photos of the hospital parking lot. A husky man took Kevin. Trying to get facial rec now."

"Thanks Carly. Send what you have to the FBI agents and us. Has the Captain's phone moved?"

"No, it's still somewhere in that area," Carly confirmed. "I hope it wasn't dumped there."

"Me too. I have a bad feeling about this." Reese wrung her hands, her woman's intuition overwhelming her.

"Wait a sec." Carly's voice broke into Reese's thoughts, "I have aerial photos of the cell tower. Not much around, except a few homes and an abandoned gas station."

"Aerial photos?" Reese asked.

Carly continued, ignoring the question. "There is no camera on the old gas station, of course, but there appears to be a ring system on a house a few hundred yards from it."

"Where the hell did you come from, Carly Brennen?" Emerson joked.

"My mother and father," she teased.

"Copy that, Officer Brennen."

"Detective Clayton," Carly got serious, "I've got that facial recognition."

"And?"

"It's Benito Rossi."

"Are you fucking kidding me, Carly? The cold-blooded killer accused of murdering both the Warden and the Governor's daughter?"

"Shit!" Lake exclaimed. "Wells, did you get that?" He hoped the FBI agents were still with them on speaker. "I guess the prick isn't in the concrete of a high rise after all."

Wells put in his earbuds in so he could talk hands free. "Yes, we know it's Rossi. We already have his photo out on the wire. We are at the gas station where Captain Brown's phone was pinging. This place is abandoned. Captain Brown's phone was retrieved from the bathroom. It's in route to our headquarters to pull what we can off of it. Neither of the sisters is here. It appears they were, but maybe they don't want to be found. Or, maybe they are being held captive?"

"There's something else, isn't there, Michael? I can hear it in your voice." The hair was standing up on the back of Reese's neck.

"I'm afraid so," he paused. "We found the body of a little boy. We believe it to be Kevin Brown. He's been shot multiple times in the head and face."

Reese quickly rolled down the window and vomited before Lake could stop the car. "Oh my God," she sobbed, her head hanging out the window, gasping for air. "No! Not that sweet little boy!"

Lake grabbed the phone from Reese's hand. "Officer Brennen, can you get anything from that ring system?"

"Working on it, detectives. I'm so sorry about that little boy.

I heard everything."

Lake muted his call with Wells and Olden momentarily.

"Carly, I want everything you find and I want it first. Do you understand me?" Emerson ordered.

"Yes, detective. I got it." She put her fingers to the keyboard, trying her best not to cry. Focusing on the screen in front of her, conversing through the computer with her nameless team. Getting them to do what they do best. Locate the bad guy.

"Reese, we need you to focus. I can't stop to console you right now, partner. Pull yourself together. Drink some water."

She closed the window and wiped her face off with a few tissues. She guzzled an entire bottle of water in seconds. Reese knew what she had to do, "I'll be fine," she finally replied.

But in the back of her mind, she knew. *I'm not fine. I'm going to be the one to kill that cowardly prick.*

CHAPTER 92

"Sorry, Wells, I had to mute the phone while I consoled my partner. She's okay now. What else have you got?"

"A mess is what we have. Medical examiner is just pulling in. I'll catch up with you both shortly. Lake, tell Reese I'm sorry. I know how attached she was to Kevin. I saw how she protected him, quieted his fears. It's bad enough seeing a child murdered. It's a hundred times worse when you know him."

Reese heard every word Michael Wells said, but she chose not to respond.

Lake ended the call with the FBI and turned his attention back to Reese's phone on the dashboard. "Tell me you got something Carly."

"I got something. The captain's vehicle was last seen headed toward the Reservation. Detectives, it appears this Benito Rossi character is driving her car. We only see one passenger."

"We don't know for sure if the passenger is the captain or if it's her sister, do we?"

"No, the image is too far away."

"Either way, where's our missing twin?" Lake asked.

"She could be in the back seat, but I'm not seeing it. Possibly the trunk. They're on the toll road about six miles from the Reservation. Those cameras are pretty damn good, by the way."

"Why the hell would he take the chance of being seen by cameras on a toll road?" Lake wondered aloud. "Doesn't make any sense."

"Yes, it does," Reese interjected, "if you're going after the Governor. Rossi is holding the captain and her sister as hostage to get to Cramer. He probably doesn't know which one is which. Benito Rossi got away with the murder of the governor's daughter all those years ago, but I'm guessing he's out for revenge."

"Why?" Lake was searching for answers.

"Think about it, Emerson. Who was next in line to take over the Rossi *family*?"

"Alessandro Rossi. Our deceased groom. His nephew."

"Exactly. And who do you suspect might have been involved in Alessandro's murder?"

"So, you think…"

"Yes, I think. I'd bet the farm that the Governor had Alessandro killed. Emerson, you better step on it. Benito Rossi doesn't think twice about killing small children, so he has zero fucks to give about killing Captain Brown and Zitkala."

Emerson hit the gas a little harder knowing Reese was right. "Carly, how close are they to the Bur Oak Casino?" he asked.

"Close. Entering the Reservation property line. Detectives, you can't go any further."

Emerson grabbed his cell and dialed Sheriff Maka.

"Jimmy, we need your help. There is an active threat against the Governor. If he is at the casino, you need to get there fast.

The suspect has already killed someone and we believe he has abducted Captain Kimimela Brown and possibly her twin sister, Zitkala. The suspect's name is Benito Rossi. Sending a photo now."

"I'm pulling into the Casino lot now," the Sheriff responded. "Looks like the FBI is going in the front door as we speak."

Emerson and Reese looked at each other, wondering how the hell they got there first.

"Carly," they both said at the same time.

"I'm headed to the side entrance," Maka said. "The two of you take off the trench coats and act like normal casino guests. Go to the front. Head for the staff staircase, about five feet from the kitchen at Solera café. The suite is on the top floor. I'll take the elevator."

Emerson held Reese's arm as they entered the Bur Oak Casino attempting to impersonate a couple searching for a fun afternoon. As they headed toward the café, it surprised Reese when she heard something.

"Reese," a voice whispered in her ear com. "Go outside. Use the front door. Left side of the parking lot, third row back past the dumpster. Captain's car is there. Movement inside the vehicle."

"Who are you? How are you in my ear? How do you know my name?"

"Does it matter?"

"Yes, it matters," she whispered.

"You better hurry, before it's too late."

Reese grabbed Emerson's hand. "Let's go honey," she said, pulling on him to follow her back down the stairs.

"What the hell is going on?" he whispered.

"I need some fresh air, honey," she gritted her teeth dragging him back out the front door.

"Look for a dumpster over there," she ordered.

"I see it," Emerson said. "Now what?"

"Three rows in back of it. What do you see?"

"It's the captain's car," he looked at her in shock. "How the hell did you know it was there?"

She looked up toward the sky, "I think we had a little help."

"A drone? Carly?" he asked.

"Not her, but guessing she knows who it is."

They cautiously went around to the back of the vehicle. Guns drawn.

"Hold it right there," Lake yelled. "Hands up, where I can see them!"

There was no answer.

"I said, hands in the air!" Lake could see the car rocking back and forth. He got down low while Reese approached the opposite side of the vehicle. The car door suddenly flung open, grazing her partner, knocking him off balance. "Hold it right there!" Reese demanded as a man jumped out and ran.

Lake quickly popped up to his feet and began chasing the suspect across the asphalt parking lot. Out of nowhere, the familiar buzz of bullet slicing through the air whizzed past his head. He instinctively ducked and shouted, "Shots fired!"

Another projectile hissed past him. "Who the fuck is firing?" Emerson weaved between parked cars using them as cover as the shots kept coming. For a split second he turned back to see his partner back at the car staring into the back seat of the captain's car. Her hands coated in blood.

The barrage of bullets came to a halt when the suspect went down. Lake cautiously approached Rossi's body. Still not seeing who fired the shots. He bent over the body, checking the guy's neck for a pulse. When he raised his glance, Sheriff Jimmy Maka and his deputy were standing in front of him. "He's gone," Lake said.

Emerson turned to head back toward the captain's car hitting the com in his ear, "We need a bus. Now!"

The voice in his ear replied, "EMT's are on their way, Detective."

"Rez ambulance is closer. Who's in the car?" Maka asked.

"I don't know," Lake shouted back as his walk turned into a sprint.

Once he reached the vehicle, he could tell Reese was shaken. He put on Latex gloves and opened the front driver's side door.

"Zitkala Brown," Reese said. "Looks like she has been beaten. There's a rope around her neck. I tried to revive her but she was already gone. There's a lot of blood, I don't know whose."

"Reese?" Emerson approached the love of his life. "Reese," he repeated. "Come with me." He took her by the arm and led her away from the scene.

"She sure looks like the captain," Maka said when he made his way back to the car to investigate. "Are you sure it's her sister?"

"Yes, I'm sure," Reese said. "She has burns on her torso. Looks like she fought like hell."

Wells and Olden finally arrived on scene. "What are the two of you doing here?" Olden asked not knowing how they got the info to follow Rossi to the Reservation.

"We got a tip the Governor's life was in danger," Lake said.

"That's when they notified me," Maka said, waiting for flak from the Feds. "We didn't even know if the governor was actually here at the casino today."

"He's not here," Wells said. "He's being held for questioning at our office."

"No, he's not," a voice whispered in Lake's ear. "He is at Jade medical, detective Lake. You didn't hear that from me." Lake tried not to react to the news from his unknown informant.

Reese explained to the agents what happened when they arrived. "We told Rossi to exit the vehicle, but he ran. Zitkala was in the car, brutally beaten." Reese choked on her words, visibly shaken. "She didn't have a pulse."

The ambulance and the coroner arrived simultaneously, pronouncing Zitkala Brown dead at the scene. The FBI positively identified Rossi by his fingerprints taken at the scene.

"Agent Wells, can I see you for a moment?" the coroner asked, after assessing the suspect's body.

"What is it?"

Everyone, but Reese, followed the coroner and encircled Rossi's lifeless body. He had gunshot wounds to his head and face.

"Look at this before I transport his body to the morgue," the coroner said, carefully pulling open Benito Rossi's bloodied shirt.

A gold shield impaled his chest.

It read:

CAPTAIN CROMWELL POLICE DEPARTMENT.

CHAPTER 93

"Any sign of the captain?" asked Olden.

"No." Reese was trembling. "I don't know where she is. He could have dumped her anywhere."

"And there was only Zitkala in the car when you arrived?"

"Yes, Zitkala and Benito Rossi."

"And no sign of Captain Brown, you're sure?"

Reese shook her head.

"Lake, what about you? Did you see Captain Brown anywhere?" Olden knew he was treading on thin ice but needed to get the statement.

Lake shook his head silently as well.

"Fan out everybody," Olden commanded. "We need to cover as much ground as possible before nightfall. She could be anywhere. Get the K9s out here."

Sheriff Jimmy Maka approached agent Olden. "This is the land of the Sioux Nation, Agent Olden. Be respectful of that and of Captain Kimimela Brown when you find her. I will expect the body of Zitkala Brown and her son to be returned to us as soon as they have completed the autopsies. We will bury them here where they belong. Do you understand, agents?"

"Yes, Sheriff." Wells shook Jimmy Maka's hand. "We have no desire to interfere with your laws. We have great respect for Captain Brown and her sister. You will notify us if Captain Brown..." Wells left it at that.

"Reese," Emerson asked, "are you okay? What's going on? You know something, don't you?"

"Not here," she whispered.

The FBI shut down the casino, to the dismay of the patrons, while they completed their search. Nothing. Even the dogs came up empty.

There is a tremendous amount of shell casings out here," Agent Olden commented. "Lake, how many times did you fire?"

"None. I never fired my weapon. I couldn't tell where the shots were coming from. Here, check my weapon."

"Reese, may I have your weapon?" Olden asked as he approached her.

"Why?" she asked.

"How many shots did you fire, detective?"

"None. Here take it," she said handing it over.

"Then who was firing at Rossi?" Wells asked.

"I have no idea," Reese replied.

"And did you see anything, Lake?"

"Nothing. I was just trying to do my best not to get killed in the line of fire."

"Sheriff Maka, I will need to see your weapons as well," Wells said. "These shell casings are definitely police issued bullets."

"Well, they aren't from my service pistol, either," Maka said handing over his weapon.

"Which means one thing, Detectives."

"And what might that be Agent Wells?" Reese shot him a look that could have burned a hole in his soul.

"We have another killer on the loose. My guess," he added. "Someone from the Rossi crime family that did not want old Benito to spill his guts. I'm guessing whoever it was might have been trying to frame one of you. Are you thinking the same, Detectives?"

"Anything is possible, Agent Wells." Emerson replied.

"Anything." Reese softened, knowing he was on their side until the end.

"We need to find where Rossi took your captain. The outlook isn't good. I'm guessing she wouldn't leave her sister alone with this animal. Not if she had anything to say about it. Thoughts?"

"Emerson and I will go back to where Carly first picked up Benito Rossi driving the car. Possible he left her somewhere between the gas station and the Reservation."

"Sounds good, Clayton. We will be in touch. Fingers crossed she's alive." Olden shook their hands. "Don't worry, we have your back on this one."

CHAPTER 94

"Okay Reese," Emerson said once back on the road. "What do you know you couldn't tell me before?"

"The captain," she exclaimed. "Pull off the road! Way off so no one can see the car."

"What are you talking about?"

"Just do it Emerson!" she yelled.

He hit the brake and pulled off to the shoulder under the cover of some brush. Reese jumped out before the car barely came to a stop. She yelled. "Pop the damn trunk. Hurry!"

Captain Brown gasped for air, extending her hand for help out of the trunk. She fell to the ground. Visible injuries covered her face and extremities.

"My sister, my sister, I am here!" She continued repeating those words. Emerson sat down beside her. Reese on the other side, stroking her hair as she lay face down in the grass.

"Zitkala, Zitkala, find me in the mirror. I'm there Zitkala. No, please, not Kevin. NO!" A blood-curdling scream erupted from her body. Reese went to the car for water and something to wipe the face of this once powerful leader, for whom the entire department had such respect and admiration. Now she was a grief-stricken woman, sister, aunt, and mother to be.

"Shit!" Reese said. "Captain! Captain! We need to get you to a hospital. Breathe, drink this water. Help her up Emerson," she pleaded. "Help her up!"

Emerson looked at Reese and then motioned down at the captain's legs. Reese swallowed hard and ran back to the car for some rags. She carefully lifted the captain's dress and placed them where the former life now settled. "Oh my God. Why?" she sobbed with her captain.

Reese washed her friend's face as best she could with just water and wipes. They got her sitting up and to the car. Emerson drove so Reese could help Kimimela in the back seat. The waves of dismay washing over her every few moments.

"Captain," Reese asked, "where is your weapon?"

"I don't know. I don't know."

"Why were you running away from the scene, Captain? It was a justified shoot."

"Not the way I handled it," she said, unable to stop sobbing.

"What do you mean?" Lake asked. "You are an officer of the law; your life was in danger."

"That no-good son-of-a-bitch slaughtered my nephew. I was going to kill him, no matter what the consequences. Then he beat Zitkala to death. She suffered terribly. I will never forgive myself for allowing her to go with me when that ugly prick sent me a photo of Kevin. He was carrying him like a sack of potatoes!" She screamed into Reese's shoulder.

Reese grabbed a paper fast food bag lying on the floormat, not knowing how long it had been there. She squeezed the top together making a cup, and held it for Captain Brown to breathe in and out of, soothing her hyperventilation.

"Why did you stab Rossi with your badge?" Emerson asked. "That was like leaving a calling card. I don't know how we can protect you from that."

"I didn't."

CHAPTER 95

"Reese, we need to help her. It's too far to Cromwell medical center."

"I know. Our safest bet is probably Sheriff Jimmy Maka. Get him on the phone. Tell him we are bringing a friend over. Tell him to have a doctor there when we arrive. He'll understand."

They arrived at the address Sheriff Maka provided. Maka and Emerson helped Kimimela out of the car and into a gracious home.

"We can take it from here, Detectives."

"I told you!" Reese yelled, "we are not leaving her side. If that's not ok with you, tell us now, we will go elsewhere."

"It's okay, detectives," Jimmy Maka said. "Thank you. I really do appreciate what you are doing for Kimimela." He paused. "I promise we will take good care of her. She's carrying my child."

Emerson and Reese were stunned.

"Jimmy," Emerson whispered barely able to get the words out, "I think she may have lost the child in the struggle. I'm sorry, my friend."

"I know," he whispered back, "but I do not want her to go

deeper into trauma than she is in right now. I will let the doctor handle this."

"It's okay, Reese," Captain Brown said. "I trust Jimmy with all my heart and soul. Please don't tell anyone where I am, at least not yet. I have many things to think about and some I never want to think about again. Take whatever evidence you need from your trunk, do what you must do. Cromwell Police Department's captain will no longer be me. I belong here on the Reservation. I should never have left my home."

"Captain, that's not true," Emerson said. "You made a vast difference in all our lives. Great strides in how others treat us as law enforcement. New programs allowing us to grow with the times."

Jimmy Maka helped position Captain Brown on an examination table. "Please let us take care of her, detectives. We can figure later what will happen."

"He's right Emerson. We need to get back to the station and sort all of this out." Reese added, "We will stay in touch on our private lines, Sheriff. We hope you will do the same."

They exchanged numbers before saying goodbye, for now, to their beloved captain and friend.

Emerson stroked the captain's matted locks. "We won't let you down. I promise."

Reese, a tear running down her face, kissed the check of her loyal captain. "See you soon. Do what the doctor says."

Kimimela Brown squeezed their hands. "I know you will do what you can. Please be sure they return my sister and Kevin to the Reservation for burial." She sobbed uncontrollably once again.

"We should leave, Reese." Emerson took her by the arm and led her out to the car. "Now," he said as they got in the car, "would you care to elaborate on how the captain got in the trunk?"

Reese, not a tear left to cry, stared straight ahead as they drove toward Cromwell.

"It's a simple story really. She was crouching directly across from Rossi, near a Chevy SUV. She saw me and the blood on my hands. I shook my head to let her know Zitkala was gone. I believe she knew that, anyway. She began firing toward you guys over and over, moving around the other vehicles in the lot. I motioned for her to get down. She was a different person, Emerson. She was wild with anger and fear. I have never seen a woman with such a pure look of hatred in her eyes. When Rossi went down, I motioned toward our car, reached in my pocket for the keys, and popped the trunk. I don't know why I needed to protect her, but I did what I thought was right."

"And that was?" he asked.

"To get her as far away from that awful scene as possible. She was no longer the captain at that point. She was a woman who wanted to kill the bastard that took the lives of her family."

CHAPTER 96

Carly and Manning were waiting when Reese and Emerson walked into the precinct.

"Well?" Carly asked impatiently, "where is the captain? Is she all right?"

Emerson responded. "She will be. We hope."

"That still doesn't answer the question," Manning said. "Where is she?"

Reese ignored Allen. "We should get the captain's attorney on the phone. Set up a meeting. Manning, do that on your private phone. Got it?"

"Sure, I'll do it right now."

"Carly, any video you have from the drone we saw flying over-head, I want it now." Carly knew there was no time to waste by the tone in Reese's voice.

"Yes, ma'am."

"I want video from that ring system on the house near the abandoned gas station too. And if you can get it, we need to find out if the FBI pulled anything off of the captain's phone that was left in the bathroom."

Emerson added, "And we really don't give a rat's ass how you get all of this, but I want it on our desks A.S.A.P. Got it, Brennen?"

"Got it. But I can tell you," Carly's fingers raced over the keyboard, "the ring system showed nothing at all."

Reese seemed disappointed. "Well grab it anyway. What's going on with the prison? Any word on Steven Daniels?"

Manning walked back to the desk. "Yea, he resigned his position as Warden."

"Really?" Emerson asked. "What happened?"

"He had a breakdown. I guess the guilt was too much for him after he heard that Judge John Orrick bequeathed a scholarship in his and the governor's daughter's names. He folded like a house of cards and admitted to their involvement in Timothy Cole's escape. He is currently at a psychiatric facility for observation until the trial date is determined."

"Wow, that's a shocker," Reese said.

"And the Governor?" Lake turned to Carly. "What was that message in my ear about him being at the hospital? Who was talking to me?"

"The governor had a medical emergency while in the FBI's custody. They took him to Jade medical where he died *of a stroke*. As for your second question, I can't divulge my sources."

"Well," Reese said, "you better divulge that drone footage."

"I will Detective. Not sure you are going to like what you see though. Can we go into the captain's office instead of out here in the open?"

"Good idea."

Carly set up a laptop on the desk in Kimimela's office.

Manning popped his head in the door. "Hold on, Mr. Hollingsworth is here."

"Come in and have a seat counselor. Sorry, no popcorn," Lake said.

No one was in the mood for Emerson's jokes.

Carly started the video. It showed Captain Kimimela Brown firing at Benito Rossi as he fled, She emptied several clips until the suspect went down. It also revealed the events right after his demise exactly as Reese had explained it to Emerson.

"Stop the video for a moment." Denton moved closer to Reese. "Do you realize this implicates you as an accessory to murder?"

Reese hung her head.

"Detectives," Carly interrupted, "I just received a message from my contact at the FBI labs. The captain's cell phone at the scene had a message for you, Mr. Hollingsworth."

Denton looked confused, "Really? What did it say?"

"*Denton, Benito Rossi just murdered my nephew*. She gives the address of the gas station."

"Mr. Hollingsworth, you just asked me if I realized I might be implicated as an accessory to murder." Reese paused for a moment biting her lip. She finally looked the attorney in the eye, "Murder was too good for that guy."

"Reese!" Emerson scolded.

"No, Emerson, I'm sorry. After what he did to Zitkala and Kevin? He was a monster. What he did to the captain has destroyed her. She lost her baby from the trauma and beating she took."

"What? Oh my God." Denton was overwhelmed with

emotion. "Is she ok? Where is she?"

"Strictly off the record, Denton?" Reese asked.

"Yes, of course"

"She's with the father of her unborn child. Sheriff Jimmy Maka. He arranged for her to see a doctor at his home practice just inside the Reservation. We thought it was the best option to keep her hidden until we can figure out next steps."

Denton Hollingsworth hung his head, placing his hands over his face. "We need to go get her. Now, damn it!"

"What?" Lake jumped from his chair. "Are you out of your mind? We can't do that. She is being cared for and we need to secure her safety for the time being. Only the FBI has jurisdiction on the Reservation and I'm fairly sure they are on our side regarding the captain."

"Except for one major factor," Denton said.

"What's that?" Emerson asked.

"Jimmy Maka isn't the father of Kim's baby. I am."

CHAPTER 97

"Detectives, I think you need to take a look at this." Carly motioned to the laptop where the drone video continued to play.

They all huddled over Carly's shoulder as she dragged the video back a few frames and hit play.

"Whoa!" Lake jumped back. "Why the hell would he do that?"

Standing over the body of Benito Rossi, as Detective Lake ran back toward Reese, the footage showed Jimmy Maka holding a gold shield. He mouthed a few inaudible words and then plunged the badge into Benito Rossi's chest.

"Kim told me she had gone to see Jimmy a while ago, asking for his help with finding her brother and Zitkala." Denton began to pace the floor. "They used to be a couple when Kim was younger, before she became captain of Cromwell P.D. Jimmy never accepted the fact that Kim left the Reservation and moved on. But her priority was to find her missing siblings. He tried to re-kindle the relationship when she sought his help. Kim wanted no part of it. I'm guessing this little act was symbolic for Jimmy. His way of hurting the man who hurt Kim."

"I suppose, but where did he get her shield?" Emerson asked.

"I have no idea."

"So, how did you and the captain get together?" Reese asked.

"We became friends while she was investigating Zitkala's boarding school. As time went on, we became something more. When she fainted recently, I learned she was pregnant. While she was in the hospital, I peeked at her charts. I know that's not legal, but she was right there. The blood work matched mine." Denton smiled. "We were happy about it, but agreed it was best to keep it quiet until we cleared her name. You know, conflict of interest."

Denton reached into his pocket and pulled out a diamond ring that would light up a room. "I planned on giving this to her when all was clear with Zitkala." He stared at the sparkling gem half smiling, lost in the thought about how he intended to propose. He finally snapped out of his daydream, remembering they had serious problems to deal with. "How long ago did you leave Kim at the doctor's home office on the Reservation?"

"About an hour and a half ago. Maybe two," Lake replied.

"I think Jimmy might try to hold Kim against her will. He was so infatuated with her and never seemed to get over the fact that she didn't want a relationship with him."

"I'm contacting the FBI," Reese said.

"We also need a search warrant for the doctor's house. Do you remember the address?"

"I do," said Lake as he rattled off the house number and street. "Let's go get your girl back!"

On the way, Lake tried the private number Jimmy Maka gave him, but it was bogus.

When the detectives arrived, FBI swat teams surrounded the home of the Reservation doctor. Hovering high above was a medivac helicopter with Agent Michael Wells and Denton Hollingsworth on board. There was nowhere to run.

The medivac landed and its passengers spilled out. Michael made his way toward the swat team and grabbed a bullhorn. "Come out with your hands up!"

The door opened and Jimmy Maka appeared. "You are on the land of the Lakota Sioux," he shouted. "You have no jurisdiction here. I am the law on this land. What do you want?"

"We would like to see Kimimela Brown," Wells replied. "We are not here to take over your land Sheriff."

"She belongs here on this Reservation, with me." Jimmy surveyed the scene. He was outnumbered and out armed.

"Not if she doesn't want to be," Wells said. "We would like to hear that from Captain Brown."

"Captain Brown is not feeling well and is being cared for by her doctor. She needs rest," the Sheriff argued. "Now I suggest you leave. I will have her contact one of you when she is feeling better."

"Jimmy Maka, listen to me, we already have you on video stabbing Benito Rossi. Do you want kidnapping charges added?" Wells asked.

Knowing there was nowhere to run, Jimmy Maka turned to re-enter the house, only to find Kimimela standing in the doorway. He grabbed her arm to keep her from running.

"Jimmy, no!" Kim gently removed his grip and positioned herself close enough to protect him from harm. "I have great admiration for you, Jimmy," she whispered sweetly. "And I have great respect for you, but I don't love you in the way you want me to. I am so sorry things had to be this way." She looked at him with sorrow and gratitude. "Agent Wells!" she shouted, "Sheriff Maka was just trying to help me, not hurt me. There is no need to arrest him." Her eyes were now swollen from all the tears shed over her great losses. "This land we stand on," she continued, "needs Sheriff Maka. The people here need him. There has been enough anger and destruction of life."

Jimmy Maka looked at her with sadness and a broken heart, but he also knew she would remain his friend. He stepped in front of her, ignoring the swarm of guns pointed at him. He gave her his hand to help her off the stairs and then stepped aside leaving her to walk away on her own. Swallowing hard, he raised his hands in the air.

Denton, being cautious of Kimimela's sensitive state, stayed back, waiting to see what would happen next. He didn't have to wait long. Kim slowly walked toward Denton sobbing, grasping the robe she wore close to her battered body, and collapsed into his arms. He picked her up and placed her on the stretcher that was waiting to transport her to the hospital. He kissed her forehead while the doctor started an IV and checked her vitals.

Agent Olden approached Jimmy Maka. "You can put your hands down, sheriff," he said. "Thank you for your help with our investigation." He stuck out his hand out for Jimmy to shake.

Wells gave the signal for everyone to lower their weapons and also extended his hand.

Jimmy Maka never thought it possible. The FBI and the Lakota working together.

"Thank you, agents. Here is my real cell number. Please let me know when Zitkala and Kevin will arrive for burial."

"Of course," Olden said.

Agent Wells approached Kim on the stretcher. "We found your weapon and clips near a parked car, Captain. You did the right thing. It was a clean shoot."

Kim sighed with relief as the medivac prepared to take her to the hospital.

Denton stroked her hair. "I will be right here by your side. At all times. I love you, Kim."

She smiled and squeezed his hand, before sleep took over her body.

CHAPTER 98

The FBI sent their NYC agents to round up the Rossi crime family. It was a work in progress.

Jack Roman ultimately was convicted on three counts of murder. At his sentencing, the judge asked if he wanted to make a statement. Of course, the arrogant prick said no, showing no remorse for anything he had done. He was sentenced to death for his participation in the murders of Judge John Orrick, Zitkala Brown, and Kevin Brown.

On the way out of the courthouse, when the press asked for a statement, he raised his cuffed hands, gave them all the finger, and said, "Death cannot come soon enough."

It took a few years of abuse in a prison cell, abuse he never imagined. But he got his wish.

There were no charges filed against Sheriff Jimmy Maka. Captain Brown had Carly Brennen discreetly remove anything incriminating from the drone footage. They never mentioned it again.

The Chief of Police would find a replacement for Captain Brown while she was recuperating.

Before her leave of absence, she held one final meeting with her team. Her messages were brief. It would have to suffice until she decided what her future might hold.

"Officer Carly Brown, as much as we hate to lose you as part of our precinct, I am sure you will make a great FBI agent."

"Thank you, Captain," Carly replied. "It was an opportunity I couldn't refuse. *Really couldn't refuse.*" She laughed at their private joke. After everything she had done for the captain, some of it legally questionable, it was a given that she would put those skills to good use for Wells and Olden. In the long run, she knew it would be good for her career.

"Deputy Manning, thank you for your caring and kind demeanor and your powerful instincts. If it hadn't been for you insisting that something was wrong when I didn't pick up your call, I might not be here today."

Manning blushed. He would miss his fearless leader.

"Reese Clayton and Emerson Lake, I don't have any words to express how I feel about you both. Please be safe."

The detectives smiled and gave her a knowing nod.

"To the entire precinct, all of you gave me the chance to love, laugh, and cry with my sister, whom I never thought I would see again. When I look in the mirror though…" she paused, choking up, "all I see is death in my reflection. Even though it was a short time with Zitkala and Kevin, it was time I never would have had without your help. I am eternally grateful, and I hope someday that reflection will become my angel."

There was not a dry eye in the room. One by one, they gently hugged and said their goodbyes. Then they stood in perfect formation and saluted Captain Brown as she made her final walk out of the building.

CHAPTER 99

"Reese, what do you say we book a real vacation? Right now. No more waiting."

"Okay, what did you have in mind, my dear Emerson? Keep in mind, if you suggest a hunting or fishing cabin, I have a weapon and I will use it."

He chuckled. "No, I'm serious, sweetheart. Let's get married while we're away. And let's talk about making some commitments for our future."

"Commitments huh? Marriage isn't an enormous enough commitment?" she joked.

"It is. I've just been thinking a lot lately about changing things in our lives. Now, before you fly off the handle, Reese, I say we have a great wedding and a long, extended honeymoon."

"I like the sound of that!"

"And then let's find ourselves a house in the country. Somewhere we can call home and raise a family. Nice schools et cetera. Maybe even go into business for ourselves."

"After this horrific case, Emerson, I'm not opposed to change." She kissed him sweetly and then plopped onto the sofa with a bridal magazine. A smile enveloping her face.

Emerson quietly opened his laptop and began his search.

How to become a private detective in Vermont.

352

EPILOGUE

Standing in the shadows of the Bur Oak Tree, feeling the breeze waft across her face.

Staring at the gravesite of a young mother and child embracing as one.

Tall grasses will grow to protect the land. A stone marks the way back to Earth.

A woman dressed in Lakota robes begins her final goodbye to the mirrored vision of herself.

> *"Warm breeze, which blows upon my face,*
> *take my prayers to my sister.*
> *Allow her to hear my words.*
> *Send her love back to me when*
> *the sun is on my face.*
> *Allow her to shine in the stars, shimmering*
> *above my head at night.*
> *Allow her to be free of pain and fear.*
> *When she is once again ready to soar.*
> *Send her to me on butterfly wings, so*
> *I may find peace."*

ACKNOWLEDGMENTS

The Author may write a novel, but not without help and guidance from many people. This is where I say thank you to those in my life, brave enough to take a red pen to my work. To verbalize the right and wrongs of the manuscript throughout the entire process. Although sometimes it is difficult to hear words of criticism, I still am very grateful. Without all of you, my work would not exist.

Crystal Dovigh for the endless hours going through the manuscript asking me if this or that should be there or as she calls describes it: "this paragraph needs to be massaged a little." I would say to myself, *What?* But she was right. So, back to the keyboard. For talking me off the wall when I felt I should quit writing. There were a lot of those days. Someone truly blessed your dad and me to have you as our daughter. I am extremely proud of the woman you have become. Thank you sincerely from the bottom of my heart and soul. I love you, baby girl, and will always send you butterfly kisses.

Jeff Dovigh for being there to take a call now and then about law enforcement, from your favorite mother-in-law. We are indeed proud of you and all that you represent. I can count on you to read and critique my work with complete honesty.

Al Fournier love of my life, my squeeze forever and a day. Through this writing adventure of mine, I would like to thank you for your support and patience. I don't know what I would do without you. I thank you for listening and being by my side all these years. We have been through enough trauma together to last a lifetime, but we have also been fortunate to have the love of family and friends, and most of all, we have been blessed to have each other for 51 years and counting. I love you.

Joseph Stahl Evidence Specialist at South Dakota Forensic Laboratory Thank you for your time and wealth of knowledge about the evidence used at crime scenes and confirming for me that the FBI also uses the state labs. It was a pleasure speaking with you on the phone. Mr. Stahl, I thank you and hope you get time to read my novel.

Jeff Larson Retired South Dakota Attorney Thank you for sending me a beautiful card, letting me know you enjoyed my first novel *Now Say You're Sorry*, and how it kept you wanting to read more. Thank you for the excellent advice you gave me for this book, the next in the series. Jeff, I wish you the very best in retirement. Thank you for always being available to answer my questions.

Author David K. Wilson In a world where so many look out for themselves, you are not that guy. I know I will always be able to count on you for help and guidance, to tell me the truth when you think something is wrong. For answering my calls when I need help with something. I should say help with this vast maze called the internet. You are funny, smart, kind, with an enormous heart, and one hell of an author. My love for you is always my dear friend.

Erin Malcolm Photography Erin the day we met, there was an immediate connection. One of trust and instant friendship. My author photo is lovely and thanks will never be enough. I highly recommend you as a photographer.

Caroline Teagle Johnson Thank you will never express how I feel about you and your amazing talent. Creating, once again, the perfect cover for my novel. You always see the vision, the heart and soul of my writing and transform my words into a cover design that is truly a work of art. The entire process put me at ease, knowing you would deliver excellence. And you did my friend. Can't wait to work with you again.

Lorraine Evanoff, Award-winning Author, Screenwriter, Producer, World Traveler and Friend. I am not sure if there are words that can express what it has meant to have you as a friend and fellow author. I have been blessed to have you critique my work and do that dreaded editing. I thank you for all the suggestions, and most of all for being you, the positive to everyone's negative.

BARBARA FOURNIER grew up in a small town in upstate New York. One of eight children. Growing up in a large family without modern day conveniences was a challenge, but in spite of their tough upbringing, or perhaps because of it, Barbara and her siblings thrived. Oh, the stories they could tell!

After retiring from a 35-year career as owner/operator of two hair salons, Barbara was ready for her next adventure as an author.

She loves creating riveting stories with complicated twists and relatable characters that captivate and engage the reader.

Death in My Reflection is the second novel in the Reese Clayton and Emerson Lake detective series.

Barbara still lives in upstate New York with her husband of 51 years. They have one daughter and son in law.

Check out these other titles from Barbara Fournier:

Now Say You're Sorry
After Our First Hello

You can order Barbara's books at your favorite
bookstore or on Amazon.com.

Visit her website at barbarafournierauthor.com

Facebook: Author Barbara Fournier

Instagram: barbarafournier54

Leave a review on Amazon, Goodreads or Google Reviews.

www.ingramcontent.com/pod-product-compliance
Lightning Source LLC
Chambersburg PA
CBHW020349220726
48290CB00014B/1386